BRIDIE'S DAUGHTER

A TRILOGY

by

ROBERT NOONAN

WILDFLOWERS

While overworked child laborers of the nineteenth century might have created the grist for the Industrial Revolution, even darker abuses were committed against them.

BRIDIE'S DAUGHTER

The Orphan Trains carried homeless children westward, altering their lives and the lives of the people who took them in … for better or worse.

SECRETS

The orphan children, as well as the adults who adopted them, have secrets from their past. Some secrets are revealed; others better left untold.

BRIDIE'S DAUGHTER

The Second Story in the Orphan Train Trilogy

Robert Noonan

Author of *Wildflowers* and *Secrets*

iUniverse, Inc.
New York Lincoln Shanghai

Bridie's Daughter
The Second Story in the Orphan Train Trilogy

Copyright © 2007 by Robert J. Noonan

All rights reserved. No part of this book may be used or reproduced by any means, graphic, electronic, or mechanical, including photocopying, recording, taping or by any information storage retrieval system without the written permission of the publisher except in the case of brief quotations embodied in critical articles and reviews.

iUniverse books may be ordered through booksellers or by contacting:

iUniverse
2021 Pine Lake Road, Suite 100
Lincoln, NE 68512
www.iuniverse.com
1-800-Authors (1-800-288-4677)

Because of the dynamic nature of the Internet, any Web addresses or links contained in this book may have changed since publication and may no longer be valid.

This is a work of fiction. All of the characters, names, incidents, organizations, and dialogue in this novel are either the products of the author's imagination or are used fictitiously.

Author Photo by Matt Stary, Hatfield, Wisconsin

ISBN: 978-0-595-43629-3 (pbk)
ISBN: 978-0-595-68934-7 (cloth)
ISBN: 978-0-595-87955-7 (ebk)

Printed in the United States of America

Robert Noonan has presented us with a gift ... three extremely well written novels highlighting a desperate time for children of our past. We may not enjoy reading about some of the challenges they faced but it is important that we learn of them. These books will become memorable additions to your historical fiction bookshelf.

—IP Book Reviewers

I dedicate this novel to all of the children who rode the Orphan Trains.

ACKNOWLEDGMENTS

I wish to thank all of the officers and members of The Orphan Train Heritage Society of America for keeping alive this little-known corner of United States history.

A special thanks to the society's founder–Mary Ellen Johnson.

For information or membership in the Orphan Train Heritage Society of America

www.orphantrains.com

OTHSA
P.O. Box 322
Concordia, KS
66901-0322

(785) 243-4471

Chapter One

Harvey Blatt entered the two-story, brown brick building, looking at his watch. It was six-fifteen a.m. He passed through the wide, dimly lit corridor of the orphanage toward his office. His footsteps echoed off bare concrete walls and black floor tile. He paused at his door, listening for sounds from the children's dormitories. He didn't hear anyone stirring, so he entered the office.

Harvey stood behind an oak desk, placing adoption papers into a black leather briefcase. He slipped his short, thin body between the end of the desk and a file cabinet, retrieving blank forms from a small table. He returned to the chair behind the desk, sliding his hands across graying, black hair lining the sides of his balding head. Harvey looked up at a small calendar on the wall, as Alice Hawthorne entered. His eyes followed the tall, slender woman as she came towards him. Her youthful face belied her thirty years.

Harvey smiled at her. "Sit down, Alice," he said, politely, pointing to a chair in front of his desk. He locked the briefcase and set it against the wall behind him, then looked into Alice's eyes. "Are you nervous?"

"Not as nervous as the children, but I would be, if you weren't going on this trip. Actually, I'm looking forward to it."

Harvey sat back in his chair, clasping his hands together. "Being that you are new at the Society for Children, and this will be your first experience traveling with the children, it may take some emotional adjustment on your part. You may fall in love with some children, yet feel indifferent toward others. That is natural, but remember, all the children must be treated the same."

Alice took a long, steadying breath. "I know exactly what you mean, Mr. Blatt, especially in dealing with the wee ones. I'd like to own a ranch with a thousand acres, and fill it with playing children." She glanced at pictures on the wall behind Mr. Blatt, showing groups of children at train stations. "I ache, when the little ones look at me with fear and uncertainty in their eyes, believing not one person in the whole world loves them, or wants them."

Harvey leaned toward her again. "Through the work of all children's agencies, more than 200,000 children have been placed in homes since 1850. Most find good homes, but a few will be treated as servants or laborers, and some, I'm afraid, will be sexually abused."

Alice looked down at her hands, nodding. "I've been told that, and it makes me ill thinking about it. I wish we could eliminate that problem."

Harvey looked into her eyes, "The Society tries to visit each child every year, but with the number of adoptions increasing so rapidly, it's an impossible task." He looked up at the wall clock. "It's time for you, and Mrs. Palmer, to wake the girls. We can continue this conversation at breakfast."

Catherine Hayes was awakened by the sound of a whimpering child. Two cots away, a girl she guessed to be ten years old, had her arm around a girl about three, addressing her as Becky. They were in long gray nightshirts, sitting in the center of a canvas cot, their legs dangling over the side.

Between jerking sobs, the small girl asked, "What if I hate the people that adopt me, Jenny?"

Catherine watched Jenny slowly stroke the little girls head, hoping to console her. Yet, she was too young herself, to give a comforting answer.

"What if nobody wants me?" was her next question. Her light brown curls jiggled each time she moved her head. Becky was holding a dirty, undressed doll against her chest. Its torso was made of stuffed cloth, with pink arms, legs and head sewn to it. Two fingers were missing on one hand and half of the blond hair was missing.

"Don't worry, Becky," Jenny replied, putting her arm around her, again. "I'm sure all of us will be adopted. You just have to believe that, because it happens all the time, and by nice people, too."

Catherine rolled onto her back and looked up toward the concrete ceiling, counting the lights that hung in dark green metal shades down the center of the long room. She heard the dormitory door open and close, followed by rapid footsteps coming toward the cots.

Mrs. Palmer and Miss Hawthorne walked from cot-to-cot, waking the sleeping girls. "Time to get up and wash," they said, shaking the girls' shoulders.

Catherine swung her legs over the side of the cot and looked at the round clock on the wall. "Six-thirty," she muttered to herself. "Where will I be at six-thirty in the morning, a week from now?"

When Miss Hawthorne came her way, Becky looked up at her with pleading eyes, "Do you think someone will take me home with them?"

Miss Hawthorne didn't know her name, but she sat next to Becky and held her hand. "Don't you worry, my dear; there are many people who would love to have a little girl like you. Just wait and see."

Becky smiled, enthusiastically, completely believing what she had been told. She looked at Jenny, to see whether she had heard.

Jenny was nodding at her.

Catherine looked around the room, observing other girls getting out of bed. Most were moving at a turtle's pace. Girls who had been awake earlier were walking to and from the bathroom, wearing long gray nightshirt they were issued when they arrived at the orphanage.

Each was carrying the white towel and washcloth that had been placed at the end of their cots. Only a few seemed to be about fourteen-years-old, the same age as her. Most were younger. Catherine stood next to her cot and stretched her slim body, rising onto the tip of her toes. Her wavy blond hair contained a wisp of red, and her eyes were a blend of gray and green.

Hunger pangs gnawed at her. *The sooner I'm dressed, the sooner I'll be ready to eat,* she thought. Catherine took the towel and washcloth at the foot of her cot and started for the bathroom, the black and white floor tiles feeling cool against her bare feet. A calendar hanging on the wall outside the bathroom entrance, had a pastoral scene of a farm with rolling hills and trees. The current date had been circled in red pencil: *Thursday, June 8, 1899*, the day she and the other children would leave New York City on an Orphan Train.

In the bathroom, she counted six toilet stalls along the wall on her right, each partitioned by thin gray marble slabs. Ten white porcelain sinks lined the opposite wall. Catherine walked to the first unoccupied sink, wishing she had privacy. She estimated the girl at her left was eleven years old. She was standing on her toes, trying to get all of her hair into the water-filled sink. Her brown hair was lathered with soap and she was attempting to rinse it. A girl at her right was washing her naked body vigorously with a washcloth, mumbling to herself. Catherine wasn't sure whether the girl was talking to herself, or quietly singing.

She hung her towel on a hook between the sinks, removed her nightshirt and pushed a black rubber plug into the drain, filling the sink with warm water. Catherine took a bar of soap from the top of the sink and submerged it with her washcloth. The warm water felt good against her tacky skin. It had been three days since she'd had an opportunity to wash thoroughly. The more she scrubbed her body, the more refreshed she felt. Catherine knew she would be on a train for a few days, without being able to bathe properly, again. She soaked the washcloth with water and wiped the soapy film from her body. The excess water ran across the tile floor toward one of four large drains evenly spaced along the center of the bathroom. She changed the water in the sink and washed her hair. After drying herself with the towel, Catherine got into her nightshirt. All the sinks were occupied now, and a girl was standing behind her, waiting to wash. Catherine smiled at her and moved on. *Lead me to breakfast*, she thought.

She returned to the dormitory, sat on her cot and dried her wet feet. She got down on one knee and pulled a dark brown clothes box from under her cot. The sides of the box were thick as cardboard, made of a hard material she wasn't familiar with. Each of the children received one when they arrived at the dormitory. Catherine unbuckled the strap around the box and raised the top. The only clothes she owned were two dresses, two petticoats, three changes of underclothes, a dark blue sweater, a brown shirt, one pink hair ribbon, a white blouse and a yellow blouse. There was a second pair of black shoes and three pair of black knee stockings. Catherine decided to wear the tan dress and laid it on the cot. She liked the green dress best, but decided to save it for when they were presented for adoption.

Catherine heard her name being called from across the aisle. It was Monica Brenn, a girl she'd met yesterday, when she arrived at the Society For Children. She recalled that Monica had come from Durham, Rhode Island, three days ago. She was Catherine's age, slightly larger and well developed. Her brown hair was parted down the middle and she had one thick braid hanging down her back.

Monica waved to Catherine, holding a red and green plaid dress over her head. She put her arms through the short sleeves, letting the dress drop around her. She grabbed her black shoes and stockings from under her cot and crossed the aisle to join Catherine.

"Are you nervous?" she asked, sitting on Catherine's cot.

"Somewhat. Right now, I'm hungry. What do they serve for breakfast?"

Monica rolled a black stocking onto her leg. "My first breakfast here was flapjacks. The second morning, they had oatmeal. Yesterday they had flapjacks again, so I guess we'll have oatmeal today."

Catherine sat next to Monica to put on her stockings and shoes. "Good, I like oatmeal."

Miss Hawthorne returned, stood in the middle of the dormitory and clapped her hands twice to get the children's attention. "Breakfast is being served in the dining hall. Have your clothes box packed and be completely dressed, so we can leave for the train station by 8:30. Do you have any questions?"

Miss Hawthorne pointed to a slender girl with long black hair and nodded, waiting to hear her question.

"How are we getting to the train station?"

A tall, husky girl standing against the wall yelled, "We're taking a train there." The girls standing around her, giggled.

"Enough, enough." Miss Hawthorne looked at the jester. "We are walking. The station is only six blocks away, so it won't be a long walk. If everybody stays together, we'll be there in fifteen minutes. Any other questions?"

A fragile-looking blond girl with her hands clasped behind her back, asked, "Is it cold where we're going?"

"No," Miss Hawthorne replied. "The temperature will be about the same as here, or warmer. The coats you have now will be sufficient." Her eyes drifted from one girl to another waiting for another question. "Those of you who have washed can proceed to the dining hall for your breakfast."

Catherine put on her dress, while Monica sat waiting. When fully dressed, she tapped Monica on the shoulder. "Let's go. My stomach is anxious for food."

The girls walked quickly out of their dormitory toward the dining room at the end of the hall. They walked between tall double doors that had been pushed back against the wall, stopping at the end of the food line. It was a large room, with gray floor tile and a concrete ceiling eighteen feet above them. The sounds of the children walking and talking echoed off the yellow plaster walls.

Boys were in the line, too, whispering and giggling about the girls and whatever else they thought humorous. Bowls and spoons were on a table at the head of the food line. Once they got their oatmeal, they moved to another table with glasses of milk. Catherine and Monica carried their food to a row of tables near the windows. The bottom windowpanes were frosted glass, making it impossible to see outside, or for anyone to look in. The scarred wooden tables were long, with hard bench seats.

While eating, two boys sat down next to Catherine. They were busy talking and laughing when they dropped themselves onto the bench. The boy next to Catherine bumped her shoulder, as he sat down.

Immediately, he turned toward her. "I'm sorry. Did I hurt you?"

"No, you didn't bump me hard." They gave each other a prolonged look. Catherine turned to Monica, with raised eyebrows and a mischievous grin. She loved his curly black hair and light blue eyes. His dark blue pants appeared to be new, but his tan, short-sleeved shirt was starting to fray around the collar.

The boy sat on the bench at a slight angle, so when he leaned forward to put the spoon to his mouth, he could sneak a peek at Catherine.

Catherine shifted herself on the bench, so when she leaned forward to put the spoon to her mouth, she could sneak a peek at the boy. When their eyes met they pretended it was accidental.

"How many days have you been here?" the boy asked Catherine.

"I arrived yesterday. And you?"

"I've been here two days, most the time scrubbing floors and cleaning the yard. Where are you from?"

"Here, in New York City." Carefully, Catherine took a small portion of oatmeal so none would fall from her spoon and embarrass her.

"I'm from Gresham, Connecticut. It's a small town near Danbury, where my father worked. He made custom furniture for rich people. He was good at it, too."

Catherine watched him scoop a spoonful of plain oatmeal from his bowl. "Don't you put milk on your oatmeal?"

"I like melted butter on my oatmeal. They don't have any on the table, so I'll eat it plain. I never could understand putting cold milk on hot cereal."

"I never tried butter on oatmeal. I'll try it next time and see if I like it better." Catherine watched him scrape the last of the oatmeal from his bowl. "What's your name?"

"Brian Hampton." He examined Catherine more closely and was surprised by the soft green of her eyes. Brian had never seen green eyes before. Her complexion was smooth and creamy, like he'd seen on dolls. Her pink lips looked soft, and inviting. Brian found himself wanting to kiss them. "And your name," he asked, with raised eyebrows.

"Catherine." She leaned back and pointed to her friend. "Monica is from Rhode Island."

Monica smiled and waved once, by rocking her forearm on her elbow.

Brian leaned back, so the girls could see his thin little friend. "Jason is from New York City, too."

Jason corrected Brian. "Actually, I'm from Brooklyn." He pushed his empty bowl and milk glass forward, resting his folded arms on the table. "The big question is, where will we be living a month from now?"

At a small table near the entrance door, Harvey Blatt was eating breakfast with Alice Hawthorne. He talked as she looked down at her bowl of oatmeal, stirring it slowly. "The history of these children is quite varied. Some had normal, pleasant lives until their parents died, while others have experienced years of abuse, or lived on the streets. I will explain the background of three of these children, so you can understand any unusual behavior they may exhibit on the train." Harvey stopped and took two bites of his oatmeal. "Look over your right shoulder to the second table. Near the center, facing you is fourteen-year-old Sally Sumner. She's wearing a blue dress, with a white sailor-boy collar."

Alice took a sip of milk and casually looked in that direction. "Yes, I see her." She took a long look at Sally, longer than she had intended. "She doesn't smile, or show any emotion. It's as if she were numb." She looked at Mr. Blatt again and said, "I've heard many stories about abused children and I'd rather you don't tell me more. I'll just love them and wish them good luck."

Harvey smiled at her. "You have a tender heart. Don't let it control you."

Mrs. Palmer entered the dining hall and stood at the front of the room by the serving tables. She clapped her hands to get the children's attention. She was a large woman, with a gruff voice. Her gray hair was combed to the top of her head, crowned with a braided ring. "Please give me your attention," she began. "We are leaving for the train station in fifteen minutes. Finish your breakfast, then get your coats and clothes boxes and meet by the front door." She stepped forward and stood among the tables. "We have only 37 children today, so chances of all of you being adopted are very good. There have been times when we've had as many as 150 children on a train. We will ride for two days before stopping in western Illinois, a very nice place to live. The train will stop in big towns and in smaller communities. Where you're adopted shouldn't concern you. What is important is who adopts you. It's a kind person who will take a child into their home and care for it. But there are times when a child doesn't like their new home, or the people are not satisfied with the child. So remember this: you do not have to stay at a home if you are being mistreated. The Society for Children will try to find you another home. Be honest with yourself as to whether you, or the people who adopted you, are the problem. Try to make your adoption a success. More likely than not, you'll be getting a new life in a fine home."

Thirty-seven faces were looking up at her, listening to her every word. Most of the children were wearing clothes that were too big, or too small. Some clothing was frayed and threadbare. "I wish all of you the best of luck and a wonderful future. May God bless you and keep you."

A rumble of 37 voices filled the room, as the children left their tables and filed out through the double doors of the dining hall. Sunlight began to shine through the clear glass at the top halves of the windows.

Brian looked at his three friends, "Actually, I'm not worried about being sent somewhere. It's got to be better than what we have now." He looked at Catherine who appeared pensive. "Are you nervous?"

"A little. But I think you're right. I should accept this as a new adventure and look forward to a happy ending." She paused a moment. "I wonder if we'll get brothers and sisters with our new home? And will they like us? That's what I worry about."

"We'd better get our clothes," Jason suggested. "See you girls by the front door."

Catherine and Monica left the boys in the hallway and entered their dormitory. Girls were at their beds talking, while buckling their clothes boxes, putting on their coats or tying shoelaces. Catherine grabbed her clothes box by the strap and put her coat over her arm. She looked across the aisle and saw two small holes in Monica's stockings. Catherine examined her own stockings, but there weren't any holes. She crossed the aisle, as Monica put on her coat. "I'm ready," she said. "Good luck to us."

They entered the hallway, walking toward the crowd of children at the front door. "It looks like we're one of the last to be ready," Catherine said, switching her clothes box from one hand to the other. The children appeared to her, as black silhouettes, against the sunlight beyond the entrance doors. Catherine looked back and saw Brian and Jason coming up behind them.

Miss Hawthorne was counting the children. She pointed her index finger towards Brian and Jason as they approached her. She was holding a piece of paper, listing the children's names. "Four missing," she mumbled, then took quick, long strides toward the dormitories. She stopped abruptly, as two girls came out of their dorm and into the hallway. Miss Hawthorne made two checks on the paper and continued on to the boy's dormitory. "Move along," she said, passing the girls.

Mr. Blatt came out of his office carrying a brown leather suitcase and black briefcase. He was humming, "Oh, Dem Golden Slippers" loud enough for others to hear. As he approached the waiting children, the ceiling lights reflected off the washed skin of his head. He stopped next to Mrs. Palmer, buttoning her coat. "Are they all here?" he asked.

Mrs. Palmer tipped her head toward the dormitories and said, "Miss Hawthorne is coming with two boys now. They complete our list of twenty boys and seventeen girls."

Mr. Blatt turned and saw Miss Hawthorne hurrying the boys toward them. The boy's coats were unbuttoned and one boy's gray shirt hadn't been tucked into his pants. The other boy's shoelaces were untied and swung around his feet, as he walked.

"Finish dressing immediately," Mr. Blatt shouted, pointing to the two boys. "We must leave now." He faced the other children. "Line up, two abreast, the boys in front and girls behind."

When they were aligned in double rows, Mr. Blatt pushed down on the two brass bars that unlocked the doors, leading the children out onto the sun-filled sidewalk. He and Miss Hawthorne walked with the boys, while Mrs. Palmer attended to the girls.

Catherine turned to see who was behind her. It was little Becky, the youngest of the group. She wasn't crying now, but she had a troubled look on her face. Catherine smiled at her and said, "In a few days, you will have a nice home. We all will." Catherine looked ahead at Brian and Jason, talking and smiling as they marched off to an unknown destination.

Suddenly, the braying of a horse startled Catherine. The horse's head was less than three feet from her. They were passing a vendor, selling fruits and vegetables from the back of his wagon, touting the freshness of his produce. She assumed the horse was facing the sidewalk so it wouldn't be scared by noisy street traffic. Occasionally, one of the children reached out to pet the horse's nose in passing.

The clanging bell of a horse-drawn trolley rattling past them irritated Catherine's ears. At the corner, a newsboy was screaming the headline news, holding a newspaper high over his head. A policeman in a dark blue uniform, his nightstick hanging at his side, stopped traffic, so they could cross the street as a group. He realized they were orphans on their way to the train station.

Catherine could see an open area two blocks ahead that was clear of tall buildings. She knew it was in front of the train station because she'd been there before. One Sunday last year, her father took her for a train ride to Fulton, New York, thirty-eight miles west of New York City. They both wanted a train ride into the country and eat dinner at the Golden Harp, a popular Irish restaurant. While they were on the train, he told her stories of when he was a boy in Ireland; how he'd met her Scottish mother at a Welsh wedding in England. "There weren't any fights at the wedding," he told her, "but the makings were there."

The columns of boys and girls stopped in front of the train station. On entering, Mr. Blatt counted them. A network of arched steel beams supported the glass-paneled ceiling that seemed twenty stories high. Most of the children had never been in a train station. They stood with their faces turned toward the ceiling, the sound of voices and footsteps echoing off the stone, walls and marble floor.

Mr. Blatt went to a ticket window, signed a document and returned to the group with forty tickets.

The man behind the brass bars of the window made a sign of the cross, as the children carried their clothes boxes toward the train tracks.

There was a long wall with openings leading to tracks numbered, one through twelve. Large black signs with white numbers hung over each entrance, the smell of soot from the train engines permeated the air. A large round clock high on the wall showed it was eighteen minutes before the train was scheduled to leave.

They walked under sign number "seven" and proceeded down the platform between two trains, until they got to the last coach. Catherine noticed, *New York and Central* was printed in gold letters on the side of each of the brown passenger cars. Ahead, she saw a man from the Society for Children. He had two large cardboard containers filled with box lunches. He unloaded them from a flatbed cart, stacking them on the enclosed platform at the front of their coach.

"Boys sit in the front seats, and the girls behind," Miss Hawthorne shouted, pointing to the coach entrance.

A conductor, standing next to portable steps he placed at the coach entrance, assisted the children up the steps. He took clothes boxes from the younger children and slid them forward on the metal floor for them to take.

Once inside, the smaller children stood on the seats or arm rests to put their clothes boxes on the overhead racks. Mrs. Palmer helped some, while controlling the flow of children into the coach.

"Stay close to me, so we can sit together," Monica said to Catherine, climbing the steps.

Mrs. Palmer stood in the aisle, making sure there were two children to each seat, before anyone could move on to the next row.

"Aaawwww! I wanted a window seat," one of the boys pouted.

"Take turns with the other boy," Mrs. Palmer said, guiding him into a seat.

Catherine and Monica were two of the first four girls to board the train. They waddled down the aisle, their clothes boxes bumping against armrests of the seats. They were directed into a seat two rows behind Brian and Jason. Catherine placed her clothes box in the overhead rack and slid across the soft, brown velour covering the seat.

When everyone was in place, Harvey Blatt walked through the coach, counting the children. "They're all here," he announced to the women.

Edna Palmer and Alice Hawthorne sat in seats at the front of the coach. Harvey Blatt sat in the back, so he could observe everyone.

Edna stood and faced the children. "Listen to me," she said, loudly. "The train will be moving very soon, and I have a few things to tell you." She paused and glared at a boy laughing and whispering to his seat partner, until he saw her and sat at attention.

"First of all," she continued, "I want to thank you children for your good behavior this morning. We will be riding for two days before arriving at our first destination in Illinois. It will be a nice ride through the countryside, enjoying the scenery and animals we'll see along the way. There are two blankets in the rack above you, to cover yourselves at night." Edna stepped back to the door of a small compartment in the corner of the coach. She placed her hand against the door, "This is a water closet, for our use only. This is where you will wash and change clothes when necessary. Are there any questions?"

"When do we eat lunch?" a little boy in front of her asked, sheepishly.

Edna smiled. "For those of you who didn't hear the question, I was asked, 'when do we eat lunch?' " Edna took three steps down the aisle. "Box lunches will be passed out at 11:30. If you are interested, we do have bags of apples at Mr. Blatt's seat. You can take one whenever you want."

The train jerked forward, knocking Edna off balance. Quickly, she sat in her seat so she wouldn't fall. Edna was glad Alice was thin, or sitting together would be a problem.

As the train backed out of the station, most of the children looked out the window, amazed at the number of train tracks spread across the rail-yard. Four tracks away, another passenger train, billowing clouds of black smoke, pulled into the station.

After ten hours of rolling past open fields and small towns, the children were restless and bored. Monica noticed two boys across the aisle looking at her repeatedly, then put their heads together and giggle. She knew they were making jokes about the size of her large breasts.

She had experienced it many times before, so she turned toward the window and ignored them.

Catherine stood to sneak a peek at what Brian was doing. He was in his seat looking down, as though he was reading something. She was weary of sitting, so she went to the water closet to wash her hands. On her return, she brushed against Brian's shoulder, continuing on to the back door of the coach. Catherine looked behind her, in the reflection of the door's window and smiled. "It worked," she mumbled. Catherine hung on to a horizontal brass bar below the rear door's window, leaving enough room for Brian to stand next to her.

"Jason is sleeping and I was tired of sitting," Brian said. He leaned against the door with his shoulder and looked out the window.

"I was bored," Catherine said, rolling back on her heels. "I thought I'd look out the back door and watch the miles slip away. Notice how the rails seem to come together in the distance." While still gripping the brass bar, she moved to the center of the door, nearer to Brian. "The rails appear to be pointing to our past."

Brian grabbed the brass bar on the door, pulling himself closer to Catherine. "We must be rolling over hundreds of railroad ties, every minute." He looked down at the ties, as they shot out from under the train, getting lost in the distance. "Clickity-clack, clickity-clack," he groaned, imitating the train wheels. "It sounds as though the train is counting off the miles." Brian moved behind Catherine, while still gripping the brass bar with one hand. "I wonder what Illinois is like? Does it have mountains, or big lakes? It's south of New York, but I don't think it's far enough south to be hot all year."

"Chicago is in Illinois," Catherine informed him. "It's a big city, but I don't think we're going there, or we would have been told that." It was getting darker and the sun had turned into a red-orange ball, sinking towards the horizon. As it got dark, Catherine could see Brian's reflection in the window more clearly.

"Big cities have enough orphans," Brian said. "We'll probably go to small towns." He reached around Catherine and put his other hand on the brass bar.

Being so close, Catherine wondered whether Brian was pretending he had his arms around her.

"It'll probably be difficult to sleep tonight," he said. "I'm sure these seats won't be comfortable."

Monica looked over the back of her seat for Catherine. *My goodness. They don't need me.*

"Look. There's a full moon," Brian whispered. "When it's completely dark, we will be able to see it better."

Catherine looked at Brian's reflection in the window. He wasn't looking up at the moon. He was looking down at her. She was elated.

Jason woke from his nap and searched the coach for Brian. He saw him standing at the back door with Catherine. Jason wasn't as intuitive as Monica, so he slid out of his seat and joined them. After a few minutes, Monica could see that Jason wasn't going to leave them alone, so she joined them.

Jason was talking in a serious tone. "I thought about living on the streets hustling coins, then I decided, if I'm lucky, I might get a nice home. If not, I could run away and get a job, or steal my living in a big city."

"I don't want to live on the streets," Brian said. "I want to finish school, to become an engineer and construct bridges and buildings. Had I stayed in Gresham, working in the cigar factory, I would never have gotten a chance to go to school. Then again, whether I'm adopted or not, I might not be sent to school. If I hate where I'm living, I'll leave. But I hope I don't have to."

Harvey Blatt was sitting in the last seat near the back door, listening to their conversation. He smiled. He'd heard that kind of talk many times before.

Edna Palmer sat with her hands folded on her lap, rocking gently with the movement of the train. Alice slept next to her, her head on a small, white pillow wedged between the back of her seat and the window. It was almost 11:30 p.m. and the coach was dark, save for a row of four dim lights built into the varnished wooden ceiling. Except for three teenage girls, whispering about a home they hoped to find, the girls were asleep.

There were also boys pointing to objects of interest beyond their window. If it weren't for clear skies and a bright moon, they wouldn't have been able to see anything, except for an occasional streetlight as they sped through small towns.

From time-to-time, they saw a person walking or driving a horse-drawn wagon down a dirt road, or a tree-lined street. Most of the houses in the towns were totally dark inside, except for a random few with lantern light flickering in one of its rooms.

Edna liked sitting in the dark, looking out at the country scenes. She would get goose bumps each time the train whistle wailed into the darkness, approaching a sleepy town.

Edna stood and faced the back of the coach, investigating all the children. The teenagers who had been whispering were now pretending to be asleep. The darkness and rhythmic, klickity-klack, klickity-klack of the train wheels had lulled the younger children to sleep. A foot, arm, or leg, jutted out from a seat into the aisle.

Edna walked to the end of the coach where Harvey Blatt was sleeping, looking at every child along the way. When she began working with orphans fifteen years ago, she cried for them occasionally, knowing that some would continue to be unloved and abused, one way or another. To shed those thoughts, Edna recalled letters orphans sent to the Society, thanking it for finding them a good home and a wonderful new life. Some would write of being given a dog or a pony, and the most unimaginable gift of all, a bedroom of their own. One little girl wrote them a letter telling of how her new parents treated her like a princess. *Who decides their destiny?* Edna wondered.

Chapter Two

At 9:40 a.m., the train stopped in Stockton, a small town in central Ohio. Miss Hawthorne stood at the front of the coach and clapped her hands. "Listen to me," she said in an assertive tone. "The train is stopping here to get water for the engine. Meanwhile, we will cross the street to the Covenant Church and eat breakfast." She paused, while the children turned their heads to look at the church. "We have only forty-five minutes to eat and return to the train, so follow me *now* and line up on the station platform.

Brian followed Jason toward the front of the coach. Placing his hand on Jason's shoulder, and whispered firmly, "Do *not* tell Catherine or Monica, about us bedding with women to earn our living. They would never understand how desperate we were, living on New York's streets."

Jason looked over his shoulder at him. "Relax. I never intended to."

Within two minutes, the hungry children were off the train and lined up in random order. With the help of her index finger, Edna Palmer counted the children walking toward the street. She led them past Harvey Blatt, standing in the center of the dirt and gravel street, swinging his arm to hurry the children along.

The white frame church was small, sitting on a stone block foundation. Three concrete stairs led to a pair of varnished doors. Above the doors was a round window of blue glass, a white cross at its center. Next to the church was another white frame building of equal size. *Christ's Hall* was written in black letters above its opened doors. Women volunteers waited inside to feed the children. Filing into the hall, sparrows and robins chirped in the surrounding trees, creating a pleasant atmosphere.

There were five rectangular tables, with eight chairs around each. All place settings had a glass of milk and a plate filled with homemade applesauce, scrambled eggs and two fried sausages. A plate of sliced potato bread was at the center of the tables. Next to each plate, there were three freshly baked cinnamon cookies on white paper napkins.

Before eating, a volunteer led the children in a short prayer of thanks. "May the King of everlasting glory make us partakers of the heavenly table, Amen."

One volunteer, a heavy-set grandmotherly type, with her white hair combed into a bun at the top of her head, came to their table with a big smile. "There is plenty of milk, so if you want more, just ask." She stood there a minute looking at each child. The expression on her face altered between *How sweet* and *Poor things*. She gave out with a sigh and walked away.

After one bite, Brian remarked, "I like this sausage. I bet it's made with pork."

Catherine pushed her plate toward him. "You can have one of mine, if you like. They're so big, one is enough for me."

Brian smiled at her. "Thanks!"

As though it were something evil, Catherine picked up a sausage with her fingers and dropped it on his plate. "I wonder who will be adopted tomorrow morning," she questioned in a concerned tone.

Brian was cutting the sausage into small pieces. "I don't think there are many people who want to adopt kids our age, so there's a good chance we'll be together tomorrow night."

Her question didn't specifically mention Brian and herself, but his answer referred to them staying together. *He is concerned about us being separated*, she thought. *He must like me.* She was delighted for the moment and then realized they would probably be separated forever. She stirred her spoon in the applesauce, listening to the birds singing outside.

Monica looked at the round clock on the wall. "The train leaves in ten minutes. I wish we could walk around town for a while. I'm tired of sitting."

Jason tilted his head back and drank the last of his milk, accidentally banging the glass on the table. "One day on the train already," he said, wiping his mouth with his shirtsleeve. "How many more I wonder? I can't wait to sleep in a bed."

Alice Hawthorne stood between the tables and clapped her hands once again. "Back to the train boys and girls. Be sure you don't leave a coat or sweater behind … or your cookies."

As the children prepared to leave, sounds of numerous chairs sliding on the floor echoed through the room. The volunteers who served them breakfast were standing like pillars, watching the children walk toward the doors, each women quietly sending love and hope with them.

Edna Palmer counted the children as they hurried across the street. The engineer watched the children board the train and tooted the whistle, signaling the train was about to leave. The children scampered back to their seats, then watched trees, light poles and buildings slide behind them until they rolled past farmers' fields.

Monica stood on the seat to get her clothes box from the overhead rack. "Today is cooler than yesterday, so I'll wear a sweater," she said to Catherine. "It won't be a difficult choice, since I only have one." Monica raised the top of the box and set it on the floor. There was a photograph standing on end against the side of the box. She pulled it out and showed it to Catherine. "This is my father. Isn't he handsome?" Monica's father was standing on wooden stairs of a frame house. He was slender, wearing a white shirt with sleeves rolled up to his elbows, and dark pants with suspenders. His eyes were like black peas, and he had a five-inch beard.

Catherine didn't think he was good looking at all. "He is handsome," she remarked, leaning back into her seat. "You must be very proud of him."

Monica pulled her brown sweater from the box. "I am. Father delivered milk house-to-house and he had the biggest route in town. His boss said he was perfect for that kind of work." Monica placed the picture in the box and put her arms through the sleeves of the sweater. "After my mother died of pneumonia, my father started drinking heavily. One night, when he was drunk, a man killed him and took his money. So here I am, riding the orphan train."

"Do you have a picture of your mother?" Catherine asked.

"No. This is the only picture I have. I'd die, if I lost it." Monica buttoned the bottom three buttons of her sweater and put the lid on the clothes box. "Do you have pictures of your parents?"

"One of my parents together, and one of just my father," Catherine answered. "My mother died of pneumonia when I was ten. Three months ago, my father died in a garment factory fire. He was a supervisor and stayed in the fire, helping women and girls to a safe stairwell. Eventually, he was overcome by smoke. After that, I stayed with neighbors. They couldn't afford to keep me because they had three children of their own." Catherine stared into space for a moment. "I'll show you the pictures later, when I go into my clothes box."

They remained in their seats, looking at the scenery. Small towns came and went. Catherine stood on the seat to get a blanket from the overhead rack. She spread it across her and Monica's lap, and settled back in her seat. A few minutes later, both girls were almost asleep.

"Look! Indians!" a boy yelled. "Eight of them." Children rushed to the left side of the coach, to see where he was pointing. They were approximately eighty feet from the train. Three Indians were riding bareback on brown and white ponies, while five Indians walked alongside them, raising dust in the open field. Two of the braves on horseback looked toward the train, as if they hated its presence. Those walking looked straight ahead, as though the train didn't exist. All but one was wrapped in a blanket, and one brave had a single feather in his hair. Two squaws carried a wicker basket, with a bright red cloth covering its contents.

"I can't believe I'm seeing real Indians," a girl gasped. "Miss Hawthorne! Miss Hawthorne! Are those real Indians?"

Alice stood behind the wall of children looking out of the window. "My goodness! They certainly are. I've never seen Indians before." She had, but she wanted the children to feel special.

"I saw them first," the boy announced, with pride.

"Who cares," a girl responded.

"Wow! I never saw Indians before, either," Jason gasped. "I wonder whether there'll be Indians where we're gunna live?"

A little girl standing in the aisle turned to the boy behind her. With a deep frown, she said, "Stop pushing. You're squishing me."

"Think they'll attack us?" a wide-eyed boy in denim pants asked.

"What kind of Indians are they?" Jason asked Miss Hawthorne.

"I can't be sure, but they could be Chippewa or Shawnee," Alice answered. "They live in this territory. But then, other tribes live around here, too."

Little Becky was sitting at a window watching the Indians, quietly, staring. As the train moved on, forty heads turned slowly toward the rear of the train until the Indians appeared as dots on the landscape.

"Back to your seats and clear the aisle," Edna yelled from the front of the coach. The children dispersed and returned to their seats, still chattering about the Indians. A half hour later, Edna and Alice passed out box lunches consisting of corn cakes filled with minced beef, two carrots, hardtack, one apple, a small bottle of apple cider and a chocolate bar. When they finished eating and the garbage had been collected, Alice and Edna used the next hour telling short stories, jokes, and riddles to the children.

That evening, Catherine and Monica stood by the back door of the coach. Brian and Jason eventually joined them. Catherine waited to see if Brian would stand next to her. She was pleased when he did.

"We're in Indiana now," Brian stated. "Mr. Blatt said, we'll be eating supper in a town called Muncie." He paused before continuing. "Tomorrow we wake up in Illinois." Brian glanced at Catherine. "Half a day and we'll be at our first stop for adoption."

Catherine understood he was referring to them being separated. She gave him a faint smile, "We're in God's hands."

"Like I said before," Jason repeated. "If I don't like where I'm at, I'll run away."

"You'll probably like your new home," Monica assured him. "It would have to be awful for me to run away."

Chapter Three

Bridie McDonald stood on a park-like strip of grass between the cobblestone street and the railroad station, waiting for the train to arrive. The station was at the end of the town square with a statue of Abraham Lincoln in the center of the street. Well-maintained brick and frame buildings lined the other three sides of the square, each with tidy little shops and apartments above.

She closed her eyes and turned her face to the sun, concentrating on its warming effect. The sounds of buggies and heavy wagons, and the clop, clop, clop of horseshoes pounded the brick street behind her. There were colorful flowerbeds at each end of the lawn. It was almost mid-June and the white daisies, blue flax and red salvia bloomed to full glory. The name, *Newberry, Illinois,* was displayed handsomely in gold letters on a forest green sign mounted on the tan brick wall of the station.

Bridie wore a pale yellow dress, with small printed flowers and round pearl buttons running up the center of her bodice to a white lace collar. Her strawberry-blond hair was rolled to the top of her head, with two curved green combs holding it in place. She stood erect, an olive-green parasol hanging from her wrist. Bridie was thirty-seven years old and came to the station with a purpose.

Bridie opened her eyes and looked down the silver rails into the distance, hoping to see a train. The only movement she saw were birds, chasing erratically under a blue sky, with occasional puffs of white clouds. The other side of the tracks was flat land that spread endlessly in both directions. Young corn was making its presence known. "Knee high by the Fourth of July," she recited to herself.

She was startled when someone called her name. Bridie turned toward the street and saw Margaret and Tom Holmgren, sitting in their black buggy, its black canvas top folded back. Their horse, Dandy, was a soft gray color that contrasted nicely with the black buggy.

Bridie walked slowly through the grass, as Margaret and Tom stepped to the ground. Tom tied the horse to a hitching post, while Margaret advanced toward her. She was wearing a new, dark brown waistcoat and ivory blouse. Her black curly hair was cut shorter than what was socially acceptable by some people's standards. When they met, and faced each other, their eyes exactly parallel.

"Trying for a son again?" Bridie asked, with a big smile. "I hope you have better luck this time."

"We haven't succeeded on our own, and I don't believe we will. I'd take a boy or a girl, but Tom wants a son. We'll see what the Orphan Train brings this time."

Tom was brushing dust from his blue short-coat and gray slacks as he caught up to the women. He stood a head above them, his hazel eyes looking down at Bridie. In a soft-spoken voice, he greeted her.

Bridie smiled at him, "How are your nerves on such an important day?"

"A little shaken, I must admit. All we can do is try."

"You must find someone, too," Margaret added. "If not, who would you leave your money to?"

Tom interrupted. "I think a train is coming. Isn't that black smoke in the distance?"

Margaret agreed. "Shall we walk toward the station?"

Strolling across the grass, Tom folded his hands behind his back. He looked at Bridie. "What kind of girl are you looking for? Any special characteristics?"

"I really don't know," Bridie answered. "I assume I will know intuitively when I see her. You know, I'll hear chimes and bells, or something."

"This is only the third Orphan Train to stop here in two years, so our chances aren't abundant," Margaret said. "Let's face it, if St. Louis wasn't forty miles away, that train wouldn't stop here at all. With only 1,800 people in the community, they would probably roll past us."

"No need to panic," Tom said. "This is an important decision and we must do it carefully. We don't want to be sorry later."

"The train is getting close," Bridie said. "Let's walk faster, so we don't get engulfed in black smoke." Bridie watched other couples, young and old, coming to look at the children, each for their own reasons. There were people who wanted to give love and a home to a child, while some came out of curiosity. Others, still, were looking for laborers.

Margaret tapped Bridie's shoulder. "Look," she whispered, so Tom couldn't hear. "There's Nerine Booker walking past Morton's Shoe Store. She's walking toward her apartment. I wonder where she slept last night?"

"She's an, 'Angel of Mercy,'" Bridie responded, softly. "Nerine tends to the needs of the community."

"The male community," Margaret stressed. "And every Sunday, she has the loudest voice in the choir."

"Could be her ecstasy is slow in arriving." Bridie replied.

They climbed five wooden stairs to the platform and entered the station. To their right, bench seats had been pushed back against the walls, so children could be displayed. A table, chair, and wire wastebasket had been set in the corner of the room for conducting the adoptions. Polished brass cuspidors stood against the walls in various locations throughout the room. The ticket window at their left was protected with black iron bars. A large calendar with a picture of a passenger train hung on the wall next to it.

Two more couples walked into the station. Bridie counted sixteen couples waiting for the children. She looked out of the east window, as the train approached the station. The engine was big and black, with a cowcatcher pointing the way. The building vibrated slightly, as it slowly rolled past with its bell clanging. Clouds of black smoke whipped around the building and the smell of soot filled the room. Bridie looked at the small pendulum clock mounted on the wall. It was forty-three minutes past ten, when the train came to a stop.

Heads of prospective parents began to bob about, anxious for their first glance at the children. A man in a wrinkled, inexpensive black suit stepped down from a passenger car, carrying a black leather briefcase.

A tall, slender woman got off the train behind him and stood on the platform, looking back into the passenger car. A husky woman in a gray dress led the children off the train and lined them two abreast along the platform. The children were carrying a brown case, with a strap buckled around it.

The man in the black suit went ahead of the others, pushing through the two doors on the trackside of the station. He went to the table in the corner of the room and took papers from inside his briefcase, placing them into three stacks on the table. The woman in the gray dress came through the doors, with the children following. She lined them against the wall—the smaller children in front. Thirty-seven poorly dressed orphans stood erect, their names printed in large black letters on white cards pinned to their shirt or blouse.

The man in the black suit stepped in front of the children and faced the crowd. "My name is Harvey Blatt, an agent for the Society For Children. I want to thank you dear people for coming here today to meet these lovely children. My experience these past twelve years has shown me the glorious rewards people like you and the children have gained through adoption. To give a hapless child a home is about the kindest deed a person can undertake, a lifetime commitment that can be gratifying until your dying days. We also know that not every match is made in heaven, so you do have the opportunity to return a child to the Society if the relationship is not working. But let me tell you, less than ten percent of the children adopted have been returned. This is an opportunity for you to fulfill a dream, or a need, or simply perform a kindness. If that child you desire is here, please step up to the table where I will be sitting, and we can fill out the necessary papers. Bless you, and thank you for coming."

A low rumble of voices spread through the room, as couples leaned sideways or stood on their toes to examine the children. A nicely dressed man and woman burst out of the crowd and ran to the smaller children standing in the front row. The woman quickly swept Becky into her arms, so no one else could claim her. She smiled and said something to Becky, who stared at her momentarily, then fully realized what was happening and flung her arms around the woman's neck, still clinging to her ragged doll. Becky's eyes gleamed with excitement, as she brandished a broad smile. She sat back in the woman's arms, looking over her shoulder at Jenny and the other children, as if saying, "Look, these people want me." The couple, obviously thrilled with their find, smiled at each other, while tears trickled down the woman's cheeks.

Catherine was elated for Becky. She watched the three of them go over to Mr. Blatt sitting at his desk. Catherine looked at Brian standing at her side, then at the crowd staring at them, as if they were livestock being auctioned. She decided to search the crowd for a kind face and try to gain attention by smiling.

Catherine noticed Jason being looked over by an elderly couple with gray hair. The man was in overalls, the woman in a white bonnet and gray cotton dress. He stepped up to Jason, and with his dirty hand, squeezed Jason's biceps and thighs. When he reached for Jason's mouth to look at his teeth, Jason frowned and jerked away. "Too skinny," the old man said, walking away.

Monica watched the eyes of the people looking at them, hoping to find someone showing interest in her. She wanted to find a home *now*, rather than ride the train from town to town and possibly return to New York City.

Bridie looked quickly at the girls, while Margaret and Tom talked with excitement. Bridie didn't hear what they were saying, because she was busy conducting her own search.

Tom stepped out of the crowd and walked to a boy at the end of the second row. The name printed on the boy's card read *Brian Hampton*. Tom was smiling and talking to Brian, as though they were old acquaintances.

Brian was lean and muscular. His curly black hair and light blue eyes were an appealing combination with his sharp, linear features.

Tom said something that made Brian smile. Margaret and Bridie watched.

"Is he handsome, or is he?" Margaret asked. "Look at his beautiful blue eyes. He seems alert, intelligent, and healthy. We both like him." She watched Tom go to the table in the corner of the room. Margaret became excited, watching him sign papers. When Margaret turned to face Bridie, she noticed her looking toward Brian. "Can't keep your eyes off him, eh?"

"I'm not looking at the boy," Bridie responded. "Look at the girl standing next to him. Her name is Catherine Hayes." The two women examined her the best they could at that distance. Bridie took Margaret by the arm and they stepped forward through the crowd, so they could get closer to Catherine.

"My dear Bridie, she is precious. She has the same strawberry blond hair as you, the same complexion, and her face is much like yours. Looking at her is like looking at you twenty years ago. Is there something you haven't told me about your past?"

"I hear chimes," Bridie said, nervously. "She's the one. The girl I've been looking for."

They watched Tom return to Brian and talk again. Tom took his arm to lead him away.

Brian looked at Catherine.

She grabbed his other arm, as if to hold him back and let go immediately, knowing she didn't have the right.

"Did you see that," Margaret said. "They didn't want to be separated. According to their name tags, they aren't brother and sister."

"I saw it clearly," Bridie replied. "Did you see the look on their faces. Obviously, their feelings are mutual." Bridie knew first hand how it felt to lose someone she'd cared for.

"If you hear chimes, why are you waiting?" Margaret asked. "Oh! Oh! Too late, the Porters are back. They seem to like her."

"Too late, hell," Bridie snapped. She walked directly to Catherine and interrupted their conversation. "Catherine Hayes. That's a fine Irish name. Were both your parents Irish?"

"Excuse me, Bridie," Martha Porter said, indignantly. "We were talking to this young lady and we are quite interested in her."

"I can appreciate that," Bridie responded, "But I don't want to talk. I would like to take her home with me."

Catherine was embarrassed, yet flattered to be of interest to two families. She looked to the floor to avoid eye contact with the women.

Martha Porter turned to her husband and glared at him. "Henry," she said, sharply, then nodded toward the table in the corner of the room

Bridie raised her hand to stop Henry. "I'm sure we can settle this in a friendly manner," she said, firmly. "Since all three of us are interested in Catherine, why don't we let her choose where she would like to live? After all, her interests are our foremost concern, are they not?"

"Of course." Martha nodded, with pursed lips. She looked at Henry for his approval and faced Bridie again. "I guess that would be fair." Martha took a handkerchief from her purse to wipe her glasses.

Bridie walked up to Catherine and smiled. "Pick up your clothes box, my dear, and we'll go where we can have privacy."

They moved along the wall, away from the other children. Catherine set her box on the floor and faced the three adults.

Bridie spoke to Catherine, so the Porters could hear everything she was saying. "You are about to make a very important decision, my dear, but please, don't be nervous." Bridie pointed toward the Porters. "Mr. and Mrs. Porter are fine people and can give you a good home. My name is Bridie McDonald and I would do the same. So, you really can't make a bad decision. Listen to what we have to say, then make your choice."

Catherine's arms were hanging down in front of her, hands clasped together. She smiled and nodded. Catherine looked at the Porters and Bridie, and said a silent prayer for guidance.

Bridie stepped away from Catherine and turned to Martha. "You go first, and say what you have to say. I'll say my piece when you're finished."

"Thank you," Martha said, stepping forward. She looked into Catherine's eyes to affirm the sincerity of her words. "First of all, I want you to know we are not looking for a girl to slave for us. Mr. Porter and I are looking for a daughter we can love and treat as our own. We never had children, that being the Lord's decision, but we would like to have a daughter before we're too old." Martha's hands were fidgeting with her handkerchief, as she talked. "We would expect you to attend school and you could study a musical instrument, if you like. You would have your own bedroom and a closet full of clothes. Our home is only five miles from town and we come into Newberry quite often. With us, you would have two parents to care for you. You appear to be a fine girl and we would like to have you come live with us."

Catherine smiled, her hands still clasped in front of her. "Thank you, Mrs. Porter. You must be nice people, or you wouldn't be willing to take a stranger into your home."

Mr. Porter nodded and smiled to Catherine, as though agreeing with his wife's words. Martha stepped back and stood next to her husband.

Bridie stepped forward, determined to have Catherine. "As I said before, my dear, the Porters and I can give you a nice life. Both of us would be good to you, and we would expect you to be good for us.

With them, you would have a nice home in the country. With me, you would live here in Newberry. The decision is yours."

Martha nodded to Bridie, implying she appreciated the kind words and fair play.

Bridie stepped back and stood next to the Porters. Smiling at Catherine, Bridie added, "By the way, that boy Brian, the one who was standing next to you, he was adopted by Mr. and Mrs. Thomas Holmgren. I know he will have a good home with them because they are very good friends of mine and live only two streets from me."

Catherine understood Bridie's implication and tried not to smile, but failed.

Bridie glanced at the Holmgrens at Mr. Blatt's table. Margaret was bent over, signing papers. *Don't go away folks*, Bridie thought, *I'll be there in a minute.*

Catherine was silent, looking back and forth at Bridie and the Porters, making it appear it was a difficult decision.

How kind of her to pretend, Bridie thought. *Catherine and I are going to get along just fine.*

Catherine took a deep breath and looked at the Porters. "Thank you for considering me, but I think I would rather live in town, if you don't mind."

Bridie maintained a calm exterior, while screaming for joy within. She was falling more in love with Catherine every minute. Bridie turned to the Porters who appeared unsettled. "I want to thank you for being gracious about this. Catherine must be a city girl."

Bridie waited until the Porters walked away, then took Catherine by the hand and led her to Mr. Blatt. "We are going to have fun together," Bridie assured her.

Catherine looked at Bridie. "I don't know what to say at the moment. Give me time and I'll express what I feel."

"Take all the time you need," Bridie replied. They arrived at the table, as the Holmgrens were leaving. They were obviously very happy, unaware of anyone around them. Bridie tapped Margaret on the arm with her olive-green umbrella. "Wait for us. We'll be out in a few minutes." Bridie looked at Brian, "It appears Catherine and I will be your neighbors."

Brian noticed Bridie holding Catherine's hand. "I'm sure you'll like Catherine." He didn't smile, but his eyes showed he was delighted with the turn of events.

Margaret took Brian's arm. "We'll wait for you outside."

Catherine watched Brian and the Holmgrens walk away, then turned her eyes to Bridie. "I guess I'm yours."

Bridie smiled, "And I'm yours."

Mr. Blatt placed three documents in front of Bridie. "This will just take a few moments," he said, filling out the forms.

Catherine looked back at the rows of children. "Could I say goodbye to friends?" she asked.

"Yes, my dear, but don't take too long."

Catherine went back to Monica. "I didn't want to leave before saying 'goodbye.' I think I'm going to like it here. Miss McDonald, the lady adopting me, seems very nice. Brian will be living here, too."

"I can't believe you and Brian have been adopted in the same town," Monica said. "I hope you have a great life." Monica was jealous when Catherine was chosen, but she truly wished her happiness.

"You can write me and let me know where you live," Catherine said. "Remember, I will be living with Bridie McDonald in Newberry, Illinois. If you address it that way, I should get your letter."

"I can't write," Monica replied, with embarrassment.

Catherine was surprised. "Then have someone write it for you." Catherine kissed Monica on the cheek. "I must go. Good luck!" She ran past Jason. "Goodbye and good luck," she said, waving to him.

Jason forced a smile and waved back, pretending it didn't hurt to be left behind.

When Catherine returned, Bridie was putting the folded adoption papers in her drawstring purse. "Come, daughter," Bridie said.

"Lead the way ..." Catherine paused. She couldn't say the word. She buried her face in her hands and began to cry.

Bridie rushed to Catherine's side and apologized, putting her arms around her. "I'm sorry, my dear. That was insensitive of me. You don't have to call me "mother." I could never take her place." Bridie began slowly stroking her head. "Bridie will be good enough for now."

Bridie took a handkerchief from her purse and handed it to Catherine. "I have a cure for that. Let's walk out into the sunshine."

The Holmgrens were waiting on the lawn near their black buggy. Margaret waved, filled with excitement and glowing with pride. She began talking to Bridie, long before she was within range to hear.

Crossing the lawn, Bridie noticed Brian's eyes focused on Catherine. When they got closer to him, his vision became less selective, so his true interest wouldn't be obvious.

"Let's celebrate," Margaret said, eagerly. "We need to get acquainted."

Tom put his arm around Margaret and gave her a hard tug. It wasn't an affectionate gesture, but one suggesting she calm down.

"I agree," Bridie said. "But first, I think Catherine and Brian should remove their name tags."

They all chuckled and smiled at the oversight.

"You may want to keep those name tags," Bridie continued. "You know, something to look at thirty years from now. I also suggest you keep the clothes boxes for the same reason." Bridie looked at Catherine. "These are my friends, Margaret and Tom Holmgren. I believe you know the other fellow."

Catherine smiled and nodded meekly. "Nice to meet you."

Margaret gripped Brian's arm, leading him two steps forward. "This is Bridie McDonald. You won't have trouble liking her. She's easy to get along with and has been a good friend for many years."

Brian smiled. "It's a pleasure to meet you. You people are so friendly, I'm starting to feel at home already."

"You appear to be a nice boy," Bridie responded. "I think all of us are going to have a good relationship." Bridie looked toward Margaret and Tom. "May I suggest we go to Kitty's Confectionery to celebrate our new relationships?"

"Good idea," Tom agreed. "I have a lock box under the buggy seat. We can put their luggage in there."

Margaret stepped up to Catherine and took her hand. "When I first saw you, I was amazed at how much you resemble Bridie when she was a girl. One would think you were related."

Catherine faced Bridie. "When I first saw you, I noticed we have the same hair color. If you have pictures of when you were a school girl, I'd like to see them."

"I'd be delighted to show you what pictures I have of myself and my family," Bridie assured her. "There aren't many, but enough to show a few years of our McDonald clan." Bridie removed her umbrella from her arm and pointed it at the buggy. "There is only room for three, so Catherine and I will walk to Kitty's."

"That's true," Margaret replied, heading toward the men.

"We go this way," Bridie said, leading Catherine in the opposite direction. "Kitty's is in the second block beyond the square." They stopped at the corner and watched the Holmgren's buggy circle around Abraham Lincoln's statue and proceed down Main Street.

Before crossing, they waited for a farmer and his wagon of potatoes to pass. Then came a tan horse pulling a wagon with five caged pigs, squealing and snorting. "You'll get those smells occasionally," Bridie remarked, as they crossed Polk Street."

Catherine looked around the square and beyond, enjoying the simplistic beauty of her new town. "It's very nice here. It's so clean and quiet, compared to New York City. I'm anxious to see all of Newberry."

"It isn't very big," Bridie declared. "The population is only 1,800, but it's a prosperous little town. We believe it's the nicest town in McDonough County." She noticed Catherine looking at clothes in shop windows. Catherine didn't say anything, but her eyes revealed her desire for new clothes. Bridie looked at Catherine's wrinkled green dress. *Nice color,* she thought, *but it is so New York. It will never do.*

At the end of the block, Les Jasper stepped out of his grocery store and stood under his green and white striped awning. Cases of fruits and vegetables lined the sidewalk in front of his store windows. "Good afternoon, Bridie," he said, with a grand smile. His large body was similar to that of a lumberjack. His red complexion contrasted sharply with the white curly hair and thin mustache. He wiped his hands on his stained, white apron and asked, "Who is this beautiful young lady? Is she a relative? She looks like you as a girl."

Bridie could have kissed him for that comparison. "She's my daughter," Bridie replied. She put her arm around Catherine and introduced her to Mr. Jasper. You'll be seeing him quite often."

Lester's hands stopped in place, as if they were stuck to his apron. "Daughter?" he repeated.

"Yes," she assured him. "Catherine has been my daughter for almost an hour now." Bridie watched the puzzled look on Lester's face.

Suddenly, he realized what Bridie meant. "The train came today," he shouted. "Oh! Oh! How wonderful. What a prize you have." He called into the store. "Gail! Gail! Come quick. Hurry!" He faced Bridie and Catherine again. "Finally, you have your daughter. You couldn't have done better. What a sweet child."

"What is it?" Gail asked, charging out of the store. "Is someone dying?" Gail was plump and a head shorter than Lester.

"Gail, we have good news. Eh! I mean Bridie has good news. This lovely young girl is Catherine." Lester stepped back and smiled, waiting for Gail's response.

Gail understood, immediately. "How wonderful," she smiled, with her hands over her heart. "I saw you going to the train station this morning. You finally fulfilled your dream. She's beautiful." Gail raised a hand to block the sun from her eyes and looked at Catherine again. "How old are you, child?"

Catherine was becoming embarrassed by all the compliments. "I'll be fifteen the seventh of July."

"Next month?" Bridie cried out. "Then I must have a party for you, so I can show you off to my friends. That reminds me. We have friends waiting for us at Kitty's." Bridie smiled at Gail and Lester. "We must go. You'll be seeing Catherine on a regular basis now."

"It was nice meeting you," Catherine said, politely.

"We'll be looking for you," Gail replied, waving to them.

"They are very nice people," Bridie said. "I do most of my grocery shopping there. Mr. Jasper is a member of the volunteer fire department, and Gail sews quilts in her spare time. She's won many ribbons at County Fairs."

"How long have you lived in Newberry?" Catherine asked.

"I was born here. I've had a good life in Newberry and there's no reason for me to leave. Trains take me anywhere I want to go. I'm sure you will like it here, too."

A black buggy was standing at the curb a few yards ahead of them. "Isn't that the Holmgren's buggy?" Catherine asked.

"It is. It's parked in front of Kitty's Confectionery. Margaret is inside, dying to ask you questions."

Kitty's storefront was painted white. Its large window consisted of fifty one-foot square panes of glass. A royal blue awning spanned the width of her shop to protect her customers from the glaring sun. When they entered Kitty's, the top of the door struck a tiny bell announcing their entry. The Holmgrens were reading menus at two tables they had pushed together by the window. Margaret was sitting at the end of the tables, facing the door. The tables were painted white, covered with blue and white checked tablecloths.

"Come Catherine, sit next to me," Margaret said, patting the back of a chair facing Brian. "The pastries are absolutely delicious, and you have a large variety to choose from."

Tom dropped his menu on the table, then sat back and folded his arms. "Brian told me you are from New York City. You'll find Newberry operates at a much slower pace."

"Good," Catherine responded. "I already like Newberry better than New York City. It's clean and quiet, and you people have been so nice. I feel very lucky today, and I hope I never disappoint Bridie."

Bridie beamed at Catherine's kind words. "We are a family now. I can tell by your manner that you had good parents who taught you proper ways."

Kitty came out of the back room and walked directly to Bridie. She stared at Catherine, then Bridie and Catherine again. "You are right, Margaret, Catherine could be a McDonald. Welcome to Newberry, Catherine. I'm Kitty, and anxious to get to know you. Anytime you want to stop for useless conversation, don't hesitate. I'm good at that."

"Thank you. I probably will."

"Do you like lemon?" Bridie asked Catherine.

Catherine rolled her eyes. "I love lemon."

"Then you'll delight in Kitty's lemon tart with cream. Trust me."

"Alright, I'll have that and a cup of tea."

Kitty removed an order pad and pencil from her apron pocket and began to write. "You're the other newcomer, Brian, so you order next," Bridie suggested.

"I'd like the cinnamon and apple twist and a glass of milk, please."

"Good choice," Tom said. "I'll have the same, but with coffee. Sorry ladies, I didn't mean to be rude and order ahead of you, but since Brian wanted the same as me, I thought I'd throw my order in at the same time."

"Impolite cad," Margaret said, jokingly. "For that, you can sleep in the guest bedroom tonight." Margaret paused as a person would, when suddenly surprised by something unexpected. She and Tom looked at each other, as though they had just realized for the first time that their privacy at home was going to be compromised.

Bridie sat back in the chair, folded her hands on the table and looked up at the ceiling. She understood what had just happened.

Margaret turned from Tom and looked up at Kitty. "I'll have a thick slice of raisin-nut bread and tea."

"I'd like a cinnamon bun and black tea," Bridie said. "Bring me a small piece of butter, too." Kitty gathered the menus and returned to the kitchen.

"Look!" Brian shouted suddenly, pointing out to the street. "It's Monica. She's in that wagon. Someone must have adopted her."

Catherine spun around in her chair. Monica was in a buckboard, sitting on a bench seat running the length of the open wagon. The sun was at her back, creating a red outline around her brown hair. A lean, balding man, about forty-five, and a woman dressed in a tan cotton work dress, were sitting in front. The man shook the long leather reins to keep his two black mules moving.

"It's Clay and Sona Peters," Tom said. He looked at Brian. "That girl was on your train today?"

"Yes," Catherine interrupted, watching the wagon disappear down the street. "Where do those people live?"

"Their farm is about a mile from town," Tom answered. "How well do you know Monica?"

"Not very," Catherine answered. "I met her at the Society For Children four days ago. She seems to be a nice girl." She looked at Brian. "Well, I guess we'll be seeing her again."

"Of course," Bridie said. "You can invite her to our house."

"Thank you, Bridie. Then I could get to know her better."

"We all have much to learn about each other," Bridie added, glancing at everyone at the table. "Catherine and I will start the moment we get home."

Catherine turned away from the window and looked at Bridie. "I'm anxious to see your house."

Bridie winked at Catherine. "Our house," she stated, firmly. "And by the way, there is a huge, spring-fed pond behind our house, and a dilapidated little boat house with a row boat, should two people want to go for a boat ride." Bridie glanced at Margaret. It was obvious that neither Catherine nor Brian understood Bridie's implication.

Bridie turned and hung her drawstring purse on the back of the chair, next to her umbrella. "What is Gresham, Connecticut like?" Bridie asked, Brian.

"It's nice and quiet there; good people, good country. As I said, it's about the size of Newberry, but not as fancy."

"Fancy, you say?" Bridie responded, as if surprised by his statement. "We are a clean community, but I've never heard anyone call Newberry 'fancy.' But thank you for the compliment."

Kitty came from the back of the shop balancing a large silver tray filled with colorful pastries on small white dishes with a thin blue border. She served Tom first and continued around the table. Kitty hesitated before leaving. "I'd like to say something from deep in my heart, and I hope I'm not stepping out of line."

They all paused, looking up at her, waiting for her to speak.

Kitty took a deep breath and exhaled quickly. "I believe this to be a great day," Kitty continued, with alternating glances at the five of them. "All of you has had a need for someone, and today that need was met, and so beautifully. Bridie ... Tom ... Margaret, what you did today was as kind a deed as anyone can do. You gave hope and security to two children with an uncertain future, and because of you, their lives will be better." Kitty turned to Catherine and Brian. "And at the same time, you two children will improve the quality of life for Bridie, Tom and Margaret. They need you, as much as you need them. They are wonderful people and you two appear to be fine children. I wish all of you, complete happiness."

"Thank you, Kitty," Bridie responded, with a smile and soft clapping of her hands.

Tom and Margaret looked at each other, "We appreciate those kind words, Kitty," Tom said, placing his hand on Brian's shoulder. "I, too, think we are fortunate to have Brian and Catherine with us, and I'm looking forward to a fantastic future with them."

Kitty noticed the children were silent, somewhat embarrassed by the flattering conversation. "I'll leave you people alone, so you can eat. Being that this is your first celebration together, I'm making it my treat."

"Thank you, Kitty," Tom said, as she walked away.

They ate their pastries, while volunteering information about themselves and asking questions of others. By the time they were finished eating, Catherine and Brian became more relaxed toward their new parents, as well as each other.

Tom stood next to the table, removing a slender black cigar from inside his coat, then rolled it between his thumb and index finger as the others stood to leave.

"This has been fun," Margaret said, walking to their buggy. She glanced at Bridie and gestured "Good-bye" by wiggling her fingers at her. "I'll plan a dinner for the five of us for next weekend." She kissed Catherine on the cheek and climbed into the buggy.

"Good night," Brian said, to Bridie. "If you need any chores done at your place, let me know. I'll be glad to help."

"I will remember that," Bridie responded. "Thank you for the offer." She fully understood why he was eager to do work at her house.

Tom flipped the reins and Dandy pulled them down the street. Brian leaned out over the side of the buggy and waved.

"My clothes!" Catherine shouted, as she watched the buggy turn the corner.

"Don't worry," Bridie said, "Tom will put your clothes inside our house."

"Does he have a key?"

"Most people in small towns don't lock their doors. We trust our neighbors."

"You can't do that in New York City," Catherine assured her. "People would steal everything you own."

Bridie and Catherine looked at shoes, hats and dresses in store windows, as they walked toward home. It was a sunny Saturday afternoon and Main Street was busy with shoppers and street traffic.

"I'm eager to see our house and how you've furnished it," Catherine said. She looked at Bridie, with her head tilted to the side, repeating the words, "Our house."

Bridie smiled at Catherine. "I understood your choice of words." They paused to look at a display of fabric in a store window, before she responded. "Our house is quite Victorian. I'm quite fond of Vicky and things of the British Empire. I guess it's in my blood."

Catherine looked at Bridie's reflection in the glass window. "Who is Vicky?"

Bridie chuckled and looked at Catherine's reflection. "Sorry, my dear, I guess you wouldn't know that name. Vicky is an affectionate name the British people have for Queen Victoria. The people look upon her as the mother of all Britain. She has been their queen for sixty years and it is difficult to imagine a Britain without her."

They crossed Powell Street and were in front of the Jasper Grocery Store again. Lester and Gail were busy attending to customers deep inside the store. As they continued walking, Bridie examined the expired clothes Catherine was wearing. She put her hand on Catherine's shoulder and guided her into Carrie's Dress Shop. "I think you should get a few pieces of clothing now. We can do our serious shopping after the weekend."

When they entered the shop, Catherine looked at Bridie. She didn't say a word, but Bridie knew what she was thinking.

"When I saw you at the train station, I knew immediately that I wanted you with me," Bridie said. "I know what responsibilities come with a daughter, and believe me, as Kitty said, I need you, too. Besides, I can afford to buy you anything I care to."

Catherine took Bridie's hand, "Give me time. I didn't know you this morning, and now you are buying me things. I hope I can be that girl you wanted."

Bridie was so pleased with Catherine that she could have cried, had she allowed herself to. "Follow me, Catherine," she said, pointing to the back of the room. "Your dress size is over there." Dresses were hung in bays on both sides of the shop. Bronze gas lamps with white frosted globes were evenly spaced along the walls. There were four display tables in the center of the shop filled with undergarments, belts, stockings, shawls and hair accessories. An array of hats on the back wall caught Catherine's eye. She was amused at the variety. Some were small, similar to skullcaps, while others had wide brims fashioned with colorful plumes and hatpins.

Carrie came out of the back room, carrying a black evening dress with a line of pearls two inches from the neckline. She hung it on a hook mounted under one of the bronze gas lamps, then crossed the room to assist her customers. When Carrie saw it was Bridie, she stopped in the center of the room and looked at Catherine. "Gail Jasper brought the groceries I ordered and told me about your daughter. She's charming, absolutely charming." Carrie stepped forward, examining Catherine head-to-toe. She held out her hand, "I'm Carrie Sutter, an old ... eh, longtime friend of Bridie's. We were classmates in grade school. Welcome to Newberry."

Catherine took Carrie's hand and smiled. "Thank you. I've been in Newberry only a couple of hours and I'm feeling at home already."

"Good!" Carrie replied. She gave Bridie a sly, playful look. "Catherine is a perfect size for her age. We're going to have fun helping her select a wardrobe, aren't we?"

"That was my thinking," Bridie answered. "Let's start with dresses."

Carrie swept her hand before a row of dresses hanging in a bay. "Your size would be in here, Catherine. The casual clothing is across the room."

"I'll have Jack come for the packages we don't carry home," Bridie said, while examining a row of dresses.

"Who's Jack?" Catherine asked, while appraising a beige dress she was holding against her body. She looked up and noticed Bridie and Carrie glance at each other in a strange way.

"You two look at dresses," Carrie said quickly, then walked away. "I'll be back in a few minutes."

"Jack is a mentally handicapped man who does small jobs around the house. I'll tell you about him later." Bridie pointed. "How do you like that blue dress at the end of the rack?"

Chapter Four

Catherine, thrilled with the clothes Bridie bought her at Carrie's Shop, stood with a white clothes box under each arm, admiring her new home on a pleasant tree-lined street. It was a two-story, red brick house, with a black mansard roof. A brick coach house was set back on the side. The window frames were painted white, matching the porch and railing that wrapped around the south corner of the house. Green drapes in the living room window were tied back, exposing a red and gold hurricane lamp sitting on a polished wood table. Catherine could see two pictures in gold frames hanging on a wall, and a palm plant standing near a piano. Catherine thought of the poor neighborhood and small apartment where she lived with her father. *How could I be given so much*, she wondered. *Why me? What are other orphans getting?* Tears blanketed her eyes.

"It'll take time for you to adjust," Bridie said, removing a pink handkerchief from her purse for Catherine. "My father had this house built forty years ago, and I've lived here all my life. It's filled with pleasant memories that are dear to me."

Catherine's eyes swept back-and-forth across her new home, admiring its size and beauty. "It's a magnificent house. I never dreamed of living in such a place." She took a deep breath to keep from crying again. "Does anyone else live here?"

Bridie chuckled. "No, my dear, just you and me. There are bigger homes in Newberry, but this is big enough for us."

"I'll say," Catherine gasped, handing Bridie's her handkerchief. "How many bedrooms are there?"

"Only three." Bridie pointed to the second floor. "That window there is where my bedroom is. Your bedroom is in the back, overlooking the pond. Shall we go inside?"

"Absolutely. This is going to be fun. Welcome home to me." Catherine laughed at her joke and followed Bridie inside.

Bridie hung her umbrella and purse on a rosewood coat tree just inside the door. A wooden deacon's bench, wide enough for three people, stood next to it. Tom Holmgren had placed Catherine's clothes box on the floor. Ahead of them was an oak staircase leading to three bedrooms and a second bathroom. The parlor was on their left, the dining room to their right. Black metal gratings over the heating ducts were set into the polished oak floors.

Catherine looked into the living room and saw the palm plant and piano she had seen from outside. "I love ... *our* home already."

"Let's take your clothes upstairs to your bedroom," Bridie suggested. "Then I'll give you a tour of the house."

Bridie stepped to the deacon's bench, grabbed Catherine's old clothes box by the strap and ascended the stairs, leading Catherine to a bedroom at the end of the hallway. "The bathroom is across the hall," Bridie said, placing Catherine's clothes box next to the bed. "Newberry built a water system about ten years ago, so we had two bathrooms installed, one downstairs near the butler's pantry, and the one up here." Bridie clasped her hands together and faced Catherine. "How do you like your room? It's rather plain right now, but you can add your personal touch to it."

Catherine laid her clothes boxes on the bed, examining the room. "It's a big bedroom. I love it." A spindle-back rocking chair with curved arms and seat stood next to the window. Its dark green seat cushion was tied to the back spindles. Catherine walked over to the rocker and swept her hand across the wooden armrest. "It's a very old rocker, but in excellent condition." She pushed on the back of the rocker and watched it swing back and forth. "I like to rock when I read. Thank you again, Bridie."

"Look out the window," Bridie said, walking over to Catherine. "The pond and field are right behind us." She pushed the lace curtain aside. "See. It's big enough for rowing and picnics on the grass. That shack next to the two oak trees is our boathouse. John and I spent many ... well, that's another story, for another time. Put your clothes away and come to my bedroom. I'll start the house tour up here."

Catherine stood next to the rocker, examining the room more closely. A dresser and chest of drawers with glass knobs stood against the wall opposite the door. Two pewter candleholders with finger loops were on each side of the dresser's oval mirror. The bed, fashioned with ornamental black iron rods and brass posts, stood between the door and the dresser. The quilt covering the bed was white, with large blue stars.

Another door was in the corner of the room. Assuming it was a closet, Catherine walked across the room and looked inside. The closet was ten feet long and seven feet wide, with wooden clothes rods and shelving from front to back. "Marvelous," she whispered. She removed two hangers from a clothes rod and spun to her bed, as if dancing. She felt like a princess living in such a home. Eager to see the rest of the house, she hung her dresses quickly and went to the stairs and called to Bridie, "I'm ready for the tour."

Bridie came up the stairs, carrying two pink towels and face cloth. "I didn't expect you so soon, so I got these for you." She handed them to Catherine, "Put them in our bathroom and I'll meet you in the middle bedroom."

"Our bathroom!" Catherine repeated to herself, rushing away. "No sharing a bathroom with strangers ever again. Our bathroom!"

A white, roll-rim bathtub stood in the corner of the bathroom, with a frosted glass window above it. On her left, an oval mirror hung over a white, pedestal sink, next to a flushing toilet with a brown wooden seat. Opposite the sink was a small built-in cabinet for linens and toiletries. Catherine hung the towels over a white porcelain bar mounted next to the cabinet. She glanced at her bathroom again, smiled, and raced to the bedroom where Bridie was waiting.

Bridie was sitting on a brass bed. "This is the guest bedroom, so I keep only one dresser and a small clothes cabinet in here. It isn't used often, so if you would like a girlfriend to stay a night, she could sleep here." Bridie waited, while Catherine looked at the room, knowing there wasn't much to look at. She stood and led Catherine into the next room.

A large oriental rug covered the center of the room, leaving two feet of exposed flooring along the walls. The bedroom furniture, including a four-poster bed, was cherry-wood, with curved, cabriole legs terminating in claw and ball feet. The wood was decorated with carved foliage and scroll designs. Catherine pointed to two pictures hanging on the wall, one on each side of the dresser. They were head-and-shoulder photographs in oval cherry-wood frames, one of an elderly man, and one of a woman. "Are they your parents?"

Bridie walked over to the dresser and looked at the pictures. "Yes, Angus and Gwyneth. They died three years ago. My mother had a difficult time accepting Angus's death. He appeared healthy, then without warning, had a fatal heart attack. Four months later, my mother died in her sleep." Bridie turned to leave, "This was their bedroom. I slept in the room you have now."

Catherine looked for pictures on the other three walls. "Do you have any brothers or sisters?"

"No." Bridie answered. "I would liked to have had a sibling, but I was never consulted on the matter."

Catherine chuckled. "I wasn't asked, either."

"Follow me, it's time to show you the most important room in the house—the kitchen."

Catherine slid her hand along the top of the handrail, descending the stairs to the vestibule. The wood was hard and smooth. *Everything here is perfect*, she thought. *I wonder what Brian's new house is like?*

At the bottom of the stairs, they turned right and entered a hallway leading to the back of the house. Being away from windows, the hall was dark. "This is a butler's pantry," Bridie said, pointing into a nook with cabinets and a serving counter. "But we don't have a butler." They stepped into the largest kitchen Catherine had ever seen. Sunlight poured into the room through two windows over the kitchen sink, making the room cheerful and inviting. The back door was opposite them, and through the door's window, Catherine could see the oak trees and the pond. Along the wall on their left were varnished wooden cabinets, with beige porcelain knobs. Next to the cabinets was a wall-hung, white porcelain sink, with one silver tap for running water. Catherine looked through the windows above the sink, guessing the neighbor's house was 150' away.

Beyond the sink stood a large black, wood burning, stove with a rising black stovepipe. The edges of the stovetop, the oven doors and the legs were stainless steel. A metal teakettle, filled with water, was heating on the stove.

An oak table and eight spindle-back chairs stood in the middle of the kitchen. Catherine pulled out one of the chairs and sat down. "I'd like to learn to cook in a kitchen like this."

Bridie stood next to Catherine, placing a hand on her shoulder. "I was hoping you would feel that way. I have a reputation for being a good cook, and I would enjoy teaching you what I know. I can make just about anything, but soups are my favorite. There's nothing like a big bowl of hot soup and a slice or two of bread on a cold day." Bridie walked to the back door window and looked out into the yard.

"What are you looking at?" Catherine asked. She got up from her chair and joined Bridie.

"I'm looking to see if wood has been cut for the cooking stove. I see it hasn't. The supply is low and I want it cut before the weekend is over." She turned from the door, "I'm sure it will be done before tomorrow night." She stepped past Catherine, "Let's go to the dining room, where someday, famous dinners by Catherine will be served."

Dark wood beams spanned the dining room ceiling, and decorative wood panels covered the lower part of the walls. A polished cherry-wood table and matching chairs stood in the middle of the room, under a crystal chandelier. At its center, stood a large porcelain statue of *Apollo and Daphne*.

"If this is Victorian, I like it." Catherine looked deep into Bridie's eyes. "Again, thank you for bringing me to your home."

"Let's go into the parlor," Bridie said. "It's a good place to talk." They crossed the foyer and entered the parlor. Bridie noticed Catherine looking at the piano with great interest and decided they would discuss piano lessons later. Bridie turned and walked out of the living room. "You look at the parlor, while I see if the water is hot enough for tea."

An elaborately designed Persian carpet of mostly red, black and ivory colors covered the center three-quarters of the floor. Catherine stood there for half a minute or so, examining its complex patterns, then walked across the room. She sat on one of the two matching chairs by the front window. Between them was a small round table with bowed legs, holding the hurricane lamp she had seen from outside. It was purely ornamental now, as the house was equipped with electricity. Beyond the chair was a mahogany drop-front desk, with a brass student lamp on top. Next to it stood the black piano and palm plants. At the center of the wall was an elegant fireplace with a black marble face that matched beautifully with the colors of the Persian carpet and black piano. Across from the fireplace there was a coffee table and a green and gold striped sette'e. Catherine walked over and sat on it, pondering the elegance of the house.

She studied two large gold-framed pictures hanging on each side of the fireplace. One was of Angus and Gwyneth standing among flowers and bushes, and the other was of a youthful Bridie, in a long white dress, standing by oak trees in the back yard. Catherine was amazed at the strong resemblance between herself and a youthful Bridie. One other picture in the room was of a man. It was on the fireplace mantel in a six-by-eight inch silver frame. Catherine could see it wasn't Angus, so she assumed he was someone important to the family.

Bridie returned from the kitchen, carrying a brown wooden tray with white cups and saucers, and a teapot covered with a multi-flowered cozy. She noticed Catherine looking at the pictures on the mantel. Bridie set the tray on the coffee table and stared at the pictures, telling about the third person. "That was John McTavish, the man I was to marry," Bridie said, affectionately.

Catherine glanced at Bridie, hoping for further explanation.

Bridie volunteered the story Catherine wanted to hear. "On a Saturday, two months before our wedding day, John and his friend, Joel Moore, were surveying a parcel of land west of town. When they finished, they went to their horses tied to a tree on the bank of the Illinois River. Due to five days of rain, the water was high and fast moving. Debris of all kinds was floating downstream toward the Mississippi River.

"John and Joel saw two boys, nine-year-old Todd Bacon and his seven-year-old brother, David. They were on the river in a nine-foot, flat bottom boat, having a difficult time rowing in the fast current. John and Joel yelled to them to come ashore, immediately. Moments later, a long raft of brush and tree branches hit their boat from the side, knocking the boys into the water. Todd quickly swam toward shore, but David was overpowered by the debris and swept under.

"John had seen the debris coming and was already swimming toward the boys. John told Todd to swim toward Joel, who was in the water behind him. As John swam underwater to get David, the raft of debris turned sideways and swept over them, dragging them underwater until it lodged against the riverbank fifty yards away. John and David's clothes were entangled with the branches and sticks, keeping them under. By the time Joel got to them, it was too late."

Unable to produce a perfect response, Catherine simply said, "I'm sorry."

"I miss him. I never met a man who could compare with him—in my eyes anyway." Bridie turned to Catherine. "You will be the daughter we dreamed of having. What Kitty said this afternoon was true. I need you, as much as you need me, and I feel very fortunate to have found you to fulfill my dream."

Catherine walked to the fireplace to get a better look at John's picture, cradling it in her hands. John wore denim pants, a plaid work shirt and dark boots. One foot was on a tree stump, and his arms were crossed in front of his chest. He was a tall, powerful man, with broad shoulders, thick wavy hair and a handsome smile.

"How old was he when this picture was taken?"

"He was twenty-four," Bridie answered, softly, still disturbed by her loss. "That picture was taken five months before the river incident. I was nineteen, anxious to be married and living with him."

As if replacing a holy statue to a shrine, Catherine returned the picture to the mantle. "You have many lovely things."

Bridie ignored Catherine's statement. It wasn't where she wanted to go with the conversation. "You like Brian, don't you?"

Catherine felt a flush rise across her face, avoiding eye contact by looking into the fireplace. "Yes, but I've only known him three days."

Bridie watched Catherine walk from the fireplace to the piano. "Does he like you?"

"I think so. When we're alone, he acts awkward and clumsy like boys do, when they like someone, not sure of what to say or do."

Bridie smiled at Catherine's astute description of a boy newly in love. "Judging by what I've seen, I'd say he likes you very much. Give him time and a little guidance, and he'll express his feelings." Bridie rose from the chair. "I have two ideas you might like," she said. "Since you and Brian have birthdays only ten days apart, why don't we celebrate them on the same day? We, and the Holmgrens, could take a train to St. Louis for a day and celebrate there. Would you like that?"

Catherine thought for a moment and smiled at the offer. "That sounds nice. I'd like to see St. Louis."

"I believe the tea has steeped long enough." Bridie poured, then placed a plate of crackers and sliced cheese between them. "You said you've always lived in New York. Were your parents born in this country?"

Catherine finished sipping her tea before answering. "No. My father was born in Ireland and my mother is from Scotland."

"Your mother's a Scot?" Bridie gushed. "Doesn't that beat all? Who knows, since we look alike, we may be kin. I knew your father was Irish by your last name, but your mother—what a pleasant surprise." Bridie stirred sugar into her tea and asked, "What was her maiden name?"

"Duart. Mary Duart. I don't remember much about her, because she died of pneumonia when I was ten."

Bridie reached for a piece of cheese and a cracker. "Do you know what part of Scotland she was from?"

"Kilmarnock. I don't know where that is, because I've never seen it on a map."

"I've heard of it, but I can't place it, either," Bridie said. "We'll look on a map one day." Bridie looked at Catherine the way a mother would, examining her smooth complexion and soft hair, her delicately tapered fingers, and graceful gestures.

Catherine got up from the sette'e and smiled at Bridie. "You're giving me so much already, I feel guilty. There must be something I can do for you?"

"Don't worry about that. We are family now, and as in all families, you will have chores to do around here."

Catherine placed her cup on the tray. "When you're finished with your tea, I'll wash the dishes."

"You see," Bridie remarked. "You'll find ways to be helpful." Bridie finished the last of her tea. "I'd say we've had a good start in our relationship, and it only took a few hours. By the way, if you'd like to invite your friend Monica to come here for a day, or an overnight stay, let me know and I'll arrange it. I'm sure the Peters won't mind."

Catherine picked up the tray from the coffee table and started for the kitchen. "I'd like that. I'll let you know when."

Bridie followed Catherine into the kitchen. "Do you want to go to the Episcopal Church with me tomorrow? The Holmgrens are parishioners there, too, and I'm sure they'll be showing off Brian."

Catherine put the dishes into the sink, turned to Bridie and smiled. "I guess I should thank God for my good fortune."

Bridie winked at Catherine. "It's almost ten o'clock. I'm going up to my room and read until I fall asleep. I'll wake you in the morning."

Catherine awoke to the sound of the bathroom door closing, followed by water splashing into the bathtub. She got out of bed to look outside. Except for two v-shaped ripples made by a pair of mallards paddling along the water's grassy edge, the surface of the pond was like glass. A black Labrador was standing on the opposite side of the pond, wagging his tail, watching them intensely. Catherine got down on her knees resting her forearms on the windowsill. In their yard, to her left, she saw a husky man with gray hair chopping wood and stacking it against the coach house. She assumed it was Jack, chopping wood for the cook stove.

Catherine raised her eyes to the heavens, thanking God for her good fortune, and told her parents she missed them. Lowering her eyes to the pond, she saw the black dog leap into the water and swim toward the ducks. When it got within fifteen feet of them, they flew away. "You'll never catch them," Catherine mumbled to herself.

It appeared to Catherine, it would be as beautiful a day as yesterday had been. Puffs of gray-white clouds drifted to the northeast under a blue sky. Sparrows, robins and blue jays flew back and forth in search of food, and the black dog was back to where it started, shaking water from its coat.

Soon, there were three raps on Catherine's door. "It's just after ten o'clock and church services are at twelve. I'm anxious to show you to Newberry, so the Holmgrens don't out-do me."

Catherine turned toward the door and smiled. "I'll get ready now." She heard Bridie walk back to her room and close the door. Catherine went to the dresser, picked out new underclothes and dashed to the bathroom.

At 11:30 a.m. Bridie and Catherine walked to church under a clear sky. Bridie was wearing a light blue, full-length dress, with a white cameo broach pinned just below her throat. Catherine wore a tan skirt and an ivory cotton blouse, with heart-shaped buttons. Bridie gave her a gold, heart-shaped locket to wear for the day.

Bridie wondered how many people already heard about Catherine and Brian. Nearing the white frame church, she shifted her eyes back-and-forth to see how many people were looking at her new daughter. "Look!" Bridie said, pointing. "The Holmgren's buggy is at the side of the church. I was certain they would be here today."

"Good morning, Bridie," came a voice from behind.

Bridie looked back at Howard and Essie Mason. "Good morning to you, too."

"We heard about Catherine and couldn't wait to meet her." The white-haired woman smiled at Catherine. "Let's skip the formalities. I'm Essie Mason, and this is my husband, Howard."

Somewhat intimidated by Howard's huge body and ruddy complexion, Catherine smiled and responded with a gentle, "Hello."

"Howard is the local sheriff around these here parts," Bridie said, with a western drawl. "He keeps them bad 'uns away from our town."

Howard chuckled at Bridie's attempt at western slang, then looked at Catherine. "Good looking girls like you are always welcome to Newberry," he said. "If Bridie doesn't treat you right, let me know and I'll sit on her."

"I don't worry about Bridie. She's been absolutely wonderful to me. I feel fortunate to be with her."

People walked by, those who had already been informed about Catherine, smiled and nodded to Bridie, each taking a casual, but concentrated look at Catherine. "We'd better get inside," Bridie said, "Or they'll start services without us."

Essie decided she liked Catherine—the person, not just her good looks. "Nice to meet you," Essie said, sincerely. "I look forward to seeing you again."

"I hope so," Catherine replied, walking up the church stairs with Bridie. The Masons followed them into church and walked up an aisle along the outer wall. "Where do the Holmgrens usually sit?" Catherine asked.

"In the back half of the church. But don't look there. I'm sure Margaret has Brian front and center today." Bridie tried to appear nonchalant, walking up the center aisle, as if nothing were out of the ordinary.

Catherine heard whispering and noticed heads turn in their direction. "Where do you usually sit?" Catherine inquired, anxious to sit and be less conspicuous.

"Mostly I sit in the back half of the church. She looked down at Catherine and smiled. "But today, we're sitting front and center."

Catherine pursed her lips to keep from laughing.

Tom Holmgren looked back and saw them coming. He said something to Margaret, who in turn whispered to Brian. They slid across the pew, allowing room for two.

"You go in first," Bridie said, knowing Catherine would want to be next to Brian, and church was as good a place as any.

Brian wore a new gray suit, white shirt with a standing collar, a black tie, and shiny black shoes. He was curious as to what Catherine would think of his new clothes. When he saw her, though, all his being, centered on her. He believed she looked more mature, certainly older than fifteen.

"You look very dapper," Catherine whispered.

"Thanks. You look nice."

She decided she would accept "nice" for now, knowing he was pleased with her.

Bridie and Margaret smiled at each other, pretending not to be listening to what was going on between them.

Throughout the service, Brian wondered about the older boys in town. *What are they like? How many are good-looking? How many of them are rich? Once they see Catherine, they'll be interested in her, too.* He took casual glances around the church, examining all the boys. Brian felt a little better. He was sure she liked him, but he knew he had to be more aggressive to make them a committed couple. The minister left the altar and Brian hadn't given the service any consideration.

A third of the parishioners remained in their pew, as others filed out to the street. Bridie was convinced those who remained seated, heard about Catherine and Brian and wanted to get a good look at them. Bridie and Margaret were more than willing to oblige. They beamed with pride, walking toward the back of the church, pretending they weren't aware of being watched.

Outside, they were engulfed by warm air and sunshine. Catherine stepped down from the last stair and faced Bridie and Margaret. "One of the ladies in the choir sure had a strong singing voice," Catherine remarked. "I bet she could be heard across the street."

"That would be Nerine Booker," Margaret said. "She's the town nightingale. She performs all over town."

Bridie turned away from Margaret, so she wouldn't laugh.

A slender woman, in a frilly dress and an abundance of face-paint, approached them with quick little steps. "Congratulations," she said, with a generous smile. "I just heard." She glanced at Catherine and Brian. "Beautiful children. We must get together soon." She wiggled her fingers at them and moved on.

"Who is she?" Brian asked, frowning.

"That is Beatrice Pendelton," Tom answered, walking towards his buggy. "Her husband is George Pendelton, an executive of the New York and Central Railroad. His office is in St. Louis, but he returns most weekends."

Brian understood why Mr. Pendelton lived in St. Louis.

At the buggy, Tom gave Dandy two pats on the rump. "I'm going to the quarry and sum up last week's progress. I'll probably be home before three o'clock."

"Bye, Dear," Margaret said, blowing him a kiss.

Tom climbed up into the buggy, while Brian untied Dandy from the hitching post. "You can come with me, if you'd like, Brian?"

"Not today," Brian answered, passing the reins to Tom. "I'll go with you tomorrow."

"Can't say I blame you," Tom responded, with a wink of his eye. "She's a pretty girl." Tom turned Dandy away from the church and rode down Lincoln Avenue.

"It's quite warm today and I'm thirsty," Bridie said. "Does anyone want to go to Carlson's Drug Store for the world's best iced tea?"

"I would like an iced tea, too," Margaret said, looking at Brian and Catherine. "It's just two blocks away on Main Street."

Catherine clasped her hands behind her back. "Fine," she said. Her response lacked enthusiasm and Brian never answered.

It was obvious to Bridie what those two wanted. "If you aren't thirsty, you might want to walk Main Street and get better acquainted with Newberry." Bridie pulled her blouse sleeve back to look at her wristwatch. "It's one o'clock now. We could meet at the town square at two-thirty."

The children stood a little taller. "That's a good idea. We could get familiar with the town center," Catherine replied.

Brian faced Margaret. "I have to learn where the stores are, for when you send me for something."

Bridie lowered her sleeve and asked Margaret. "Is that agreeable with you?"

Without hesitation, she responded, "Sure." Margaret pointed to the west. "There's a nice park one block on the other side of Main Street. It has a creek running along the edge of it, so if you go there, be careful. See you at 2:30."

Brian and Catherine turned and walked away, in a controlled rush.

The women stood shoulder-to-shoulder, watching them. "Did you ever know a boy who wanted to look into store windows?" Bridie asked.

"Not really," Margaret answered, watching them run across the street. "I guess it depends on who you're with."

Bridie sighed, deeply. "I wonder if our children will marry each other someday?"

"Good chance," Margaret answered. "They're two handsome kids in a small town where pickings are slim. They obviously care for each other now, but will it last?"

"Probably." Bridie paused. "I love his curly black hair."

"They both have nice personalities," Margaret added. "They must have had good parents."

Bridie nodded. "I agree. I would like to have known them." She looked down at the cameo pin on her blouse and centered it properly. "They're a block away. Shall we go to Kitty's instead of the drug store? Her iced tea is decent and her ceiling fans make it more comfortable."

"Fine with me. Just so I'm home by three o'clock."

On their way to Kitty's, a man stood by Crumbie's Shoe Store, with a cardboard box at his feet. He was holding something in his palm for other's to inspect. When they got closer, they saw it was a tiny black and white Terrier puppy, no more than eight inches long. There were five more in the box, whimpering and squirming. He tried selling them for fifty cents. Bridie and Margaret groaned with love of them, but continued on for fear of buying one.

As they entered Kitty's, the little bell over the door jingled. A middle-aged man and woman were sitting at one table, and a man and woman with a five-year-old boy were at another. They sat at a table by the window, thankful for the blue and white awning blocking the sunlight.

Margaret tilted her head back and let the ceiling fan blow against her face.

Kitty came out of the kitchen and went directly to their table. "Two days in a row?" she said, with her hand against her chest. "I'm honored." She removed an order pad and pencil from her apron pocket. "Where are those lovely children?"

"They're walking Main Street, getting familiar with Newberry." Margaret answered. "We want iced tea."

"I'll be back in two minutes," Kitty said, backing away from the table. She continued toward the kitchen, glancing at the other customers to see whether they needed her services.

Margaret folded her hands on the table. "We're thinking of sending Brian to Illinois University in September. He wants to be an engineer and construct buildings. Tom tested his knowledge of math, and he's good at it. Brian is an intelligent boy."

"What a perfect tie-in," Bridie commented. "Being you're in the quarry business selling stone to construction companies, you'll have plenty of contacts to get Brian a good engineering job."

"Absolutely. Three years at the university and he'll graduate when he's eighteen or nineteen." Margaret rolled her eyes. "A popular marrying age."

Bridie ignored Margaret's comment. "I wonder how Brian and Catherine will respond to being separated for long periods of time?"

Kitty returned, with their iced tea in tall glasses. "Enjoy. Would you like a tart, or piece of cake?"

"Yes, we would," Margaret, answered. "But we had our weekly limit of pastries yesterday."

"I understand, completely." She returned to the display case to wash glass shelves.

Margaret sipped her tea and looked out onto Main Street, concentrating on the cool liquid bathing her parched throat. Being a Sunday, there wasn't much traffic, except for an occasional carriage, or pedestrian walking by. Margaret set her glass on the table. "I'm worried about the war with Spain. President McKinley is sending 17,000 of our men to Cuba. If the war goes on for years, Brian could get involved."

Bridie stirred her tea with a long spoon. "General consensus is the war will be over quickly. Look what happened in Manila Bay. Our ships destroyed the Spanish fleet in seven hours. I wouldn't be concerned about Brian getting into the fight, especially as young as he is."

Kitty walked past them, carrying a potted plant to place in the center of the window. She looked up the street, then to the south. She stood erect and stared. "It looks like Brian and Catherine coming this way. Are they meeting you here?"

"No!" Margaret answered. "They don't know we're here."

Bridie leaned toward the window to look down the street. "They make a nice couple, especially in their new clothes."

Kitty stepped back and watched them, too. "They couldn't walk any closer to one another, unless they were in each other's arms. Is there a relationship developing?"

Bridie smiled. "No, they came to us that way."

"How cute. I wish they were coming in," Kitty said. She watched for another moment before going back to work.

"Look at them," Margaret said. "They stop and gape into every window. What in the world is so interesting about a hardware store, barbershop, surveyor's office or dry goods store? They haven't a clue as to what's beyond any of those windows. All they have on their minds are each other."

"Watch closely. They're directly across from us now," Bridie said. "Their arms are hanging at their sides like leather straps." She stared at the children, as if under a microscope.

Margaret chuckled, "When they stop, then start walking again, Catherine taps her hand against Brian's, trying to give him a hint. At least, it looks that way. Their hands couldn't be any closer, without touching."

Bridie gave Margaret a questioning look. "Are you sure Brian is as smart as you say?"

"He's being a gentleman. We've given him good moral training."

Bridie straightened her back and looked at Margaret. "In one day? You must be marvelous parents."

Margaret took a deep breath. "Well, I had to say something in his defense." She extended her hand toward the window. "Look. They've moved on, and now they're gaping into the shoe repair shop. I mean, reeeaally."

Bridie and Margaret leaned toward the window, observing them, as they advanced down the street.

They were looking into a furniture store when Catherine started to walk away and stopped. When Brian moved forward, he bumped into her, putting his arm around her to keep his balance. When he retracted his arm, he cupped her hand in his. They were deep in smiles, looking at each other.

"Kitty!" Bridie yelled over her shoulder. "Bring us two almond tarts. It's graduation day."

They continued walking down the street, their pace increased from lethargic turtles, to one of spirited puppies. Catherine laid her head against Brian's shoulder, passing the remaining stores without glancing into a window.

"Well, they've taken the first step," Margaret said, drawing back to the table. "I wonder if they'll have their first kiss today?"

"They're so into each other right now, I can't imagine it not happening," Bridie replied. She looked at her watch. "They have only forty-five minutes for step two, then they meet us at the town square." She tapped Margaret's hand resting on the table. "We must keep our eyes open. We don't want them stepping too fast."

Margaret sipped her tea and wiped her mouth with a napkin. "I'll bet she walks him into a jewelry store one day."

Kitty arrived at their table, carrying two tarts on her trademark blue and white plates. "Who graduated?" she asked, placing two tarts on the table.

"Brian and Catherine," Margaret answered, with a sparkle of excitement. "They just held hands for the first time. We could be wrong, of course, but judging from our observation of them, we're convinced this was their first time."

Kitty took two forks from her apron pocket and laid them on the table. "I hope you hens don't smother your chicks with observation."

Bridie picked up her fork. "Not at all. Just prudent guidance, if necessary."

"Who decides if it's necessary?" Kitty smiled, walking away.

"She has a point," Margaret said. "We don't want to be overbearing parents."

"Calm yourself," Bridie responded. "We're just having fun watching them. We aren't ogres."

Minutes later, Bridie laid her fork on the empty plate. "What do you think about taking a train to St. Louis, to celebrate the children's birthdays? We could show them places of interest, then have a nice dinner at Jim Chandler's."

Margaret shrugged her shoulders, as though uninterested in the idea. "That could be nice. I'll have to ask Tom, of course, being he works some Sundays."

Bridie folded her hands on her lap. "You don't seem enthused about my suggestion. Do you have another idea?"

Margaret leaned forward and pushed her empty plate to the side. "I do, actually. I thought if we have a party at my house, we could introduce the children to some of our friends. They will have to meet them eventually, so why not then?"

Bridie smiled at her, "That sounds sensible. As a matter of fact, it's a good idea. We can have it on a Sunday after Newberry's Fourth-of-July Celebration." Bridie folded her napkin and laid it on the table. "My time is flexible, so you discuss it with Tom and let me know the time and day." Bridie stood and adjusted her cameo pin, again. "It's almost 2:30. We must meet the young lovers."

"Today is my treat," Margaret said, taking money from her brown-beaded purse. "Good-bye, Kitty," she yelled, placing a few coins on the table.

They walked toward the town square, two blocks away. The only people near them was an elderly couple walking on the other side of the street, dressed in their Sunday's best. A gray horse pulling a badly weathered wagon was moving toward them at a slow pace. The wagon was half-filled with barrels and crates, and the driver was sitting high over the rump of his horse. As he passed, the driver shook the brown leather reins and spit tobacco juice onto the street.

Margaret cringed with disgust. "How can men chew that stuff? It's horribly disgusting. Worse yet, how can a woman kiss a man who chews tobacco?"

Bridie laughed. "I'll call him back, so you can find out." She looked up the street. "Look! The lovers are passing the Lincoln Monument."

"They aren't holding hands now," Margaret said. "I guess they would be embarrassed doing that around us. I wonder where they went when they left Main Street?"

Bridie chuckled. "I imagine they were in heaven."

They walked on a little farther, looking into store windows. Margaret broke their silence and asked, "Tom and I were wondering if you've told Catherine about Jack?"

"Not yet," she answered, "In due time."

Chapter Five

That evening, Bridie was showing Catherine the proper way to cut and tear vegetables, while two bass fillets sizzled in a frying pan. Bridie went to a cabinet next to the sink and removed a small bottle of olive oil, held it high, and saw only a few drops remaining.

"Would you go in the basement and get another bottle, while I finish the plate of vegetables? It's in the white cabinet against the wall." She looked at Catherine standing at the table. "I forgot, I never showed you the basement, not that it's a thing of beauty." She waved her hand twice, signaling Catherine to come forward. Bridie opened the door and turned on the basement light. "At the bottom of the stairs, turn right and you will be facing the cabinet. The oil should be on a higher shelf."

"I'm sure I'll find it," Catherine said, starting down the stairs.

There were two light bulbs; one toward the front of the basement and one near the back door. The foundation of the house was made from blocks of white stone. Crates, barrels and cardboard boxes were stacked between her and the back door. The electric lighting was poor, but some natural lighting came through half-windows high on the stone, walls.

The white cabinet was six feet high, with doors that opened at its center. Catherine pulled on the metal knobs, revealing a variety of fruits and vegetables preserved in jars. Catherine looked at the higher shelves and saw the oil. She removed it from the shelf and examined glass jars of peaches, cherries, applesauce, green beans, corn, beets, and pickles. She began to feel an eerie presence, as if someone was watching her. She stood still, listening, pretending to be looking at the jars. She heard someone breathing, then remembered Bridie saying the people of Newberry didn't lock their doors.

Catherine slowly turned her head toward the back door, looking between the barrels and crates. She didn't see anyone, but the sound of someone breathing continued. A chill spread across the surface of her skin. *There! Between the stacked crates, someone, or something moved.* She left the cabinet doors open and darted for the stairs without looking back. Her feet barely touched the stairs, as she raced upward, past the light switch and into the kitchen. Her heart was pounding and she was pale with fear. "Bridie. Someone's in the basement!"

Bridie was turning a fish in the frying pan when she stopped to look at Catherine. "That could be," she replied, just before the basement door slammed shut. Bridie went to the back door and looked out the window. "It's Jack. I'm sure he's more scared than you are. He's running away."

Catherine sat down on a chair and took a deep breath. "Why didn't he say hello, or something, instead of standing in the dark staring at me?"

"He doesn't know you, so I guess he decided to hide until you were gone." Bridie walked over to Catherine and sat on a chair next to her. "Jack has had misfortunes through the years. He is mentally ill and is only capable of doing simple work. About ten years ago, he was removing snow from the roof of his mother's house. He fell and landed on his back, across a pile of firewood. He damaged his spinal column, causing his body to lean to one side." Bridie smiled and took Catherine's hand in hers. "He is completely harmless, so don't be afraid of him."

Catherine began to relax and leaned back against the chair, still clutching the bottle of olive oil. "I assume Jack is the man I saw chopping wood this morning?"

"Yes," Bridie answered. "He lives nearby with his mother, Doreen. I have a bed for him in the basement, should he want an afternoon nap. Sometimes, he sleeps there through a night of bad weather. If he doesn't go home at night, his mother knows he's here. Doreen and I have been friends for a long time."

Catherine placed the bottle of olive oil on the table and walked over to the stove. "I think the fish is ready."

"Move the pan to the cool side of the stove. I'll complete the salad." Bridie mixed the olive oil with salt, a little pepper and two spices she liked. "Are you sure fish and vegetables are enough for supper?"

"Definitely. Especially in warm weather."

Sitting opposite each other, Bridie began telling Catherine about the change in plans for her birthday party. "Margaret and I decided to have the party at her house. That way, you two could meet our friends. You never know when you might need one of them for an emergency, or something. We'll probably have the birthday party the first or second Sunday after the Fourth of July. If you'd like, you can call Monica and invite her."

"Thank you. I want to see Monica and find out how she likes her new home with Mr. and Mrs. Peters."

"Having this party means we would postpone the trip to St. Louis," Bridie said, in an apologetic way. "We'll do it another time." Bridie poured the olive oil onto her salad. "Where did you and Brian walk to this afternoon?" She was curious as to how much information Catherine would volunteer.

"We looked into the stores on Main Street, then we went to Winnemac Park and sat by the creek. A man and his little boy were having a great time flying a box kite, even though it crashed several times. I was surprised it didn't break." Catherine began eating, hoping to put an end to Bridie's questions about her and Brian.

Bridie cut her fish into small pieces, waiting in vain for more information. "Is Brian still shy around you?"

"Not as much as he was." She quickly took another bite of food.

Bridie realized by Catherine's abrupt answers there wasn't any interesting news forthcoming, so she changed the subject. "Every year, Newberry has a wonderful Fourth-of-July Celebration in Getty's Field, east of town. I'm sure you'll love it. John and I went every year to dance and watch the fireworks. At seven o'clock, Mayor Abernathy gives a short speech to open the festivities. He usually fills them with humor, so we aren't bored hearing about our civic responsibilities. When his speech ends, the Newberry band, which has only thirteen musicians, sits in a large canvas tent and plays music for those who want to dance or just listen."

Bridie could see that Catherine was interested, inspiring her to continue with all the details. "There will be barrels of beer for the men, and iced tea and lemonade for the ladies and children. Some women in the community have tables where they sell crafts and foods that are their specialty. Others tell stories and organize games of competition for the children. When it gets dark, which is usually about ten o'clock, there will be thirty minutes of fireworks."

"It sounds like fun," Catherine said, enthusiastically. "I've seen fireworks in New York, but they were so far away, I couldn't enjoy them properly."

Bridie pushed her plate aside and sipped her lemonade. "Do you know if Brian can dance?"

"That's what I was wondering. I guess I'll find out then."

At seven o'clock, Bridie returned to the kitchen carrying a vase filled with wilted flowers. She poured the dirty water into the sink as Catherine finished washing the dishes. "Would you like to call Monica and chat with her for a while?"

Catherine hung the wet dishtowel on a hook next to the sink. "Thank you. I would, but I don't know how to use this kind of telephone."

"That's right," Bridie said, with a chuckle. "You're new around here. Come, I'll show you." They walked over to the wall telephone next to the basement door. It was an oak wooden box, with a black metal receiver, a mouthpiece jutting from the box and a metal crank at the side. "It's quite easy. Just pick up the receiver, put it to your ear to listen, and turn this crank a time or two and wait for Cora to answer. When she does, just tell her you want the Peters' farm. It's that simple."

Catherine smiled. "I guess I'm ready for something simple." She put the receiver to her ear and began cranking the handle, almost giggling at her new experience.

Cora's voice came booming out of the receiver, loud enough so even Bridie could hear.

"Please connect me to the Peters' farm," Catherine requested. "You're right, I'm not Bridie. I'm Catherine McDonald, her new daughter ... Since yesterday." Catherine looked over at Bridie, standing by the table. "No, she hasn't punched me, or kicked me yet ... You think it would be a good hospital for me ... Yes, I'll sleep with my bedroom door locked ... Thank you. It was nice talking to you."

Bridie was shaking her head at Cora's ever-present nonsense, but was proud of Catherine's polite manner. Cora was the Paul Revere of Newberry and would report her opinion of Catherine to everyone.

Catherine was looking down at the floor, waiting for someone to answer her call.

Bridie went to the back door and looked out the window. Jack had returned and was standing at the edge of the pond, throwing pieces of bread to *his* pair of ducks. It was one of his few enjoyments in life.

"Hello, Mrs. Peters? This is Catherine McDonald."

Bridie opened the door and walked out onto the porch. She stood at the porch railing, watching Jack feed the ducks. The moon and fading blue sky reflected on the water. Jack lowered himself to the ground, flapping his folded arms like a duck.

Bridie turned and looked through the door window at Catherine. She was leaning against the kitchen wall, smiling and talking. Bridie felt the warmth of her love for Catherine settle into her body, and whispered, "Catherine is perfect for us." She faced the pond again and looked to the sky. "She is ours, John, the girl we wanted."

Chapter Six

Catherine raced down the porch stairs and waited for Bridie. She tugged and shifted her green cotton dress, so it hung properly without twists or wrinkles. Except for the threat of rain in the distance, the weather was perfect for the Fourth of July. The temperature was in the low seventies and there was a gentle breeze. Branches of trees lining Root Street, swayed to a rhythm dictated by Mother Nature, flashing green and silvery sides of their leaves. Catherine stared at dark gray clouds in the west, watching to see which direction they were going. She believed if they continued on their northerly course, the evening celebration would be rain-free.

Catherine watched Bridie shift a folded, gray blanket from one arm to the other and pull the front door shut. She was wearing a full-length brown skirt and tan blouse, complimented by a necklace made of white wooden beads. Catherine looked at the doorframe above her, where three polished brass numbers, *3-2-2* were displayed. *My new home,* Catherine pondered. *322 Root Street.*

She noticed Jack standing at the side of the house, peering at her through the white porch railing. All she could see was his round face and thinning hair. He stared at her, as though confused and curious about her. She made eye contact with him for only a moment, smiled, and then looked down the street, so she didn't have to face him.

Catherine was afraid of Jack, unsure whether his interest in her was desire or just the curiosity of a simple-minded man. She didn't mention his presence to Bridie, wanting to walk away, leaving him behind.

She turned her thoughts to more pleasant things, like seeing Brian and Monica at Getty's Field. She wanted to be alone with Brian to watch the fireworks, but knew it impossible with Monica there. Besides, she was anxious to talk to Monica and hear about her new life with the Peters. When they talked on the telephone, Monica was limited in conversation, because Mrs. Peters was sitting nearby.

"I'll carry the blanket," Catherine said, removing it from under Bridie's arm.

"Thank you. I appreciate that." Bridie lowered her arm and moved on. "I think tonight would be a good opportunity for you and Brian to make friends with some of the local boys and girls. I'm sure most of them will be there for the fireworks and dancing."

"I hope so. Brian and I had discussed that."

They walked along in silence, noticing every house on Root Street had an American flag affixed to its front porch, fluttering out over green lawns and flowerbeds. Entering the next block, they saw thirteen-year-old Carol Whipple across the street. She stomped across the porch and down the stairs of her white frame house, yelling, "Hurry up" to her family inside. She was wearing a blue dress, white knee stockings and a red straw hat.

Bridie chuckled. "That is Carol Whipple. She dresses in our flag's colors every year. She looks like a candidate for some political office." Bridie prepared to wave to her when she looked their way, as Carol always gave her a big friendly greeting. When they were opposite Carol and she looked at them, Bridie waved to her.

Carol stood in front of her porch stairs staring at them, then turned and ran up the stairs, back into the house.

Bridie was perplexed. "I'm certain Carol recognized me. I've known her since she was an infant. Maybe she was confused, being I'm usually alone." When they got to the next corner, Bridie looked back and saw the Whipple family standing on their porch, looking in their direction. Bridie gave Catherine a big smile, "Carol is a nice girl. You'll like her when you meet her."

At Getty's Field, people were coming from all directions, riding on horses, in buggies, and on open wagons, with excited children piled in the back. Just as they were about to step onto the road, a gray buggy turned the corner and dashed past them. The young driver flicked the reins so the horse would go faster.

"Idiot!" Bridie yelled, glaring at him. She looked at Catherine. "If you're ever with a young man that operates a buggy in that manner, tell him to stop immediately, then get out and say 'good-bye' forever."

Catherine wanted to laugh at Bridie's response to the incident, but kept her composure.

Volunteers were giving small American flags to children as they entered the grounds. "Thank God it's a grassy field," Bridie said, fanning her face. "Otherwise, the air would be thick with dust." Bridie held on to Catherine's arm, crossing Feller Road, carefully avoiding oncoming horses and wagons. "Watch where you step, my dear. You don't want any surprises."

Catherine giggled and surveyed the grounds of Getty's Field. She could see two large canvas tents, fifty yards ahead. In front of them were two long rows of tables, where food and crafts were being sold. "Where are we meeting the Holmgrens?"

"At the first crafts table," Bridie answered. "I hope it's a table of quilts, so I have something to look at while waiting." Bridie sighed. "I started one once, but gave up after sewing only a dozen patches together."

Catherine searched the crowd for Brian and the Holmgrens, looking to the left of the tents, where horses and wagons were tied to stakes in the ground. After a vain attempt to find them, Catherine asked Bridie, "Why do you think that girl, Carol, didn't say hello to you this evening? I'm sure she recognized you."

"Then you did sense something was odd," Bridie said, shrugging her shoulders. "I'm bothered by that incident, too."

Catherine shifted the gray blanket from one arm to the other. "If she didn't recognize you, why did she run back into the house, then come out again after we moved on?"

Bridie waved her hand at a fly buzzing in front of her face. "Go by the horses," she said, sarcastically, then placed her hand on Catherine's shoulder. "We are probably overreacting to something meaningless. Let's forget it and have a good time."

They stood near a table of baked goods, watching a steady flow of people move into the grounds. Mary Merkle, a slender woman with silver-gray hair, was describing her pies and cakes to a bulky farm couple that appeared quite fond of food.

The man pulled a red and white handkerchief from his back pocket and wiped perspiration from his face and neck. He took a step back from the table and ordered, "Two apple and two cherry."

"We should get at least one peach," his hefty wife added, quickly.

"We're here!" Brian bellowed, running up behind Bridie and Catherine. He had a broad smile for Catherine.

Catherine's smile was just as inviting, surprised by his dark blue denim shirt and pants with red suspenders. "Where are the Holmgrens?"

"They're coming," he said, pointing toward Feller Road. "I ran ahead to let you know we we're here."

Anxious to see Catherine is more accurate, Bridie thought. "Good evening, Brian. Didn't you come in the buggy?"

"No, Miss McDonald. We decided to walk since it wasn't far from our house. Besides, Tom and Margaret wanted to talk to neighbors along the way. That's why we're late."

"I would prefer that you call me, Bridie," she said, in a priggish way. "I don't need a constant reminder that I've never been married."

Brian's smile vanished, sliding his hands into his back pockets. "Sorry. Bridie it is."

"Been waiting long?" Margaret asked, approaching the trio.

Bridie turned and smiled, "About ten minutes, is all." She looked at Margaret's feet. "Are you wearing new boots?"

Margaret looked down and lifted her skirt, enough so Bridie could see all of her black boots. "They're soft leather and very comfortable. They're perfect with this brown skirt and black belt." Margaret gave Tom a peck on the cheek. "Would you believe, Tom bought them for me? I still haven't figured out what he did to feel guilty."

"Maybe he hasn't done it yet?" Bridie joked. "Keep your eyes and ears open. You may learn something."

Tom shook his head and raised his arms, a gesture of futility in trying to please his wife. "Just a purchase of love, ladies. Nothing more."

"We're just having fun with you," Margaret assured him. "Where shall we sit to watch the fireworks? By the oak trees, again?"

"I think the fireworks have already started," Bridie said, tilting her head toward Catherine and Brian, standing a few feet away. "Oak trees are fine with me, but first, I want to show Catherine the quilts, then show her around the grounds." Bridie pointed her thumb at Brian. "I'm sure the bee would like to stay with the flower, so you two go ahead and enjoy yourselves."

Tom yelled to Brian, "You stay with Catherine and we'll meet you later."

Brian raised his hand, acknowledging Tom. Just then, a woman walked past him and Catherine, handing them a little flag on a stick. They began waving them at their parents, laughing at their silliness.

Margaret took Tom by the arm and walked away. "We'll be at the oak trees, no later than 9:30. See you then."

Bridie looked at her watch. It was 7:30. "Follow me," she said, gesturing with her hand. "I want to show you some quilts."

Brian took the gray blanket from Catherine and tucked it under his arm. "I'd like to treat you ladies to a glass of lemonade this evening."

"You have money?" Catherine asked.

"Sure. Tom pays me to work at the quarry," he said, proudly. "It's just for the summer, until I go to school."

"What do you do there?" Bridie asked, examining a table of handcrafted aprons. "Something related to engineering?"

"Kinda. I'm learning about explosives and how much dynamite is needed to blow a specific amount of stone from a wall. I also help with the stone cutting. It's important for me to learn the basics of the construction business."

Catherine frowned. "That sounds dangerous. Be careful a stone wall doesn't fall on you."

Bridie led them to the next table, glanced at the pottery and walked on. "You don't need to worry about Brian. I'm sure Tom will keep his son out of danger."

"Tom said you own part of the quarry business, and sometimes you work in the office." Brian elbowed Catherine to make sure she heard what he was about to say. "I've heard the office employees work harder the days you're there. Why is that?"

Bridie gave him a feeble smile. "Because they work harder when I'm there, that's all. I'll ignore the insinuation that I'm a penny-pinching slave driver. I've heard it before, but I assure you it isn't true."

Catherine didn't want Bridie upset with Brian. "He's just having fun with you."

"I understand," Bridie replied. "It would take more than that for me to be upset with Brian. Besides, I don't want to lose my chance of him buying me a lemonade."

Suddenly, three boys and two girls about ten years old, raced between and around them, shouting and laughing, as if distancing themselves from something they shouldn't have done. "It spilled all over him," a wide-eyed boy laughed, running by.

"I don't want to know what that was about," Bridie said, watching them disappear into the crowd. "They came to have fun and it seems they are."

"Look! There's a lady selling quilts over there," Catherine said, pointing to a table up the line. "See the table with the green canvas cover?"

Bridie stepped back quickly and glanced ahead. "Josie," she muttered, affectionately. "When you said, 'green canvas cover,' I was sure it was, Josie. She wasn't here the last two years and I feared she died." Bridie placed her arm around Catherine's waist and walked her to Josie's table. "This is a very interesting lady. I call her, 'Queen of the Quilts.'"

Approaching the table, Bridie couldn't hide her excitement. "Josie, I'm so happy to see you."

Josie was sitting on a wooden crate, examining the stitching on a quilt spread across her lap. She looked up and smiled. "Bridie, I knew you'd be here tonight. You're always here on the Fourth." Josie was a chubby, sweet-faced black woman about fifty-five years old. A wide-brimmed straw hat sat high on her curly gray hair. Her white cotton slacks and shirt were similar to those worn in the tropics.

"You weren't here the last two years, and I was afraid something serious happened to you."

"Gout. Painful gout," Josie replied, glancing at Catherine and Brian. "Two years of painful walking, so I stayed home. And yourself?"

Bridie beamed with pride. "My exciting news is I have a daughter."

Josie cocked her head back like a confused rooster. "What you talkin' about woman? You had a baby?"

Bridie put her hand on Catherine's shoulder, guiding her closer to the table. "This is my daughter, Catherine. We've been a family for almost a month."

Josie rolled her eyes back-and-forth between Bridie and Catherine. "She's blue ribbon quality, but I need an explanation."

"I adopted her," Bridie answered. "I fell in love with her the minute I saw her at the train station. Fortunately for me, Newberry was the train's first stop after leaving New York City."

Once again, Catherine was feeling uncomfortable under the barrage of kind words. She looked at Brian, who was grinning and enjoying her discomfort. She knew he'd endured the same when the Holmgrens introduced him to people.

Josie stood and looked deep into Catherine's eyes. "You have my sympathies, my dear."

Bridie frowned. "Sympathies?"

Still looking into Catherine's eyes, Josie continued. "Yes, sympathies. Your loss must have been painful, chile. Keep your parents in your heart, but look to the future. Being adopted by Bridie was good fortune for you. Make the most of it." With raised eyebrows, Josie looked at Bridie. "I assume you're referring to the Orphan Train?"

"Yes," Bridie answered, taking a step back to grip Brian's arm. "Brian came on the same train, and now he's the son of Tom and Margaret Holmgren."

"Lawdy. That must have been a train from heaven. Both of them are top drawer." Josie leaned forward slightly. "My sympathies to you, too, Brian."

"I would like you to show Catherine some of your interesting quilts." Bridie turned to Brian. "Sorry, this probably won't be interesting to you."

Brian shrugged his shoulders, signifying he'd be patient.

"Do you know anything about quilts?" Josie asked Catherine.

"Beyond sewing patches of cloth together, no."

"Quilts are difficult to make. It takes lots of love and dedication, but when you're finished, you have something to be proud of." Josie raised the quilt she was holding, so Catherine could see it better. "You can make colorful patterns with squares, triangles, rectangles–whatever you like. Solid colored cloth, or cloth with a print. You can make a picture of anything you want." Josie flung the quilt over her shoulder, picked up another and unfolded it. "Here, chile, look at this one, a picture of a farmhouse surrounded by trees, black and white cows and brown horses in the field. See the farmer with the pitch-fork pilin' up the hay."

"Its recorded history," Catherine said. "I like it."

"There are stories behind many quilts," Josie said, enthusiastically. "Some are happy stories and some are sad. Lookin' at quilts is like lookin' back in time." She folded the quilt with the farm scene. "If you wanna see quilts with history, I've got something special. Ever hear about the Underground Railroad that helped slaves escape from the south?"

Catherine shook her head. "No."

Brian stepped forward. "What's an underground railroad?"

"Let's do this," Josie said. She turned around and began sliding crates over dirt and tufts of grass. "You folks sit back here, facing me, under my canvas. I'll tell you about quilts and the Underground Railroad."

She lifted the lid of the crate she was sitting on and pulled out two quilts. She glanced at the people passing her tables, before sitting down. "I keep my most important quilts in this case," she said. "I've got three more in there. All were made by slaves some forty, fifty years ago, maybe longer. They bring the best price because they were made and used by slaves involved in the Underground Railroad. The real thing, you might say."

"These were made by negro slaves?" Brian asked.

"Yes, Sir, made by the hands of negro women. Their white boss thought it was clever of them slave women, makin' quilts in their spare time. They even bought them for gifts. What they didn't know was, as some quilts hung out of a window, or over a clothesline or fence, it had a message that only the slaves understood. A message tellin' 'em what night a group was heading north, where they should meet, and who was leading the escape. They was displayed right under their master's nose and he wasn't wise to nothing."

Catherine looked closely at a quilt. "How did they do that? I don't understand."

"Did they have weapons?" Brian questioned, eagerly. "Guns and knives to protect themselves as they traveled north?"

"What about small children?" Catherine added. "Were they strong enough to make such a long trip?"

"Sometimes, they had a weapon or two, and sometimes they didn't," Josie said, to Brian. "It was difficult for a slave to get his hands on a gun. That wasn't allowed."

Josie turned her eyes to Catherine to answer her questions. "Yes, children did make the trip, but seldom babies. An infant's cry could reveal where they was hiding, when being hunted." Josie shook a fly off her arm and shooed it away. "There were times when slaves was hiding in the woods, or in tall weeds along a river bank, and a mother held her hand over her baby's face so it couldn't cry out. Then the mother would cry, quietly, holding her lifeless child."

Catherine reached out to touch the quilts Josie was holding, pondering their history.

A stretch of silence brought a need for Josie to continue her story. "Let's go back to Catherine's question, about how quilts was used as messages." She unfolded one of the two quilts she took out of the case and spread it across her lap. "See these square designs in the corners that look like pointed shoes. That's called a Monkey Wrench. It's what turns them wagon wheels. It was generally displayed at the house where they would meet the night of the escape. When slaves saw a quilt with the Monkey Wrench, it meant—gather the tools you'll need for the journey to freedom." Josie turned the quilt over and placed it on her lap again, sliding her finger over another symbol. "Now, when a quilt was showin' this round, Wagon Wheel design, it told slaves to start packin' their things for the journey."

Brian reached out and felt one of the wagon wheels on the quilt. "Where did they get all the tools and food for the trip north?"

"Some had tools of their own," Josie answered. She raised her eyebrows and smiled. "Some stole things the night they was leavin' the plantation." Josie leaned forward and laid the quilt across the laps of her listeners. "Feel this piece of history while I go on with my story."

A man and women in farm clothes stopped and fingered two quilts on Josie's table, then moved on, after a nod and a smile.

"You won't be able to sell anything, if you're telling us tales," Bridie said.

"I'm goin' to the Tyler County Fair when I leave Newberry, tomorrow. I'll have time to sell there. Besides, I want to spend time with you and these two Newberryites." Wide-eyed, she paused. "Did I say that right?"

"I think you did," Bridie answered, with a smile.

Catherine tugged on Brian's sleeve. "You are Brian, 'The Newberryite.' Did you ever imagine that?"

"Can't say I gave it much thought," Brian replied, giving her an affectionate nudge with his shoulder.

Bridie and Josie glanced at each other. Bridie tilted her head to the side, fluttering her eyelashes, as a clue to Brian and Catherine's relationship.

Josie responded with a slow nod and said, "On with the story. See the clusters of boxes on this quilt? Some people refer to them as cubes, while others called 'em boxes. This symbol is called Tumbling Boxes, or Tumbling Cubes. When that pattern was displayed, the slaves knew it was time to escape. A spiritual verse on a quilt could secretly reveal the night they would leave, and a number of stars or animals may give the hour to meet."

"They were quite clever," Brian commented. "Where did they run to? How did they find their way?"

"Some went to northern states and some continued on to Canada," Josie answered. "White folks against slavery helped them along the way. The Masons were abolitionists and they helped slaves in many ways. They had 'safe houses,' farms or homes where they'd hide slaves for a day or more—until it was safe for them to continue their journey. These safe houses were generally about twenty-five miles apart. Quilts was used as signals to help guide the slaves along the way. If a quilt with stars hung out of a window or over a clothesline, it meant slaves would be safe to stay the night. They would sleep in a barn or shed, and food was brought to them in the morning."

Music by the Newberry Band spread across Getty's Field. "It must be eight o'clock," Bridie said, looking at her watch. "They're starting with that new John Philip Sousa march, 'The Stars and Stripes Forever.'" Bridie folded her hands on her lap and smiled. "What a pity. I believe we missed the mayor's speech."

"That music is quite lively," Catherine remarked. "It makes you want to line up and march around the field."

"Not until we're finished with the story," Brian said, waiting for Josie to continue.

Josie gathered the four corners of the quilt together and held them in front of her guests. "See the set of symbols in these corners? Three triangles standin' on end, one right behind the other, like arrowheads? They're called Flying Geese; each set a different color. The black geese were the important ones to watch for, 'cause they pointed in the direction the slaves should go. Up this road, or down the other, just guidin' them the right way. Sometimes, there was a number behind the black geese, letting the slaves know which city or town was in that direction."

Brian reached for one of the corners, to examine it. "Why did they use numbers?"

"If they used names of towns, the quilt would look like a map and raise suspicion. So, the men leadin' the group had to memorize which big town was what number. They didn't need many, just five or six to guide them to where they was going." Josie leaned back and folded the quilts again. "The Underground Railroad is a much bigger story, but now you know how quilts played a part in it."

Catherine slid her hand across the quilt on her lap, trying to feel the hand of the woman who made it. "These *are* special," Catherine said, to Josie. "The one with the flying geese is my favorite. It's so colorful. The woman who made it must have been very talented."

"Thanks for telling us that story," Brian said, retrieving Bridie's blanket from the ground.

"I see a lemonade sign up ahead, and I'm thirsty," Bridie declared. "You kids go ahead. I'll be right behind you."

A minute later, Sheriff Mason and his wife Essie, walked by, waving to Bridie. "You missed the mayor's speech," he yelled to her. "It was as boring as last year's." They smiled and continued on their way.

Two girls sipping lemonade stared at Catherine and Brian, approaching the lemonade vendor. They stepped back from the table and walked away, looking over their shoulders at them. One of the girls said to her friend, "I bet they're the bastards from New York."

Catherine looked around them, wondering whether the girl was referring to someone else. The only people nearby were obviously local residents. She looked at Brian, "Do you think she was referring to us?"

"I certainly hope not." He turned to the woman behind the table. "Three lemonades, please." He placed three coins on the table.

Bridie walked up behind them. "It's been a while since a good-looking young man bought me a lemonade. I'm positively thrilled."

"He's mine," Catherine said, thrusting her nose upward.

"He certainly is," Bridie agreed, with a wink.

"Catherine! Brian!" someone shouted from the crowd. It was Monica, waving her arm over her head, sidestepping through the crowd of people. She was wearing a red cotton dress and beige knee stockings that appeared second-hand. Her black shoes were the ones she wore on the train to Newberry.

Monica grabbed Catherine and hugged her. "I'm glad we're finally together." She stepped back and looked Catherine up and down. "I like your dress. It fits you perfectly." She smiled at Brian. "It's good to see both of you."

Brian was taken aback by Monica's exuberance. "Would you like a lemonade?"

"No, thanks. The Peters bought me a root beer when we got here."

Catherine grabbed Monica's arm and turned her toward Bridie. "The first thing I want to do, is introduce you to Bridie McDonald."

Bridie extended her hand to Monica. "Nice to meet you. Catherine told me about you and the train ride to Newberry."

Monica took Bridie's hand. "It was a long ride, but interesting. We even saw Indians when we got into Illinois. That was special." She looked at Catherine. "We were nervous about where we would be living, but we never imagined we'd be adopted in the same town."

"I have a suggestion," Bridie said, glancing at each of them. "I'm sure you have much to talk about, so why don't you three wander off and get reacquainted." Bridie pointed to a group of oak trees beyond the tents. "Be at those trees before ten o'clock and we'll watch the fireworks from there." Bridie looked at Monica. "Do Clay and Sona Peters know where you are?"

"I'm to meet them at Feller Road after the fireworks. They'll be spending most of their time at the beer tent. Mr. Peters is intent on having beer and sausage, while listening to the Newberry Band. Not that I believe he's that interested in the band."

"You're probably right," Bridie agreed, nodding. "Actually, you should go over to the band, too. Boys and girls your age usually meet there to dance and do whatever young people do today. You haven't circulated around town much, so it's a good opportunity to make new friends." She stepped up to Brian and took the folded blanket from under his arm. "Go have fun. I'll meet you later." Bridie sipped her lemonade and watched them walk toward the music.

The sun was setting and exhibitors began lighting kerosene lanterns that were sitting on tables or hanging from metal rods stuck into the ground. Brian took the girls' arms and guided them down the middle of the path.

The band tent was open at both sides. The musicians were at the far end, sitting on a variety of chairs, boxes and barrels. Kerosene lamps stood among them, so they could read their sheet music. Volunteers were nearby to prevent fires. Couples stood in front of the band, waiting for another round of music. The dance floor was the best patch of grass in Getty's Field, cut close to the roots.

The Newberry Band wore colorful uniforms that were beautiful enough to be in a parade for President McKinley. Their royal blue pants had twin gold stripes down the side of the legs, and their red coats were decorated with gold piping at the cuffs and lapels. Their military style hats were white, with a black bill under a gold medallion.

Mr. Perkins, the bandleader, tapped the baton against his polished belt buckle to get the band's attention. He reached forward with his arms bowed, like the pincers of a scorpion, dipped the baton and counted, "one ... two ... three," then curled his arms through the air. The band began playing an old favorite, "Lorena." A large number of older people, who remembered the song from Civil War days, rushed to dance. It has been said, and believed, that "Lorena" was such a haunting love song it made Confederate soldiers so homesick they actually deserted after hearing it. Confederate General John Hunt Morgan called it "The cursed ballad" and ordered his officers to kill the author.

Catherine tugged on Brian's sleeve. "Do you dance?"

"Not well, but I've done it," he replied, knowing he was being called to duty. He placed his arm around Catherine's waist and led her into the dance. They held each other and rocked, not moving far from where they started.

Brian was right, Catherine thought, *he isn't a good dancer*. But she was happy just to have him holding her. "How many girls have you danced with?" She asked in an attempt to learn more about him. She kept her head against his chest, waiting for an answer.

"Neighbors' parties and school dances. Nothing special." He became somewhat uncomfortable. Five boys and four girls were standing outside of the tent watching them. In an attempt to appear friendly, Brian smiled at them, making a slow turn with Catherine. There wasn't an inviting response from any of the nine youngsters. They looked at Brian and Catherine and turned away. Brian turned Catherine again, so she could see the old white-haired couple next to them. They were dancing cheek-to-cheek, with their eyes closed.

"How sweet. They're still in love," Catherine whispered.

When the music stopped, Brian and the girls strolled slowly in the direction of the other youths, hoping a conversation would develop. The nine moved on, obviously avoiding them.

Brian took both girls by the arm and led them toward the beer tent, pretending that was where they were originally headed. "I wonder why they walked away?" Brian asked. "It's going to be hard to meet people at this rate."

Monica skipped ahead, walking backwards to face Catherine and Brian. "We're orphans. You know, kids from New York–thieves, children of drunks and prostitutes. In other words, they think we're bastards, kids with bad blood, undesirables they should stay away from. Mrs. Peters warned me this could happen."

"She right," came a youthful voice nearby. "Don't try be friends with them. Not now." A slender girl, about twelve-years-old, was sitting on the grass in the shadow of the beer tent. She stood and walked over to them. Her eyes were very dark and her straight black hair was cut even with her chin. "You come on Orphan Train, yes?"

"How do you know that?" Brian asked, wondering if they had met her before.

"I go train station when you come. I see you there," she replied. The curious looks bestowed on the girl motivated her to explain her poor English. "I, too, come on Orphan Train, five month now. I live at Campbell house. Mrs. Campbell teach school and she learn me to speak English. I not good, but better now." She couldn't help but giggle at her poor English. "I teach Italian to her."

"Why did the other kids walk away from us?" Brian asked.

"Let's sit and talk where it's more private," Catherine suggested, glancing at the people walking past them. "You can teach us about Newberry."

The girl giggled again. "I teach you? That funny."

Monica stepped closer to the girl. "You can be our new friend and we can be your friends. I'm Monica. What's your name?"

"Pina." She looked at Brian and Catherine, waiting for their names.

"I'm Catherine and he's Brian. We're glad to meet you. Now there are four of us who came on the Orphan Train."

Once again, Catherine suggested they move to a more private place, away from the tents. The others agreed, walking to a place a dozen yards off the path by an outcropping of big, black boulders.

They sat in the grass, forming a circle, so they could face each other as they talked.

Brian renewed the conversation with Pina. "Why are the kids avoiding us?"

"Monica right by what she say," Pina answered. "They no sure if we bad people, so they keep away. Some people nice to me. In time, be better, I think, when they know us more. Sheriff Howard and Essie good to me. I like them."

"I don't want anyone thinking I'm a bastard," Brian said, angrily. His pride was ruffled and he ripped a plug of grass from the ground and tossed it aside. "I had two wonderful parents, better than most of the people in Newberry."

"Me, too," Catherine chimed in. She gave Brian her flag to hold, while hooking her arm with his. "We know who we are. We just have to wait for them to like us, and they will."

Monica stuck her American flag into the ground next to her. "We're good people. If the people of Newberry are nice, they'll accept us for who we are." She turned to Pina. "Where are you from–here in America?"

"Papa die in Italy. Then Mama, my brother Marcello and I come America and live New York City for eight months, then go Alton, Delaware." Pina was staring at the ground, concentrating on how to continue the story with her best English words. "My mother die there, then me and brother live with Italian friends two weeks. They send us to Saint Mary's Children's Home in New York City. Like you, Marcello and me go Orphan Train. I stay here. He go on. Marcello see I in Newberry, but I don't know where he go. Hope I get letter soon."

The band began playing "There's A Tavern In The Town." Their conversation was interrupted by, shouts and cheers. The children looked toward the band tent and saw spectators clapping their hands and stamping their feet, while dancers spun and twirled to the music.

"They won't be dancing much longer," Catherine said. "It's almost time for the fireworks."

"Watch the fireworks with us," Brian suggested, to Pina. He pointed to the silhouette of trees, barely visible in the darkness. "We'll be sitting by those trees over there. Can you see them?"

"Yes, I see," Pina replied. "I must ask parents." They all stood and brushed grass and dirt from the back of their clothes.

"Let's all go meet her parents," Catherine suggested. "Then they will know who Pina is with."

"Yeah!" Monica cried. "Be on your best behavior."

Bridie unfolded her blanket and spread it on the ground by the oak trees. Tom and Margaret arrived moments later, placing their blanket next to hers.

"It was difficult to tell in the dark, but wasn't that Kevin McCue I saw you talking to?" Margaret asked.

"Yes, it was," Bridie answered. "He stopped for a brief chat, that's all."

Margaret sat on a corner of her blanket and looked up at Bridie. "I'll bet he was panting hard. He usually does when he's around you."

"That's nonsense."

"Nonsense? Everyone in town knows he wants to get into your bloomers."

"Margaret!" Tom shouted. "That's no way to talk to your friend."

"We've discussed this before, Tom. It's just a bit of humor between Bridie and me. She knows I'm having fun with her, don't you, dear? Of course, Kevin McCue would like to have fun with you, too." Margaret covered her mouth with her hand and laughed.

"Kevin McCue is just a lonely man, with too much time on his hands," Bridie said, casually.

"He'd like to have some of *you* on his hands," Margaret said, with another burst of laughter.

Tom looked across the dark, grassy field. "I think I see the children coming, so stop talking about sex and start talking about rolling bandages for the Army, or something."

Bridie saw four dark figures walking toward them, their black silhouettes enhanced by lantern lights behind them. "It appears they have a new friend, other than Monica." She continued watching them. A man and woman carrying a lantern crossed in front of the children, their light illuminating the four figures. "It's them, but I don't recognize the girl next to Monica."

Margaret remained sitting on the blanket, while Bridie and Tom stood above her, watching the children as they came closer.

"You're just in time," Bridie said. "The fireworks should start any moment now."

"Then I'd better hurry and introduce you to our friends," Catherine said, looking at the Holmgrens. "This is Pina and Monica. I know it's hard to see them in the dark, but … well, this is Pina and Monica."

"Nice to almost see you girls," Tom said, with a chuckle.

"Catherine is *my* daughter," Bridie said. "I'm glad that you could join us."

Somewhat uncomfortable meeting strangers, Pina responded softly, "Nice to meet you."

"Pina is a pretty, yet unusual name," Margaret commented. "What country are you from?"

"Pina is Italian. It short name for Josephine."

"Her new mother is teaching her to speak English," Catherine added, quickly.

Margaret looked up at Pina's dark image. "New mother?" Margaret turned to Catherine. "Explanation, please?"

"She came here on an Orphan Train last February."

Bridie looked at Tom and Margaret. "We were at the train station that day. If I remember correctly, only one girl and three boys were adopted." She straightened her back and thought for a moment. "I remember now. You must be the Campbell girl."

"That right. I Pina Campbell."

"I'm so glad you're with us tonight," Bridie said, enthusiastically. "I've wanted to meet you since you arrived, but we can talk later, when the fireworks are finished."

A man and woman, with two young boys, came and laid down their blanket, fifteen feet away. The man stood his glowing railroad lantern on the ground and each boy dropped a battered pillow onto the blanket.

"How nice of them to bring light," Tom said. "Now we can see each other."

"You children better sit down," Bridie suggested, patting the blanket with her hand.

Bridie looked at Pina closely, trying to make a quick character judgment. "Sweet girl," she decided.

The heads of the crowd turned skyward towards a thunderous BOOM! BOOM! BOOM! Three great balls of red and white sparks illuminated the night. The sparks drizzled downward, turning into ribbons of smoke. The screaming and laughter of little children could be heard from every direction. BOOM! BOOM! BOOM! Three more lit up the night sky. The crowd roared, with approval.

"You can feel the explosions," Bridie commented. "John liked the big powerful ones best." A dozen rockets crisscrossed high above the field in front of them, followed by the snapping of a hundred firecrackers on the ground.

"I want to go home," said a little girl nearby. She was cringing, burying her face into her mother's chest.

A dozen Roman candles shot red, white and blue balls of sparks skyward for a full minute. Twelve pinwheels swirled amid the accumulation of smoke drifting across the field in front of them. Occasionally, volunteers could be seen running through the flashing light of exploding fireworks, attempting to ignite more.

"I want to go home," the little girl repeated in vain.

"In a little while. It's almost over," was her mother's unconvincing response.

BOOM! BOOM! BOOM! The smell of burnt gunpowder filtered through the crowd of onlookers.

Bridie leaned forward to whisper into Catherine's ear. "If you care to, you can invite Pina and her parents to our party this Sunday."

Catherine turned her head and nodded in agreement.

Minutes later, a gigantic display of pinwheels, roman candles, firecrackers and rockets filled the night sky, announcing the end of the show. Hoops, hollers and applause of appreciation followed.

Tom was the first to stand and help the ladies to their feet. Following the people with the lantern, Bridie looked at her daughter, her girlfriends, and the Holmgrens with their son. She fought back tears. It wasn't just her, Margaret and Tom spending an evening together, as they've usually done. As small as it was, she finally had the family life she always wanted.

Chapter Seven

The following Sunday, Tom and Margaret were at their dining room buffet, fussing over a display of fruit and pastries for the children's birthday party. Crystal stemware, serving bowls and silverware sparkled under the chandelier's light.

Bridie and Catherine were in the kitchen, watching over a roast beef in the oven, while Millie, Margaret's housekeeper, prepared salads and cooked green beans, potatoes and corn.

A half-hour earlier, Brian brought ice from the icehouse located near the train station. Clean, and smartly dressed, he ambled down the rear stairs leading to the kitchen, wearing a dark blue suit, with a white shirt and starched collar that looked uncomfortable.

Catherine saw him first. "Well, don't you look smart," she said, with an approving look. "Your suit goes nicely with my gray dress. We must stay together all day, so people will notice."

Bridie turned away from the stove to see what he was wearing. "You get more handsome as time goes on. I may try to win you for myself."

Catherine placed her hands on her hips and stared at Bridie. "That's the second time this week you've flirted with Brian."

"It probably won't be the last time, either," Bridie responded, with a chuckle. "You'd better land him fast, or somebody else will."

Millie walked up to Bridie, "Want me to set up a gift table in the living room? It'll be easier having all the presents in one place."

"There won't be any gifts, except from the parents," Bridie informed her. "I asked our guests not to bring gifts, and the children were told that. This is not only a birthday party; it's also a gathering for them to meet Brian and Catherine. Besides, Margaret and I didn't feel it proper for them to bring gifts to children they don't know."

Catherine and Brian nodded, agreeing with what Bridie. "We prefer it that way," Catherine said. "Brian and I would be embarrassed, taking presents from strangers."

The clapper of the front door bell rattled three times, announcing the first guest had arrived. "You two sit in the living room, so Margaret and I can introduce you as they arrive," Bridie suggested, walking toward the front door.

Margaret arrived at the door via the dining room. She was the hostess, so Bridie stood behind Margaret while receiving the guests.

"Good to see you," Margaret said, with a welcoming smile. She extended her hand to the woman. "Give me your parasol, I'll put it in the umbrella stand."

Tom walked up behind Bridie and Margaret. "Hi, Bill! Hi, Jean!" He looked at Bill and said, "I received those maps I ordered from St. Louis. We can look them over and see what location you think would be best for the new foundry."

Margaret glared at Tom. "Not today. They're here for the children's party."

Tom winked at Bill. "Of course. We can examine them another time."

"We went to pick up the Hogans," Jean said, "but their son is sick and they asked us to send their apologies. They said Todd and Brian could meet another time."

"The Wagners aren't coming, either," Bridie said, leading the guests to the living room. "When I called Maxine to invite them, she said they're taking their daughters to Pittsfield this weekend. One of their nieces is getting married."

Catherine and Brian rose from the sofa when the first guests entered the room. They felt like a curiosity on display, wanting the day to end in a hurry. They both smiled politely, as they were introduced to Bill and Jean O'Neal, people who were never blessed with children, but blessed with an attitude of not giving a damn.

The telephone rang and Tom went into the kitchen to answer it. When he returned, Catherine and Brian were back on the sofa paging through books. The ladies and Bill were standing at the dining room window, looking out at Margaret's flowerbeds. "That was Natalie Shore calling to say they wouldn't be coming," Tom announced to Margaret.

"Them, too?" Bridie responded with a frown. "At this rate, Catherine and Brian won't be meeting anyone their age."

Margaret walked over to Tom at the end of the dining table. "Why aren't the Shores coming?"

"Carrie has a temperature, so they're keeping her in bed. Natalie said she doesn't have any idea what could have caused it."

Catherine and Brian listened to the conversation in the dining room and glanced at each other. They were being avoided, as Monica and Pina predicted.

"There are four of us so-called bastards," Brian whispered to Catherine. "Four friends are enough. We don't need any one else."

The doorbell rang again. Margaret and Bridie excused themselves and went to meet their guests. Looking through the sheer curtain covering the door's glass, they saw Dr. Aean Batrin, and his wife Ellie. Their son, Donald, was standing next to them, half-hiding behind his mother.

Sheriff Howard Mason and his wife, Essie, arrived moments later, eager to visit with Catherine and Brian. After inviting them in, Margaret went into the kitchen and asked Millie to remove six place settings from the dining room table.

Millie stared at Margaret, with eyebrows raised and mouth open. "Remove six," she repeated, wiping her hands on her apron. "There's gunna be a lot of food left." Millie turned and walked to the dining room, mumbling to herself and shaking her head.

When Margaret returned to the living room, Bridie was at the front door with Pina and her parents. Margaret went to them immediately, brandishing a friendly smile. "I'm so pleased you could come. Bridie and I are in love with Pina."

Bridie took Pina's hand and led the Campbells into the foyer. "You look beautiful in that beige dress, Pina. It's a good color for you." She turned to the Campbells and introduced them to Margaret. "Richard is an accountant at Fidelity Bank and Eileen is a teacher at Number Seven elementary school." Eileen was slightly shorter than Bridie and had what appeared to be a perfect figure. Her brown, wavy hair was loosely arranged and covered her ears.

"We moved to Newberry just two years ago," Eileen said. "Richard and I were born and raised in Northern Pike County."

Richard was built like Tom, and equally good-looking. A modest mustache gave him a sophisticated look. Richard stepped forward and placed his arm around Eileen. "I was offered a decent position at the bank and there was a teaching position open at the school, so we took both. We like Newberry and our roots aren't far from here, making it easy to go back and visit our families."

Margaret put her hands on Pina's shoulders and turned her toward the living room. "I'm sure you don't want to listen to us jabbering. Catherine and Brian are right around the corner."

Pina smiled, then looked at Eileen, who swept her hand toward the room ahead. "Go on, your friends are waiting. Richard and I will meet them shortly."

Margaret and Bridie took the Campbells to meet the children and other guests who were conversing in the dining room. The three children went into the dining room, looking for Donald Batryn, then went out the back door and found him in the yard. They examined the flowerbeds walking through the grass toward the front of the house, to wait for Monica and her parents.

Suddenly, Pina screamed and ran up the front porch steps.

"What's wrong?" Brian asked.

"Look!" she yelled, pointing toward Donald. "Snake in grass by you. Run!"

Donald turned around and straddled the snake. Carefully, but quickly, he grabbed it behind the head. The snake coiled its body around Donald's arm, trying to push away.

Brian walked over to Donald. "Let me see it. Is it poisonous?"

Donald held it close to his face, looking into its mouth. "No. It's just a harmless grass snake." Donald held the snake, so Brian could examine it closely and stroke its skin.

Pina's grimacing face looked down at them with disgust.

"I hear snakes taste like chicken," Brian said.

"Taaaaste?" Pina squealed, leaning over the porch railing. "How you can touch it? It bite you, maybe."

Donald frowned, giving Pina a curious look.

"She's from Italy," Catherine whispered to Donald. "Her English is a little chopped up."

Donald nodded his head.

Brian pointed up the street. "Isn't that Monica and Mr. Peters coming?"

The three children went to the edge of the street, while Pina remained on the porch. The wagon ambled slowly down the street under an arch of leaf-filled branches, stretching from one side of the street to the other.

"Get snake away," Pina yelled from the porch. "I come by you."

Brian and Donald looked back at Pina and laughed.

Donald ran to the back of the house and placed the snake in the farthest flowerbed. When he returned, Mr. Peters was pulling on the reins, stopping the mules in front of the house. Sunlight flickered through the leaves and branches, as they swayed in the gentle breeze.

Pina joined the others at the street, looking at Donald's hands to see if he still had the snake.

"Happy Birthday!" Monica shouted from the bench seat behind the mules. "Look! No presents, as requested. Good thing, 'cause I don't have any money." Monica gave Mr. Peters a peck on the cheek and climbed down from the wagon.

Brian looked up at Mr. Peters. "Good afternoon, Sir."

"Afternoon," he mumbled with a nod. He gave Monica an uncompromising look and said, "7:30." He shook the reins and drove off, surprising the other children with his unfriendly attitude.

Monica was wearing a homemade, red cotton dress and white knee stockings. Mrs. Peters had sewn on a white lace collar and a round pearl button and loop to hold it closed at the neck.

"Your parents were invited," Catherine declared. "What happened?"

"My Ma isn't feeling well and Pa didn't want to leave her alone. They were disappointed, but asked me to thank you for the invitation."

Mr. Peters was just here, Catherine thought. *He could have apologized for himself.* She believed they didn't want to come because they don't have nice clothes.

Brian looked at Monica, "This is Donald. While we were waiting for you, he caught a snake with his bare hands."

"I want to see the snake. I like them," Monica said, to everyone's astonishment. "Where is it?"

"You go see. I stay here," Pina responded, quickly.

Bridie stepped out onto the porch and called to Monica, "Where are your parents? Aren't they coming for dinner?"

"No. They asked me to thank you for the invitation, but Ma is sick, so Dad is staying with her."

Bridie believed, as Catherine did, that the Peters would feel out of place among well-dressed people. "Sorry to hear that. I was looking forward to meeting them." Bridie started to go into the house, then stepped back onto the porch. "Come into the house and we'll eat." Bridie asked Millie to remove two more place settings.

The children filed into the house, as Millie hurried around the dining room table, rearranging chairs and place settings so they were evenly spaced. When she finished, the adults seated themselves, leaving a seat at both ends of the table for Catherine and Brian.

After the main course and refills of coffee and tea were served, Millie brought in a birthday cake. She showed the cake to all the guests before setting it on a serving table in the corner of the room. It was a flat cake, with chocolate frosting and "Happy Birthday, Catherine and Brian" inscribed with yellow sugar crystals.

On Margaret's cue, everyone began singing "Happy Birthday."

Sheriff Mason raised his glass of red wine to Brian, while his wife, Essie, raised her glass to Catherine. "If I may have everyone's attention, please," Howard asked. "I'm not much at giving speeches, but I would like to propose a simple toast to both of you. This is the second time we've met you, and we have been impressed. You appear to be two nice people, and Essie and I want to welcome you to Newberry." Howard paused. "That's it." Believing he gave a weak toast, he blushed and gave a nervous laugh. Others at the table raised their glasses and made similar statements.

Catherine raised her glass of water to the Masons, then to all the guests around the table. She rolled her eyes before responding. "Thank you. I hope we can live up to your kind words. Many times, Brian and I have discussed how fortunate we are to be living with Tom, Margaret and Bridie, and how we like Newberry. I also want to thank all of you for coming this afternoon."

Brian raised his glass from the table, looking at the guests. He fixed his eyes on Tom and Margaret, then Bridie. "Actually, I can't think of enough kind words to show my appreciation, so I'll simply say—Catherine and I are lucky to be where we are, and to be living with these wonderful people."

"I hope you're as pleased as we are," Margaret muttered.

Tom winked at Brian. "Thank you, Son."

"All this mushy talk is making me sick," Bridie said. She looked at Millie. "It's time to open the presents."

Millie went into the kitchen and returned with two large, white boxes. Brian's had a wide blue ribbon tied around it, while Catherine's was tied with a pink ribbon.

Catherine's eyes widened, staring at the large gift. "The box is huge. I can't imagine what's in it." Catherine pushed her chair back from the table and glanced at everyone, wondering if they already knew what it was. She placed the box on her lap. "See, I told you they've been wonderful to us–spoiling us, actually."

Brian's arms were hanging at his sides, staring at the box on his lap. He shook his head at Tom and Margaret for doting on him, as they had.

"Somebody open something," Monica rumbled, leaning over the table.

"Maybe it's a big snake?" Donald joked, trying to get a rise out of Pina.

Pina folded her arms on the table, looking at Catherine. "We want to see."

Catherine looked across the table at Brian. "You open yours first."

Brian smiled. "Ladies first," he insisted.

"Glad to," Catherine responded, quickly untying the pink ribbon. Catherine raised the lid of the box and pushed aside white paper covering the gift. She squealed and covered her mouth with her hand, muffling her words. "The Flying Geese." Her hand remained over her mouth, staring at the quilt, unable to say anything immediately. She removed it from the box and showed it to everyone in the room, while giving a quick explanation of its involvement in The Underground Railroad. Her eyes glossed over, looking at Bridie. "You shouldn't have, but of course I'm glad you did." She didn't know whether to laugh or cry, then did a little of both.

Bridie smiled at Catherine. "I saw you fall in love with it when Josie told you its history. I had to get it for you."

Brian looked at Bridie and clapped his hands three times in appreciation for Catherine's gift. "You couldn't have given her anything better." He gazed at the quilt, knowing how happy Catherine was. Yet he, too, would like to have a relic of The Underground Railroad.

Jean O"Neal stared at the quilt. "That's a fabulous gift for a lifetime."

"It's beautiful," Monica moaned, knowing she would never receive such a gift.

"What railroad?" Pina asked, looking around the table for someone to tell her.

Eileen Campbell whispered into Pina's ear, "I'll tell you when we get home."

Catherine smiled at Brian. "Open your gift."

Brian leaned back against the chair and lifted the cover off the box. He brandished a big smile, removing a buckskin jacket he admired on a man visiting the quarry. He looked at Tom. "I guess I did comment on how much I liked it. Thanks for remembering." He smiled at Margaret, and stood to put it on.

Margaret brushed her hand against it. "It looks great on you."

"Be still my beating heart," Bridie swooned.

"Flirting with Brian again?" Catherine questioned.

Millie began serving birthday cake, tea and coffee, as conversation centered on the four adopted children. When they finished eating, everyone went out into the garden or sat on the back porch. Pina stayed near Donald in case a snake appeared.

The Campbells were on the back porch, sitting in wicker chairs when Bridie came out of the house. Eileen looked over her shoulder at her. "Tom and I are so pleased that Pina has Catherine and her other new friends. She's been bored without special friends."

Bridie was surprised by Eileen's statement. "Surely, she has friends in Newberry? She's such a nice girl."

Richard raised himself from his wicker chair, so Bridie could sit down. He leaned against the porch railing. "Nice doesn't mean anything, if people believe you're a bastard," he said, in an irritated voice. "Pina had parents and gets very emotional when she talks about her family, proving she's not making it up."

"Wait a minute," Bridie interrupted. "Do you mean to tell me that people in Newberry believe Pina is a bastard?"

"People question the parentage of all orphans coming from New York City," Eileen said. "You never considered that possibility?"

Bridie took a deep breath, looking as though she had been slapped in the face. "I realize some New York orphans are bastards, but certainly only a small percentage. How can people label a child in such a way, without having proof?"

Richard's eyebrows rose and dipped again, looking at Bridie. "Are you alright? You look kind of pale."

"I'll be fine," Bridie answered, trying to ignore the tightness developing in her throat. "I'm adjusting to this revelation. Not that I hadn't thought of it before, but certainly not about these children." Bridie looked at the couple. "Eight families with children the same age as ours were invited to today's birthday party. Five of them didn't show, for one reason or another. I'm not going to pass judgment now, but I will take note of who accepts our children into their lives and who doesn't." Bridie stared out into the yard where the children were playing. "Children are children. It's not their fault how they came into this world. They need love and understanding like anyone else."

Eileen bit her lower lip, watching Bridie struggle with her emotions. Finally, she said, "I'm not overly concerned. Being that they are nice children, I believe they will be accepted in time. There has been some improvement toward Pina already."

Bridie recalled the first Sunday Catherine and Brian were brought to church, and how, after the service, people remained in their pews to see them. *Were they happy for us*, she wondered. *Or were they curious to see what bastards look like*? She smiled at Richard and Eileen. "You're right," she said, "Everything will work out for them because I'll make sure it does." Bridie excused herself and went down into the yard to say something to Catherine, then returned to the Campbells.

Two minutes later, all of the children ran up the porch stairs and went into the kitchen and beyond.

Richard folded his arms, glancing at Bridie. "Whatever you told them, they seem to like the idea."

"I believe they did," Bridie responded, grinning like a child who just found the hidden cookie jar. "Do you want something to drink?"

It was dusk when Bridie and Catherine returned home from the party. They went into the kitchen and discovered Jack standing on the back porch, looking over at the two ducks on the pond. Not wanting to be around Jack, Catherine carried her present upstairs.

Bridie was upset Catherine was still afraid of Jack.

Catherine dropped the white box on the bedroom floor, kicked off her shoes and removed the blue comforter from her bed. She folded it a few times before placing it on a shelf in the closet. She started humming, "Old Man River," and removed her 'Flying Geese' quilt from the box. Catherine slid her hand across the quilt, again trying to feel the soul of the woman who'd made it. Remembering Josie's words, she began thinking of slaves sneaking from one town to another. To preserve the quilt, she knew she couldn't keep it on her bed. It would have to be stored carefully. She would sleep under it this once.

Catherine laid the quilt across the bed, centering it perfectly. She saw herself in the dresser mirror across the room, then stood on her toes and examined herself from every angle. "Thank you, God," she whispered.

On the Fourth of July, Bridie told her there was a picture book, *Slaves On The Plantation*, in the living room bookcase. She decided to go down and look at some of the photographs before going to sleep. When she got to the bottom of the stairs, Bridie was standing in the hallway by the butler's pantry, just outside the kitchen. She was about ten feet behind Jack, watching him eat. Bridie didn't hear her coming because she was in her stocking feet. Catherine hesitated a moment, wondering why Bridie was standing quietly behind Jack, then moved on to the living room. She was puzzled about their relationship, wondering why Bridie was so concerned about Jack's welfare. Catherine believed feeding Jack and having a bed for him in the basement was odd, especially since his mother lived nearby. *Surely, they couldn't be doing anything sexual?*

Catherine went directly to the bookcase and began searching for the book. All the books were standing on end and the title she wanted was in bold black print on a white jacket. She pulled it from the bookcase and pretended to be reading, making her way back to the stairs. Without turning her head, she looked laterally and saw Bridie, still standing in the hall, unaware of her presence. Quietly, she made her way up the stairs and back to her room.

Chapter Eight

The next morning, Margaret walked into the kitchen as Brian finished the last of his flapjacks and molasses. "It's Monday, the day I do bookkeeping for Tom, so please take his black boots to Mr. Kinnaird's shop and have him put new heels on them." She stepped toward the dining room, "Before I forget, Tom said you'll be working with him at the quarry tomorrow."

"Good!" Brian replied, carrying his breakfast dishes to the sink. "Tomorrow, they're blasting a big stone wall at the south end of the quarry. It should be quite a sight."

"Stay far away, so you don't get hurt," Margaret insisted, entering the dining room. She sat at her desk overlooking her yard and flowerbeds.

Brian decided it was too much bother hitching up Dandy for the short ride to Main Street. He picked up Tom's black boots from the vestibule floor and went outside. He jogged the first two blocks under the green, leafy arches formed by tall trees lining both sides of Harper Street. Sunlight flickered between their leaves and branches.

When Brian got to Main Street, he stopped and leaned against a lamppost, watching a slow moving, green and gold Keeler's Beer wagon roll by. The driver, a burly man with a handlebar mustache, was wearing black pants and a sleeveless undershirt. The barrels in the back of the wagon were shaking and rattling, as the wagon bounced over the cobblestone street. Brian gripped the boots firmly and darted across the street.

Most of the stores along Main Street had colored awnings stretching out over the sidewalk, sheltering customers and merchandise from the hot sun. Brian passed Billaby's Drug Store, New Perth Tobacco and The Inverness Dram Shop, before arriving at Kinnaird's Shoe Repair. He entered the shop and placed the boots on the counter, the smell of leather filling his nostrils. He saw Mr. Kinnaird sitting on a stool, holding a short, curved knife, trimming the edge of a leather sole he was attaching to a man's brown shoe.

The man lowered his head and squinted over his glasses at Brian. "What ya got there, Laddie?"

"I need new heels on these boots. They're for Mr. Holmgren."

"Tom Holmgren?"

"Yes, I'm his son."

Mr. Kinnaird looked puzzled, until he realized who Brian was. "Praise be Jesus," he mumbled. "You the lad Tom took home?"

"That's one way of saying it," Brian responded.

Brian examined Mr. Kinnaird, walking to the counter. He wore a black leather cap and a work apron over gray denim work clothes. The leather apron had many brown and black smudges of shoe polish streaked in every direction.

"Eeeyy, and a sturdy lookin' lad ya are. Welcome ta Newberry." He presented his dirty hand to Brian. "Ya canna go wrong with parents like Tom and Margaret."

Brian shook Mr. Kinnaird's hand firmly, in spite of the glue and polish and whatever else covered it. "They're very nice people and I'm lucky to be living with them." Brian pushed the boots closer to Mr. Kinnaird. "When can I pick these up?"

Mr. Kinnaird turned the boots upside-down and examined the bottoms. "Come back in two days," he replied, with a wink.

Brian winked back, "Thanks, I'll see you then." He left the shop and returned to the intersection he had crossed moments before. Sixty feet away, a woman was struggling with two canvas bags of groceries. A strap had torn away from one and she was having a difficult time carrying them. Brian ran up behind her, taking the bag resting on her hip. "Let me take this one."

Brian guessed her to be in her late thirties. His eyes followed the pleasant curves of her body. She was about six inches shorter than he, with wavy, honey-brown hair that reached her shoulders.

She gave a sigh of relief. "You're an angel. I have only one block to go, but I don't think I could have managed both bags by myself." She wrapped both of her arms around the one bag and looked at the helpful stranger. She was immediately captivated by his good looks. "I've never seen you before. Do you live in Newberry?"

"Yes, I arrived here seven weeks ago."

She maneuvered herself away from Brian, just enough so she could see all of him. "What's your name?"

"Brian Hampton." He paused a moment, "Brian Hampton-Holmgren." He looked at her and laughed, knowing he must have confused her.

She shifted the grocery bag in her arms and smiled at him. "I don't know any people named Hampton, but I know Tom and Margaret Holmgren. Not personally, mind you, but I know of them because we attend the same church. I sing in the choir," she added with pride.

"They're my parents. They adopted me."

"Then you're not a blood relative?" She examined Brian's physique again. "Did you come on that Orphan Train a few weeks ago?"

"Yes. I'm fifteen and happy to have a family again."

In her thoughts, she agreed. She didn't want him somewhere else, either.

Brian waited for a noisy carriage to pass before asking her name.

She liked his self-confidence and how relaxed he was with her. He appeared mature beyond his fifteen years. She gave her name with a flirtatious smile. "My name is Nerine." She removed a key from a slit pocket in her green skirt, stopping in front of a two-story, red brick building. "This is where I live," she said, in an informative way. "Number 170, Temple Street."

"I like living across from Winnemac Park. I get plenty of sunlight and I don't have to look at a neighbor's brick wall." Nerine led Brian up the three stone steps and into the hallway where there were twelve brass mailboxes. "I would appreciate it if you would carry that bag into my apartment. It's right here, first floor, front."

Brian watched her unlocked the door and walk directly to the kitchen table where she let the grocery bag slide out of her arms. He enjoyed the way her body moved when she walked, and the friendly warmth of her voice. She reminded him of Renny, his frequent, and favorite customer in New York City. He enjoyed making love to Renny, and believed he could enjoy Nerine, too.

Nerine went to a sky blue cabinet standing next to the kitchen sink hanging on the wall. She hurried to get two glasses of ice water, hoping to stall Brian's departure. "It's so hot, both of us could use a cold drink," she said, chopping at a block of ice with an ice pick.

The apartment consisted of two rooms and Brian could see into the bedroom from where he was standing. It had flowered wallpaper and a bed covered with a blue bedspread, the same blue as the dish cabinet. The kitchen made up half of the room they were in; the other half was a sitting area, with a brown sofa and two stuffed green chairs.

Nerine walked up to Brian, closer than necessary, handing him a glass of ice water. "This will quench your thirst," she said, looking directly into his eyes. She slowly backed away and leaned against the sink. "Where did you live before coming to Newberry?"

"New York. I'm really from Gresham, Connecticut, but after my father died, I tried to find work in New York City."

Nerine watched his eyes survey her body. "What kind of work did you find there?"

Brian drank some water before answering. "Pay was poor at the factories, so I worked the streets doing one thing and another. I got by, but I wanted a home and schooling, so I could be an engineer. Besides, I prefer to eat every day."

Nerine was amused by his attempts to sneak quick glances at her body without being obvious. "How did you earn your money?"

Brian decided not to answer that question completely. "No special way, just odd jobs." He set his glass on the kitchen table. "I suppose I should be going."

"Don't go. I'd like to know you better. You're a very interesting young man." She placed her glass in the sink and walked over to one of the stuffed chairs. "Come, sit with me awhile. I want to know more about you and your work in New York City." Brian's mature attitude toward her convinced her he'd had sexual encounters with women. She decided to be direct with him. "My guess is you made money pleasing women."

Brian was surprised by her accurate diagnosis and stared into her eyes. "Why would you say that?" he asked, calmly.

"Because both of us are thinking about having sex together and you aren't nervous at all, and that comes with experience."

Brian walked to the door and opened it.

"Whatever we do together would be our secret," Nerine said. "Once a person has enjoyed sex, there's a need for more, and you are ready for more."

"How can you be sure I'm ready now?"

Nerine crossed her legs and leaned back against the stuffed chair. "Easy, my dear. I can tell by the way you've been looking at me since we came to my apartment. Your breathing has become labored, and you've developed a bulge in your pants. Our secret," she repeated.

Brian turned his back to her and closed the door. Nerine smiled, as he walked toward her.

Chapter Nine

The second Saturday in August, Brian was taking Catherine for a buggy ride to show her the quarry where he worked. He spent the morning feeding Dandy, washing the buggy and greasing the axles. When finished, he ran into the house and raced up the carpeted stairs, two at a time.

Margaret came out of her bedroom humming "The Emperor's Waltz," picking a loose thread from her brown dress. Her curly black hair had a slight spring to it when she walked. She stopped, waiting for Brian to come closer. "I had Millie put clean towels and a new bar of soap in the bathroom."

Brian gave her a passing peck on the cheek. "Dandy and the buggy are ready to go, so I'll leave in a half-hour.

Millie came up the stairs carrying Tom's newly laundered shirts. "Tom sure is proud of that boy."

Margaret smiled, "We both are."

At 12:10, Brian was in the shiny black buggy approaching Catherine's house. He shook the reins one last time, while looking ahead at 322 Root Street. He saw Catherine standing on the sidewalk talking to a young man he had never seen. When he got closer, Brian saw he was wearing a tan tweed suit and highly polished brown shoes. His brown hair was slicked back, with a part down the center. Brian guessed him to be twenty years old, and his massive smile showed he was enamored with Catherine, who was also smiling freely. Brian's heart sank. He pulled on the reins to stop Dandy. He climbed down from the buggy, holding the reins in one hand.

Catherine walked over to him, her sober-faced friend following. "You're right on time," Catherine said, still smiling, dramatically. She pointed to the young man. "This is Charles Belcher, a biology teacher at Knox College." She looked at Charles and introduced him to Brian."

Slowly, he extended his hand to Brian. "You're the young chap Mr. and Mrs. Holmgren adopted at the train station, right? I hope the match is working well for you."

Brian gave Charles a less than hardy handshake and responded, defensively, "Were you adopted?"

"Heavens, no," Charles answered, quickly, as though being adopted were degrading. "My family has been …" He suddenly remembered that Catherine was adopted, too, and changed his attitude. "Let's say, I've been fortunate to have parents with good health."

Aware of the tension developing between the two boys, Catherine interceded by taking Brian's arm. "We should leave, or we won't have enough time for our ride." She smiled at Charles. "It was nice meeting you. I hope we meet again."

"I'm sure we will," Charles replied, sliding his hands into his pants pockets. "I live nearby." He took two steps backwards and watched Brian help Catherine onto the buggy.

Brian sat next to her, flashing an insincere grin at Charles, then shook the reins. Neither Brian nor Catherine said a word until they turned the corner and headed toward Main Street. "Why do you hope to meet him again?" Brian asked, irritated by her statement. He looked ahead at the passing traffic on Main Street, waiting for an answer, deliberately avoiding eye contact with Catherine.

Catherine leaned forward to look into his eyes. "I was just being polite. I don't care if I ever see him again."

Brian stopped the buggy at Main Street, waiting for two horsemen to amble by in front of them. The men rocked in their saddles, looking at window displays and the young women passing them. Brian pulled the right rein and Dandy turned, quickly passing the two men.

"You two were doing a lot of smiling when I arrived at your house. It was as though you were interested in him." Brian was certain Catherine wasn't interested in Charles, but he wanted her to say it.

Catherine leaned close to Brian and whispered in his ear. "You know you're the only man for me ... and that's what you wanted me to say." Brian laughed and pulled on the reins, so a woman could cross the street in front of them. The woman turned her head and looked at Brian. It was Nerine Booker. Brian's laughter ceased. He squeezed the reins between his fingers, more from fear than from restraining Dandy. He watched Nerine glance at Catherine before walking on as though she hadn't recognized anyone. *Our secret*, he recalled her saying. He began to relax, but not completely.

Ten minutes later, they were on a country road leading to the quarry, quietly enjoying the surrounding scenery and small animals fleeting about. Brian broke the silence. "We've signed the papers for school, so I'll be leaving for Illinois University in three weeks."

Catherine locked arms with him, laying her head on his shoulder. "We knew that day was coming. I don't want you to leave me, but you must, if you want to be an engineer."

"What about you?" Brian asked. "Are you definitely going to Bradbury Finishing School?"

"Yes. Bridie is quite taken by the school's programs. She said it has an excellent reputation for producing accomplished young ladies ... like herself." She chuckled. "I believe she's somewhat prejudiced. Besides, being that it's right here in town, I won't be leaving the comforts of our home."

"Won't be leaving *her*," Brian stressed. "Now that she has a daughter, especially one she loves, she doesn't want you to leave."

"I prefer staying in Newberry, too. Only fifty-five girls attend the school and fifty are from out of town. Some girls come from as far as St. Louis, Chicago, Galena, and Springfield."

They came upon a big dip in the road where they couldn't be seen by anyone. Brian pulled on the reins, stopping the buggy.

Catherine gave Brian a questioning look. "Why are you stopping here?"

Brian put one arm around Catherine's waist and looked into her eyes. "Because I love you." With his other hand, he supported the back of her head and kissed her. Catherine slid her arms around his neck and kissed him with equal commitment, again and again. Brian felt her warm body against his and wanted to make love to her. But he knew he couldn't now, afraid he might frighten her and turn her against him. She wasn't a playmate like the mature women he had experienced. He would have to wait.

Catherine looked up and down the road and laid her head against his shoulder. "We'd better go to the quarry before someone sees us."

A few minutes past five o'clock, Brian stopped the buggy in front of Catherine's house. They looked at each other longingly, wishing they could hold each other and kiss again, but neighbors could be watching from behind windows. Being alone on a buggy ride into the country could be enough reason for people to question Catherine's virtue.

"It was a beautiful afternoon," Catherine said. "I'll write about today in my diary."

Brian walked around the buggy and took Catherine's hand to help her to the ground. "If our parents take us to church tomorrow, let's try to think of a reason to get away."

Catherine giggled. "I agree." She gave his hand an affectionate squeeze, then turned and ran up the porch stairs, looking back at Brian.

Bridie was in the parlor standing by the fireplace, holding the framed picture of John McTavish. She placed it on the mantle and walked over to a glowing Catherine. "By that look on your face, I'd say you had a grand afternoon. Is he as inspired?"

Catherine clasped her hands together under her chin, as if acting on the stage. "Yes, he is. And yes, it was a grand afternoon. And yes, I love him."

"And yes, I'm anxious to hear about your ride to the quarry," Bridie responded. "Let's sit in the parlor and tell me everything. Mothers are insufferably nosey beasts, you know." Bridie followed Catherine into the parlor, examining her dress for grass or dirt stains, or bits of leaves and other ground cover. There weren't any, and her dress wasn't wrinkled. *She's still my girl*, Bridie sighed.

They sat on the sofa and Catherine began pouring her heart out about loving the boy who loved her, and how wonderful she felt. Then, unable to hold her secret in any longer, she said blissfully, "Brian kissed me today."

Confused, Bridie batted her eyelashes, staring at Catherine. "Today? What do you mean, today? Certainly, he's kissed you before?"

Catherine tilted her head and looked at Bridie. "No. Today was the first time."

Bridie leaned back and folded her hands on her lap. "I'm delighted that both of you are happy. Does this mean I can't flirt with him anymore?"

Catherine gave Bridie a sympathetic look. "You can try, but I suggest you save yourself that embarrassment. He's all mine." She sprang to her feet and began walking out of the parlor. "I'm going upstairs to wash this road dust off of me."

"You do that, and don't forget to wash your hair." Bridie wanted her in the bathtub as long as possible, giving her time to tell Margaret about the first kiss. She went into the kitchen and sat at the table until she heard water running into the bathtub. Bridie stepped over to the telephone and cranked it vigorously. She heard a couple of clicks echo through the receiver before Cora's voice appeared.

"Hello, Bridie, how are you and Catherine this pleasant evening?"

"We're doing fine. How come you're working on a Saturday?"

"Sarah and I traded two days this week, so she could attend the Fred Stell and Edna Whitaker wedding today." Cora chuckled before continuing. "Turns out, everybody but the bride and groom showed up at the church this morning. The way I heard it, Edna left her parents' home yesterday evening and wasn't found until two o'clock this morning in a dazed condition. She was found walking down Claremont Street, near to where her former boyfriend lives. Edna couldn't give an accounting of herself, so Fred jumped out of that wedding like a cat in a tub of hot water."

"Just as well," Bridie commented. "Better they split now than live a life of regrets."

"Whom do ya want me to ring?" Cora asked, "Fred Stell, now that he's available?" Cora laughed again. "Oh! I sure enjoy me."

"I do, too," Bridie said, unconvincingly. "Please ring Margaret Holmgren for me."

"Shall do."

Three rings and Margaret answered. "Holmgren residence."

"It's Bridie. Are you in the kitchen?"

"Yes, I just sliced an apple to munch on."

"Then pull a chair over to the telephone and make yourself comfortable. I have some news about Catherine and Brian."

"I hope the news is pure, innocent and wholesome. Be right back."

Bridie could hear Margaret dragging a chair across the kitchen floor, followed by her clearing her throat.

"Do I need smelling salts?"

"Not hardly," Bridie answered. "We don't have to worry about how fast those two are walking through their romance. I found out they're walking real slow."

"Good. How slow?"

"Well, when Catherine came home from their ride to the quarry, she was all aglow and walking on clouds. We sat in the parlor and she told me Brian kissed her today, and it was their first kiss."

"Oh, how painful," Margaret gasped. "Catherine must have been frustrated with him all these weeks. First time? Today? Their romance isn't walking, it's standing on a corner somewhere."

"What about Brian? Is he walking on air, too?"

"Brian isn't home yet. He probably went for a ride down Bennett's Road to the abandoned gristmill. He likes to go there and explore the old building."

"It's a boy's thing," Bridie said, leaning against the wall. "They're inquisitive and like to explore."

Brian rode across Main Street and along Winnemac Park. He tied Dandy to a hitching post around the corner from Nerine's building. He stood for a moment, debating whether he should go to Nerine. His body was tense from being with Catherine and he wanted relief, yet he wanted to be faithful. The truth was he wanted to make love to Catherine. Brian recalled Nerine's words, "Once you've had sex, there's a need for more." He knew how true that was, but he also knew he would never cheat on Catherine, if they were married.

Brian searched the street for anyone he knew, before walking to, 170 Temple Street, first floor front. He passed the mailboxes, then hesitated at Nerine's door, listening for a presence inside. He heard a soft shuffling sound, like slippers moving across the floor. Brian looked down the hallway and up the stairs to the second floor. He didn't see anyone, so he wrapped gently on the door. He heard Nerine walk toward him and unlock the door.

Opening the door, she stared into his eyes, smiled, and said, "That girl is adorable." Nerine tied the belt around her white satin robe, dotted with purple roses. She stepped back, so Brian could enter the apartment.

Brian glanced down the empty hall before stepping into the apartment. "I hope you don't mind me stopping by."

"Not at all. I gave you an open invitation." She studied Brian's disposition, convinced he was in need of sexual gratification. "That girl I saw with you, is she your special girl?"

"Yes, and I want to thank you for keeping your promise about, you know ... our secret."

"A promise is a promise. Besides, I'm looking forward to a long relationship with you."

The scent of her lilac perfume increased Brian's desire. His hands explored the curves of her body. "I enjoy your company, too. You're the first woman I've wanted to return to ... voluntarily."

Nerine tilted her head and gave him an appreciative smile. "I'm sure your beautiful, young girlfriend is a virgin and intends on being one until she's married. That poses a problem for you. But being the Good Samaritan that I am, I can be your salvation." Nerine slowly slid her hand across the swelling in his pants and began unbuckling his belt. "Your young love will get you excited, then you can come to me for relief. A nice arrangement for you and a lonely spinster."

Brian parted Nerine's robe and began fondling her breasts, gently rolling her nipples between his fingers, kissing her neck and lips, indulging himself in his willing partner.

Chapter Ten

The next morning, Catherine was lying in bed, looking at a bright blue sky and white clouds drifting beyond her window. Chirping robins and sparrows darted back and forth, searching for a morning meal. Her bedroom was getting warmer each minute, a sure sign it would be another hot day. She grabbed the bed sheet covering her and whipped it aside, rolling off the edge of the bed and landing on her feet. She walked on her toes and stretched her body, strolling toward the window to inspect the new day. Catherine knelt at the window, looking down at the pond. The black Labrador was lying in the shade of a bush, waiting for the ducks to return. After weeks of watching him, she decided the dog was more interested in playing with the ducks, than eating them.

Catherine looked over her shoulder at the round brass clock on the dresser. It was ten minutes past eight o'clock, later than she expected. She quickly washed her face and hands and put on a gray cotton work dress for the morning's chores. Bridie asked her to clean the flowerbeds, pulling weeds and snipping off dead blossoms. Bridie was borrowing the Holmgren's buggy to take Catherine to the Peters' farm for an afternoon visit with Monica.

It was almost nine o'clock when Catherine hurried downstairs to join Bridie for breakfast. She was startled when she saw Jack standing by the back door, staring at her. He was holding a brown leather cap in his hand, his lips parted, moist with saliva.

Bridie was sitting at the table watching her, too, waiting for her reaction to Jack's presence.

Catherine got a good look at Jack in the sun-lit kitchen. She could see he wasn't menacing, just a pathetic man who needed kindness and understanding. What fear she had of him faded. Catherine smiled and said, pleasantly, "Good morning, Jack," as though she greeted him that way every morning.

Somewhat nervous, Jack fumbled with his cap, gave Catherine a fast nod and mumbled, "Mornin," forcing the word from deep within his lungs. Jack looked at Bridie, then at Catherine again, before stepping out to the porch, leaving the door open.

Bridie got up from the table and closed the door. "If his mind was together, he would have closed it." She turned to face Catherine, "He forgets everything when he's nervous, and you make him nervous."

Catherine slapped her hand against her chest. "Me? Why would I make him nervous?"

"It appears he likes you. He may be feeble, but he's a man and he can still appreciate a pretty girl." Bridie looked out into the yard. "Have you bathed yet?"

"No. I'll do that after I finish the garden work." Catherine looked inside the icebox. "I think I'll have a glass of milk and … is there any fruit left?"

"Come here," Bridie snapped, looking through the door window. "Look at Jack by the boat house."

Catherine walked over to Bridie. They began laughing, watching Jack running about, trying in vain to catch a butterfly with his bare hands.

"That's *our* Jack," Catherine quipped, to please Bridie.

Catherine had a small wicker basket of gardening tools and a soft rubber pad to kneel on. She kept a careful watch for snakes, remembering the one they saw the day of the birthday party.

"Good morning," came an unfamiliar voice from behind her.

Startled, she turned quickly and saw Charles Belcher looking down at her, brandishing a broad smile. She took a deep breath. "Good morning," she responded, standing to face him. "I didn't hear you coming."

"There isn't much sound when a person walks on grass," he answered. "Besides, I enjoyed watching you work with the flowers. From my observation, I've decided you're prettier than the flowers."

"Thank you," Catherine replied, cautiously. "I didn't expect to have company while I was digging in the dirt." She dropped her pruning shears into the wicker basket and wiped her hands on her apron. "When do you return to Knox College? I'm sure you're scheduled to arrive before the students."

"True," Charles answered. "I leave in two weeks and I'm looking forward to this semester. Besides teaching, I will be doing research on amphibians with two renowned professors. With luck, we'll discover a new connection between sea animals and land animals. If we succeed, I will be writing a paper on the results of our study, which, if published, will be a big boost for my career."

"You must be excited," Catherine said, satisfying his already inflated ego. "You must let me know how it turns out."

Charles interpreted that invitation as a sign of interest in him. He stepped closer to her, "I was hoping I could call on you one evening, before I leave town. I would like to know you better."

Catherine was uncomfortable with him standing so close. She turned and walked slowly toward the back porch, with Charles following. She noticed Jack watching them, with his back to the pond. "I'm flattered by your offer, but Brian and I are seeing each other quite regularly."

"Oh! Yes, Brian. I remember that young lad; the fellow who took you for a buggy ride."

Catherine nearly laughed at his pretending to forget about Brian, labeling him "young lad," implying Brian hadn't attained his maturity. She stopped at the porch stairs and turned to him. "Brian leaves for Illinois University in three weeks. He wants to be an Architect and Engineer. He's good at mathematics, which helped him pass the entrance exam."

"Fifteen is a young age for a freshman, but it's been done before. He won't be near Newberry, so he won't be coming home very often. I return from Knox College every weekend." Charles moved close to her, again. "We could go on picnics together, or boat rides and dances."

"Thank you, but I don't think so," Catherine replied.

Charles was getting frustrated with Catherine's continued rejections. "We could attend concerts that come to town."

Catherine raised her hand to stop him from coming closer. She wasn't sure if he was near-sighted, or just being rude. His persistence was beginning to scare her.

Charles heard a grunt from behind him. Jack was a few yards away, his fist gripping a mallet. He understood that Jack's glare was defying him to move closer to Catherine.

"There isn't much sound when a person walks on grass," Catherine repeated.

"He appears angry," Charles said, walking away. "I'll talk to you again, when the fool isn't around."

Catherine liked Charles even less, for calling Jack a "fool." She hoped Jack scared him enough he would stay away forever. Catherine yelled to Jack, walking back toward the pond. "Thank you, Jack."

He turned his head, enough to let her know he heard.

After cleaning the flowerbeds, Catherine went inside to bathe and dress. When she came downstairs for lunch, the *Newberry Times* was on her chair. Catherine picked up the newspaper and laid it at the center of the table.

"You'll want to read today's paper," Bridie said, entering the kitchen.

"I usually do, but I'll read it later."

"I'm sure you'd like to read it now."

"What's special about today's paper?" Catherine asked.

"The only way you'll find out is to read it."

Catherine gave Bridie a side-glance and reached for the *Newberry Times*. "Should I read the entire paper, or is there a special page I should go to?"

"Try the Society page. Page eight."

Catherine turned to page eight and began reading. The more engrossed she became in what she was reading the closer she raised the paper to her face.

> *NEWBERRY WELCOMES NEW MEMBERS TO OUR COMMUNITY. Since January of this year, Newberry has been blessed with the arrival of four children that are proving to be an asset to Newberry. Being that family history is an important part of all families and society, the following information will reveal the backgrounds of these wonderful children. This information was gathered through the cooperation of the Society for Children, The New York Times, The Durham Chronicle and The Gresham Post.*
>
> *Pina (Sasso) Campbell–adopted daughter of Richard and Eileen Campbell. Born in Lucia, Italy, April 10, 1885. Father, Angelo, died in a mining accident, 1897. Pina immigrated to New York City, 1898 with mother, Maria, and brother, Marcello. Moved to Alton, Delaware, 1898, where all three worked at the Alton Textile Mill. A year later, Pina's mother died of pneumonia and the children were placed with the Society for Children, which arranged passage on an Orphan Train. Brother's location is unknown.*
>
> *Pina, like Eileen Campbell, intends on becoming a schoolteacher.*

Catherine (Hayes) McDonald– adopted daughter of Bridie McDonald. Born in New York City, July 7, 1884. Mother, Mary, died of pneumonia when Catherine was ten years old. No siblings. Father, John, was killed in a garment factory fire, March of 1899. New York City awarded him a medal for bravery, guiding women and girls out of the factory through dense smoke. He is credited with saving 87 lives. Society for Children arranged passage on an Orphan Train.

Next month, Catherine will follow Bridie's footsteps and begin studies at The Bradbury School in Newberry.

> Brian (Hampton) Holmgren– adopted son of Thomas and Margaret Holmgren. Born in Gresham, Connecticut, July 17, 1884. Mother, Esther, died from heart disease when Brian was eight years old. No siblings. His Father, Karl, was employed as a master craftsman making custom furniture for businesses and private estates in the New England area. He died of tuberculosis in 1898. The Society for Children arranged passage on an Orphan Train.
>
> Since his arrival in Newberry, he has been working with Thomas Holmgren, learning the business of excavating stone. His main interest is to construct buildings. Soon, Brian will leave for Illinois University to study Mechanical and Structural Engineering.
>
> Monica (Brenn) Peters–adopted daughter of Clay and Sona Peters. Born in Durham, Rhode Island, May 22, 1884. Mother, Joan, died from a ruptured appendix when Monica was nine years old. No siblings. Father, Henry, delivered milk to homes in their community. He was robbed and killed on Monica's last birthday. The Society for Children arranged passage on an Orphan Train.

Catherine leaned back in her chair and looked at Bridie. "So this is why you wanted personal information from us."

"Absolutely! When so many people chose not to come to your birthday party, I felt I had to do something. This article will show you children are not bastards, which is their only concern, and you won't infect their children with anything evil … or whatever else they can imagine."

Reading it again, Catherine rocked slowly in her chair, pondering the affect this information would have on the community. "Thank you, Bridie. I hope it works. I'll take this to Monica this afternoon, so she can read it."

"She can keep it," Bridie said, flashing a grin. "I have extra copies. Remember, I own part of the newspaper."

That afternoon, Bridie borrowed Margaret's rig, to take Catherine to the Peters' farm for a visit with Monica. Outside of Newberry, Bridie stopped the buggy on the side of the road. She was amused by Catherine's befuddled glance, when she was handed the reins. "Now that we're out of town, I want to give you a lesson in driving a buggy. I have Margaret's permission. You'll have to learn sooner or later, so you might as well start now. When you become proficient at it, I might buy us a buggy."

Catherine's frown faded and a smile blossomed in its place. "Really? You'd let me drive? I've been wanting to do this, but I didn't have the nerve to ask." She leaned towards Bridie and kissed her cheek. "I would be able to run errands for you, and drive you places."

"Don't get too excited, Jack will do most of the fetching for us. If I took chores from him, he'd feel he wasn't doing a good job, and that would make him sad."

"I understand. He must feel needed and loved too."

After getting basic instructions, Catherine started down the road. An occasional giggle or laugh along the way validated her enjoyment in flipping the reins to keep Dandy moving.

It was an easy one-mile drive, without sharp turns or deep ruts in the road. When they got to the dirt lane leading to the Peters' house, Catherine turned toward the farmhouse.

Monica came rushing from the kitchen door at the back of the house. Her thin, gray cotton dress clung against her body, as she ran toward them. "Aren't you special, driving a buggy like that," she yelled, with excitement. "You'll be a proper lady in no time."

"She handled the buggy quite well," Bridie commented, with an approving nod. She looked toward the house and into the field. "Are Mr. or Mrs. Peters home?"

"Clay is fence mending and Sona is at the McCutcheons, helping with their new fat baby."

"Another McCutcheon?" Bridie questioned. "When did this one break into daylight, and how many is it now?"

"Two days ago, and eight," Monica answered, swiftly. "I was told Mrs. McCutcheon promised her husband it would be the last one, but you can't be sure about that."

Catherine thanked Bridie for letting her drive the buggy, then jumped down to Monica. "I didn't know I would be driving a buggy today. It was a complete surprise."

"You looked like an old hand at it," Monica said.

"Have you forgotten something?" Bridie asked, handing a copy of *The Newberry Times* to Catherine. "You girls have fun and be careful. See you in three hours." Bridie flipped the reins and looked over her shoulder at Monica. "Say hello to the Peters for me." Bridie rode off, raising a cloud of dry earth behind the buggy.

"What's the newspaper for?" Monica asked. She listened intently as Catherine opened the newspaper and began reading page eight. Monica's smile got wider, as she listened. "This should make a difference. I'll put it in my room, now. Let's make sure Pina reads this."

Monica took Catherine's hand and lead her to the house. "That's the henhouse over there. We sell eggs in town and people come out here and buy our eggs, figuring they're fresher if farm bought." In front of the kitchen door was a five-foot square platform of rough-hewn boards, three inches high. A boot scraper was nailed at the corner, next to the door. When they stepped inside, Monica saw Catherine frown, unintentionally, looking around the kitchen. Monica didn't mind. She did the same when she first saw it. "It isn't much," Monica said. "The iron stove is coming apart, the scarred oak table and chairs rock on the uneven floor and the small flowers on the peeling wallpaper are almost faded from view. But it's home."

Looking at the rooms, Catherine became overwhelmed with her own good fortune. She was adopted well, and Monica had only this. "Yes," Catherine agreed, "It's a home and you are not living on the streets." She put her arm around Monica and gave her an affectionate hug. "This house may be old, but it appears comfortable."

"You don't have to be polite," Monica insisted. "At first, I wondered why the Peters adopted me, being they don't have much money, and the farm isn't that big. Then, I learned Mrs. Peters has a bad heart and she could die at any time. I guess they figured I could learn the chores around the farm, especially the cooking and laundry, in case she passed on."

Catherine smiled at Monica's casual attitude. They crossed the small kitchen and entered a little room with a tiny closet in the corner. A sturdy wood bed of raw pine and a black dresser were the only furniture in the room. The wallpaper was the same as in the kitchen.

"This is my bedroom. It's small, but it's mine. And it's close to the kitchen stove for heat in the winter." Monica threw the newspaper on her bed. "Their bedroom is on the other side of the stove. You saw the living room from where we stood in the kitchen, so now you've seen the house. What I really want to show you is outside."

"Show me what?" Catherine asked, following Monica out of the house.

"Have you ever been on a farm before?"

"No."

Crossing over brown tufts of dry grass, Catherine was careful not to turn an ankle in ruts made by wagon wheels, or wide cracks in the ground. Monica pointed ahead at the fenced-in yard next to the pigpens. "What I'm going to show you will be hard to believe. We have a feisty boar chasing a dozen sows and … well, wait to see what *he's* got."

When they got to the fence, they leaned over the top, draping their arms down the other side. "Where's the boar?" Catherine asked.

"There," Monica said, pointing across from them. "The biggest pink blob you'll ever see. He's following a sow … of interest, you might say. Look between his hind legs."

"Eeeyyeeew," Catherine wailed. "His thing is ugly, like a pink corkscrew."

Monica laughed at Catherine's distorted face examining the boar. "You'd think the sow would spin around when he put it in." They laughed until tears covered their eyes. "Come," Monica said, flapping her hand for Catherine to follow. "We've got two boy-oh-boy horses on the other side of the barn."

Catherine examined the weathered, gray wood of the barn, as they passed it. Rusting next to it was an old reaper and a dilapidated buckboard surrounded by tall weeds. "The barn doesn't look very strong," Catherine remarked.

"I thought that, too, but it appeared sturdy when I banged things on it and jumped on the floorboards in the hayloft. It had a solid sound to it." Monica stood on the bottom board of the corral fence, resting her arms across the top.

"That one is Homer," Monica said, pointing to a dark brown horse with a black mane and tail. "Clay named it after a cousin in Missouri. That gray and white horse is called Frosty, because of its color."

"They must be well fed," Catherine remarked. "They look big and strong."

"They are. Clay rents 'em out to get his neighbors' mares pregnant." Monica turned to Catherine and chuckled. "I was hoping their thing was hanging out, so you could see it. They almost touch the ground. Honest! They're that long."

"I can't believe you're showing me sex organs of animals."

"Don't you think it's interesting?" Monica asked, dropping from the fence. "I've never seen such things before I got here."

"Yeah, I guess, but I'd rather sit and talk about us for a while."

"You're right," Monica agreed. "Let's sit in the hayloft and talk there." She ran toward the barn door, with Catherine following. Monica went straight for the ladder and climbed to the loft.

Catherine was behind her, climbing at a slower pace. She looked up to see how much farther she had to climb and laughed. "I can see up your dress," Catherine giggled.

Monica stepped onto the loft and turned to look down at Catherine. "So can Mr. Peters."

Catherine stopped at the top of the ladder. "What do you mean, so can Mr. Peters?"

"It's not hard to figure out," Monica answered. "I'm always wearing a dress and he's below me every time we're going up or down the ladder. All he has to do is look up, and there I am ... almost."

Catherine stared at Monica. "Do you really think he's doing that?"

They sat on a bale of hay. "I'm not completely sure, but he's always second when we go up the ladder, and first when we go down–and I mean every time."

"Ask them for work pants."

"I have. Clay says he'll buy them when cooler weather comes. I guess he'll decide when that is." They were silent for a moment before Monica continued. "I can tell by the way he looks at me, he wants me."

"That would scare me," Catherine remarked.

"What about Brian? Has he tried anything with you?"

Catherine jerked her head in Monica's direction. "Of course not. I know he loves me and wants me, as I do him, but we can wait until we're married."

"It must be difficult to love and want someone, but do nothing."

"It is, but we can get married in two years when he graduates. Then, we can indulge ourselves in each other for the rest of our lives."

Monica looked to the blue sky and began rocking from side to side. "Indulge, indulge, indulge. I wonder what doing it is like?"

"I suggest you keep an eye on Mr. Peters, so you don't find out."

Chapter Eleven

Two days later, Catherine and Bridie were preparing supper when Maxine Wagner telephoned. Catherine was removing a roasted chicken from the oven, so Bridie lifted the receiver.

"I wanted to tell you how disappointed I was that my niece's wedding in Pittsfield caused my daughters to miss Catherine and Brian's birthday party. I'm so anxious to have my girls meet them, that I'd like to plan a small party at my house this coming Sunday, or the one after, whichever is good for them. Of course, Pina and Monica will be invited, too."

Bridie looked at Catherine carving the chicken on the table. "That's very nice of you, Maxine, I appreciate it. I'm sorry for making this conversation so short, but we are starting to eat dinner. I'll talk to Catherine and Brian soon and let you know which Sunday is best for them."

With carving knife in hand, Catherine looked up at Bridie. "I heard my name. What was that about?"

Bridie walked back to the table and sat down. "That was Maxine Wagner, apologizing for missing your birthday party a month and a half ago. She wants to have a party this coming Sunday, or the following one, so you can meet her daughters and some of their friends. You and Brian get to pick which Sunday."

"Do you think the newspaper article has anything to do with this?"

"Absolutely. That's why I printed the information. Most people in Newberry are nice people. It's just that I didn't like the attitude of some."

Catherine sat opposite Bridie, pushing the platter of chicken toward her. "Maybe they really did go to a wedding that day?"

Bridie reached for a piece of chicken. "Oh, I'm sure they did, but if she was so anxious for her daughters to meet you and Brian, why did she wait so long to call?"

"They had to be convinced we were good people?" Catherine questioned.

"Exactly! Brian and you can decide which Sunday you'd like to go … or if you want to go."

After eating, Bridie walked up behind Catherine and put her arm around her. "Thank you for being you," she said, affectionately. "I love you, and you have never disappointed me. Jack loves you, too. I can tell."

Catherine looked up at Bridie, curious as to why she included Jack at this moment. His inclusion didn't seem appropriate. "And thank you for being you, Bridie."

"I believe you children will become more involved in Newberry's social life from now on."

The Wagner party was to begin in less then an hour. Instead of it being for seven children as planned, Maxine invited fifteen boys and girls. In spite of the short notice, all would be attending. Bridie interpreted that as acceptance for Catherine and her friends, or at least it appeared so.

"You don't have much time," Bridie yelled upstairs to Catherine. "Pina and Brian should be here any minute."

"I know," Catherine shouted back. "I'll be down in seconds."

Bridie looked out the living room window and saw Brian ride up in the Holmgren's buggy. He was wearing a dark blue suit, with a light blue shirt and white, starched collar.

Brian tied Dandy to the hitch in front of the house and jogged up to the door, which Bridie opened. "You give good service," he said, walking through the doorway.

"I'm glad I could be of service," Bridie said, with a half-bow.

At that moment, Catherine started down the stairs, wearing a dark green dress with gold piping around the neck and sleeves. Her descent was somewhat dramatic.

Brian watched her, with an enthusiastic smile. He glanced at Bridie. "She looks beautiful, doesn't she?"

Bridie placed her hand over her heart. "Don't tell me, tell her."

"Of course," he snickered, turning to Catherine. "You look beautiful."

"Well, I guess a second-hand compliment is better than nothing," she joked. "But I understand … you're a man."

The telephone rang and Bridie went into the kitchen, with Catherine and Brian following.

"McDonald residence."

"Hi, Bridie, it's Essie. I'm calling to be sure that Catherine knows about the dance next Saturday at the Masonic Hall. It's a fundraiser for new textbooks for the elementary school. Yesterday afternoon, the committee decided on this and the members asked me to be sure Catherine and her friends knew about it."

"A dance on such short notice?" Bridie questioned.

"We decided to have it before some of the children went off to school. There will be another fundraiser for us old folks, later on."

"Hold on, Catherine and Brian are here now." She handed the telephone receiver to Catherine.

They agreed to attend the dance and bring something for the confection table. When Catherine hung up the receiver, Bridie raised her hands above her head and began dancing around the kitchen table. "The committee wanted to be sure you kids were invited," she repeated.

"Why are you so pleased?" Brian asked.

"Catherine will explain later."

They went to the door to greet Richard Campbell and Pina in her gray party dress. Her black, hair, which was normally straight, swirled about her head, giving her a pixie look.

"You look adorable," Catherine squealed at her. "The boys will be drooling over you."

"She's always adorable," Bridie said.

"I like her hair this way, too," Richard commented. "It's perfect for her."

Pina smiled at the compliments. "I like, too, but be gone tomorrow. My hair too straight to stay like this. Hillary, my friend in Delaware, have hair like this, but she blond."

"Your English is improving all the time," Catherine said, enthusiastically. "Soon, you'll be speaking perfect English."

"Thank you. I … I'm determined to improve," she said slowly.

"Determined!" Brian repeated. "You certainly are improving."

"That is one of the big words Eileen teach me. She's the principal lady in my life," she said deliberately and carefully, as if fighting a stuttering problem. "Exacerbate … multiple … colorful … complicated … unified. See, soon I speak good, I hope."

They all laughed and praised her again. Pina's smug expression showed she was pleased with her progress.

"You'd better leave for the party," Richard suggested. He turned to Bridie. "Eileen and I are going to Motch's Steak House for dinner. Would you care to join us?"

Bridie thought for a second. "I can't think of any reason why not."

Ten minutes after two o'clock, they arrived at the Wagner house. Mrs. Wagner opened the door and introduced herself, welcoming them with great enthusiasm.

"Nice to meet you. I'm Catherine McDonald." She stepped to the side and introduced Pina and Brian.

"I'm so pleased you could come. Is Monica coming?"

"Yes," Catherine answered. "Mr. Peters will bring her soon, I'm sure."

Mrs. Wagner backed into the house. "Some of the guests are already here. Follow me and I'll introduce you."

"You have beautiful home," Pina said, walking to the parlor.

"Thank you. Mr. Wagner has lived here since he was a boy."

As they entered the parlor, Patricia Wagner was at the piano playing, "Oh My Darling Clementine." There were seven boys and girls standing around her, their arms across each other's shoulders, singing along. They were between the ages of fourteen and eighteen. When they finished their song, they turned to look at the new guests.

A plump, blond girl stepped toward them. "Welcome. I'm Gretta Wagner and that's my sister, Patricia, at the piano. We're glad you could come." She proceeded with a round of introductions before returning to the piano.

"Can you sing?" Todd Hogan, asked. "You don't have to be good. As you can tell, we aren't."

"Of course," Brian replied. "We can mess up a song as well as anybody."

"Good! Join us." Todd turned to Patricia, "Play 'Camp Town Races.'"

As they sang, another boy and a girl arrived and began singing with them. Two songs later, Monica arrived and Catherine introduced her to the other guests, as her "good friend." Again, she noticed Monica wearing a dress that was obviously homemade. As the party progressed, Catherine could see Monica was uncomfortable around this group of well-dressed people. Some of the guests were being polite to Monica, but not overly receptive.

Through the course of the afternoon, Catherine and Pina received the lion's share of attention from the older boys, a fact that was not missed by the other girls and Brian. Catherine stayed close to Monica, keeping her involved in the activities, while Brian stayed close to Catherine.

The following Wednesday morning, Brian worked at the quarry. He returned home by 12:30 to run errands for Margaret and drive her to

Mrs. Tomitz's home for pinochle and poker with her lady friends. He was to pick her up at 4:30.

After hitching Dandy to the buggy, he took a bath and dressed for his afternoon activities. He dropped Margaret at the Tomitz house and hurried to the bakery for two loaves of bread, the grocery store for canned fruits and vegetables, and finally to Carrie's dress shop for three pairs of gloves Margaret had ordered for the coming winter. He was allowed plenty of time to explore the old gristmill by the river, one of his favorite activities. But Brian wasn't going to the mill this day.

Brian secured his purchases in the lockbox under the buggy's seat. He rode west past Winnemac Park to Dillard Street, turned left, then tied Dandy to a hitching post. He walked back around the corner and entered 170 Temple Street. He knocked on Nerine's door and waited. It took only seconds for her to open the door. He looked at her and wondered whether she was going out, or had just returned. She was wearing a green and yellow striped dress and a necklace of green and brown wooden beads.

Brian looked disappointed. "Are you leaving?"

"I was," she smiled, "But I don't have to. I was wondering if I would see you before you went off to school. I'm going to miss you."

Brian stepped in to the apartment and closed the door. "I'll miss you, too."

"I'm sure you'll miss Catherine much more than me. It's our lovemaking that we'll miss." She pointed her finger at him and said, "Whatever you do, don't send me a letter. The people at the post office can gossip, too."

Brian smiled. "Our sex has been good and I do have feelings for you ... eh, not like Catherine, of course, but you are more to me than a casual friend."

"I know what you mean." Nerine stepped to the center of the room and opened the clasp of her necklace, letting it fall into her hand. "You appear to have guilt when you come to me. Am I right?"

He paused. "I feel I'm cheating on Catherine when I come here. But, I believe this is better than trying to force her to do something she isn't ready for."

Nerine snickered. "I see—you're being a nice guy. You shouldn't worry about it. Everybody has a life before marriage."

Brian sat on the arm of her stuffed chair. "It feels like there are two parts to me. One part is my heart for Catherine, and the other part is below the belt. When I lived on the streets, I supported myself by having sex. It's not like you can stop, like you'd stop chewing tobacco."

"I'm curious," Nerine asked, with an inquisitive smile. "Where do the Holmgrens think you are when you come here?"

He grinned at her. "I tell them I'm exploring the old gristmill outside of town. If you're not home, I go there."

Nerine laughed. "I'm not sure I like being referred to as, 'The Old Mill.'" She walked up to Brian and took his hand, leading him to the bedroom. "Enough conversation. I'm sure you have only so much time to be here, so let me take care of that part of you below the belt."

Chapter Twelve

The first Saturday in September, Brian was leaving for Illinois University. He had his arm around Catherine, waiting for people to disembark from the train.

Bridie and Margaret stood back in silence, waiting for their loving goodbye.

Tom was standing behind the women, more interested in the mechanics of the train than the children's "goodbye."

Brian and Catherine looked at each other, pledging to write often, that they would miss each other and love each other, and numerous other promises.

"For God's sake," Margaret yelled. "Kiss her. We're going to watch you, no matter what, so you might as well get started."

They glanced sheepishly at their parents and kissed, kissed again, holding each other tightly. Tears slid down Catherine's cheeks. Brian waved to the others, kissed Catherine again, then grabbed his luggage and boarded the train. They waved to Brian, as the train chugged away from the station.

"The last time all of us were here at the train station, we were starting a new chapter in our lives," Bridie said. "It was a wonderful day."

At the Peters' farm, Monica and Clay Peters were working in the loft of the barn while Sona Peters drove to town for groceries and fencing material. Clay handed Monica a broom. "Sweep up the loose hay and push it to the horses below. I'll go down and water them."

Monica hummed, "Camp Town Races" and "Rosalie," gathering two piles of hay. She brushed one of the piles through the loft door and watched it drop to the horses below. She could see Mr. Peters had already filled the water trough.

Clay appeared at the top of the ladder with a new horse blanket over his shoulder.

Again, Monica swept hay out of the loft and watched it drop to the ground.

Clay threw the horse blanket over some of hay bales. "Put the broom over there," he said, pointing to a wooden post near the blanket.

Monica did as he asked. When she turned to face him, he was unbuckling his belt.

"Take off your dress," he demanded, staring into her eyes.

Monica backed away from him, her face pale. "Please, no, Mr. Peters. I'll do whatever work you want me to do, but not that."

"If I'm going to support you, I'll do what I want with you." He stepped closer to her, still looking into her eyes. "You're a mature young lady, developed enough to receive a man. Now take off your dress."

She looked frantically for a way to get around him, but was walled-in by bales of hay. "Don't! I'll tell!" she screamed.

Monday evening, Sheriff Howard Mason telephoned Bridie. "By any chance, is Monica at your house?"

"No!" she responded. "Why are *you* looking for her? Is something wrong?"

"She ran away. Gone since Saturday morning. Clay Peters said he was working in the barn for a couple hours and when he went to the house, Monica wasn't there and all her belongings were gone."

"Saturday? And when did they tell you she was missing?"

"This morning. Clay said they waited to see if Monica would return."

Bridie pulled a chair from the table and sat down. "My God, that poor child. I haven't heard of any trouble at their house. Have there been problems reported before this?"

"None," Howard shot back. "Is Catherine there?"

"Yes. She's on the back porch reading. Do you want to talk to her?"

"Yes, but don't say anything to her now. I'm coming over. Keep her there."

Bridie heard Howard hang up his telephone, then walked to the back door and looked through the window at Catherine, reading peacefully. She went to the living room and waited for the sheriff.

Fifteen minutes later, Sheriff Mason appeared on his horse, Teddy. He tied Teddy to the hitching post and walked straight to Bridie's front porch.

She opened the door, as he was about to ring her doorbell.

"I find this confusing," Bridie said, as he entered the house.

Howard stopped in the foyer. "I don't," he replied, looking at her. "This is not unusual when dealing with orphans. They disappear for many reasons and my job is to learn the reason."

"How bad could it be?"

"I'm not guessing at anything. What I do know is, the land around their farm is flat for miles, and I can't imagine him not noticing her in the amount of time it would take to walk out of sight, especially carrying luggage. It's possible, but unlikely. Besides, I questioned him for a half-hour and he appeared nervous. His answers seemed rehearsed. Something smells."

"Follow me," Bridie said.

When they stepped out onto the porch, Catherine looked up at them and closed her book. "Howdy, sheriff," Catherine said, jokingly. "What brings you to these parts?"

"A beautiful young lady named Catherine," he said, smiling. "I'm sorry for interrupting your reading, but I have a few questions I want to ask you about your friend, Monica."

"Monica?" she questioned. "Why Monica?"

"Don't get excited, but Monica is missing. Mr. and Mrs. Peters said she ran away last Saturday."

Catherine rose quickly and faced Howard. "Ran away?"

"I was hoping you could help me. Do you know of any reason why she would leave the farm? Did Monica tell you anything that would cause her to run away, you know, private talk between you girls?"

"No! She seemed … content." Catherine's pause showed she thought of something.

"What is it?" Howard asked. "Any little statement she may have made could be helpful. Do you remember anything?"

"Yes!" She sat in her chair again and stared at the porch floor. "Monica said she was nervous about the way Mr. Peters always looked at her, you know, not like a man would look at a daughter." She glanced up at Howard. "Monica also said, he was always under her when they went up or down the ladder to the loft in the barn. Monica believed he looked up her dress." Catherine looked at the sheriff again. "That's all, but she wasn't sure if he was looking."

"Anything else?"

"No."

Sheriff Mason looked at Bridie. "That could be enough. I'll get a couple of men and we'll search the farm and surrounding area." Howard squatted in front of Catherine. "Don't get upset imagining crazy things. Children run away all the time, especially an orphan who isn't happy with their new home. If she comes to you, let me know right away, but do it without her knowing."

Wednesday morning Catherine started classes at The Bradbury School. It was a colonial-style building of red bricks and white trim, with a bell tower above the front entrance. The faculty and business offices were just inside the front door. The rest of the first floor and the second floor were classrooms. A chemistry laboratory was in the basement.

The function of the school was to give the girls a well-rounded education and prepare them to be suitable ladies for upper society. Catherine was happy to be getting a good education, but she wasn't too concerned about upper society. In time, she learned that most of the other girls believed as she did. They just wanted to be girls, marry some day and have children. By Friday's end, Catherine was feeling comfortable with all her new teachers and classmates.

Saturday afternoon, Sheriff Mason was talking to Bridie in her kitchen when Catherine returned from grocery shopping. She set the bag of food on the table and saw a photograph lying there. At first glance she didn't know who it was, then remembered. Her eyes shifted to Sheriff Mason, "This is a picture of Monica's father."

"I know. Mrs. Peters said, Monica left it behind and she wanted you to have it. She assumed if Monica were to get in touch with anybody, it would be you."

Catherine looked disturbed. "Oh, Sheriff, she never would have left his picture behind. She adored her father. Something has happened to Monica."

"Monica left in a hurry," Bridie interrupted. "It would be easy for her to forget the picture. Don't worry until there is something to worry about."

Howard pulled out his pocket watch and glanced at it. "I'd better go. I have another stop at the other end of town." He started for the front door and Bridie followed.

"What do you really think happened?" Bridie asked.

Howard opened the door. "I'm going to get a couple of men and some hounds. We'll search the farm and outlying area."

Bridie returned to the kitchen. "Are you going to write a letter to Brian now?" Bridie asked.

"Yes, especially about Monica." She picked up her stationery from the kitchen table and started for the back door. "I hope Charles Belcher doesn't come around."

"I met his mother at the bank two days ago. She said Charles called to tell her that he wouldn't be coming home this weekend, or many weekends this school year. He's doing a lot of research that will keep him from coming home as often."

Catherine paused, with the door partially open. "He seems to be very ambitious. I'm glad he's busy. That way, he'll stay away from me."

"I'm not sure it's all ambition. His mother seems to think he's met a girl he likes and she's the real reason for not coming home."

"Bless her," Catherine said, walking out to the porch. She sat in one of the wicker chairs and laid her stationery on her lap. It was sunny and warm. Catherine closed her eyes for a moment, concentrating on the warmth of the sun and gentle breeze wafting her hair, then looked out at the pond and other fine homes bordering it. *How lucky I am.* She began thinking of other children that rode with her on the Orphan Train. *What happened to them? Were they blessed? Is Jason happy? And little Becky with the bouncing curls. I'm sure she has a good home. God, where is Monica?*

Chapter Thirteen

Thanksgiving was celebrated at the Holmgren's house, and during dinner, Brian explained his Architectural Drawing and World Architecture classes. When he cited landmark buildings in Scotland as excellent examples of brick and stone architecture, Bridie glowed with Scottish pride.

Bridie waited until he finished explaining his classes, then mentioned the Annual Scottish Festival that was held every summer, two counties north of them. The others seemed interested, but no one was enthused enough to discuss attending.

Christmas was celebrated at Bridie's house and she began discussing the Scottish Festival again, but with more fervor, hoping to get a commitment from all to attend. Her eyes shifted back-and-forth between her guests seated at the table. "Beside all the athletic competitions I mentioned, and the Scottish music and dancing, you'll see how the clansmen are dressed in their clan's colorful plaids. Being that it will be a Centennial year, 1900, it should be especially eventful."

Brian looked at Tom and Margaret. "It sounds like fun. Catherine and I would like to go. What do you think?"

Tom leaned back in his chair and looked at Margaret. "I agree. It should be interesting, and we haven't taken a trip together in quite a while."

Margaret smiled at him, "You're right, we are due for a vacation. Let's do it."

Bridie folded her hands on her lap, pleased with her Christmas.

Early June, Brian returned after his first year at Illinois University. Monica was still missing and Pina had finally mastered the English language.

Bridie was excited. She hadn't attended the Scottish Festival since she and John McTavish, went three years in a row. Her memory of John winning the caber toss and log cutting contests heightened her enthusiasm to return to the festival.

Catherine was in her bedroom storing schoolbooks on a closet shelf, when Bridie walked in. "Have any idea what you'd like for your sixteenth birthday?"

She looked at Bridie from within the closet. "I don't believe I have a right to ask for anything."

"But I want to buy my daughter a birthday present. After all, if I don't buy you something, people may accuse me of being stingy."

Catherine smiled, walking out of the closet. "We know that isn't true." She sat on her bed and folded her arms. "If you feel you must do something for me, I do have an idea. Rather than buying *me* a gift, I'd like to take Pina with us to the Scottish Festival. I don't think she would ever be able to go, otherwise."

Bridie pretended to be pondering her suggestion. "I certainly couldn't refuse an unselfish request like that. Besides, I was thinking about inviting her myself."

"Really?"

"Yes, really. The fair is just three weeks away, so I'll talk to her parents today. As a matter of fact, I'll call Margaret now and see if they have any objection to Pina coming. I'm sure they won't, but I should extend that courtesy."

Catherine flew from the bed and threw her arms around Bridie. "Thank you so much. I won't say anything to Pina until you've talked to her parents."

"You'd better not. Her parents may say no!" Bridie went downstairs to the telephone and gave it three cranks.

"Queen Victoria here, how can I help you?"

"Queen Victoria?" Bridie questioned. "Newberry certainly is improving."

"Sorry, I thought you might be Catherine. It's a long story so don't ask. With *whom* do you wish to speak?"

"The Holmgrens, please."

In a matter of seconds, Margaret answered. "Hello?"

"It's Bridie. You answered so fast you must have been standing near the telephone."

"I was walking past it, as it rang."

"What have you been doing this morning?"

"I'm sorting my summer clothes, trying to decide what to keep and what to get rid of. Brian is shopping for summer clothes now, then he might explore the old gristmill for an hour or so."

"Catherine needs summer wear, too. I love shopping with her, so she can model clothes for me." Bridie moved her mouth closer to the transmitter. "Enough about clothes. I called to ask you something about the Scottish Festival. Would you mind if Pina Campbell came with us? I doubt her parents will ever take her."

"Not at all. She's a sweetheart."

"I didn't think you'd mind. I'll ask her parents before we say anything to Pina. If they have a reason to say no, Pina would be very disappointed. Tomorrow, I'll let you know what they decide."

"Don't hang up," Margaret shouted, quickly. "I keep forgetting to ask if you ever told Catherine about Jack?"

"No, not yet. I hope no one else has."

It was almost two o'clock when Catherine walked into the kitchen for a drink of water. She wondered why Bridie was sitting at the table with a curious grin on her face. Jack was standing behind her, with his back to the door, clutching a small bouquet of yellow and white wildflowers. "What pretty flowers," Catherine commented. "Are those for Bridie?"

Bridie looked up at Catherine. "No, he brought them for you."

"For me?"

With staid face and moist lips, Jack raised the flowers toward Catherine. She stepped forward and took them from him, giving him a kiss on the cheek. He gave a shallow nod and backed away.

"They are beautiful, Jack. Thank you."

He nodded again, muttering, "Welcome." Not sure what to do next, Jack backed through the doorway and out to the porch.

"I said, he likes you," Bridie insisted, maintaining the sly grin.

"You had him do this. He couldn't have done it on his own."

"He certainly did," Bridie assured her. "Early this morning when we were in the yard, he pointed to the flowers along the pond and said, in his arduous, slow way, 'Lowers, Catherine.' I told him it was a good idea and it would make you happy. He kept them in our cool basement until now."

"That was sweet. I'll have to do something special for him." Catherine took a narrow crystal vase from a cabinet and filled it with water. "I should display them in an appropriate place, so he'll know I appreciate them."

"Jack thinks the parlor is a special room. Why don't you put them on the fireplace mantle. Then he would believe you thought they were important."

Bridie followed Catherine into the parlor and watched her place the flowers at the center of the mantle. Bridie glanced at the flowers, then her eyes drifted to the picture of John McTavish at the end of the mantle. *The Scottish games are in three weeks. I miss you.* She smiled at Catherine. "Yes, perfect."

Catherine went to the window and searched the street. "Brian said he would be here at two o'clock and it's almost that now." Beaming, she looked at Bridie. "One year of his schooling is over. In two years, he'll graduate."

Bridie knew what Catherine was thinking. "Yes, in two years you and Brian could be married." Bridie could feel Catherine's excitement at the prospect of living with her man. She was happy for her, but as for herself, she was cheated of that bliss.

"Thinking ahead, are you?"

"Of course, marrying Brian is my destiny … and his."

"Has he told you that?"

"Not verbally, but in many other ways."

Bridie sat on the sofa. "I'm sure you're right, and it would make me and the Holmgrens very happy. You'd be living in Newberry and Brian would be working with Tom, so then, Margaret and I would have grandchildren to play with."

Catherine spun away from the window and waited by the front door. "I saw him walking across the street."

Bridie looked over her shoulder at Catherine and laughed. "My God, girl, you look like a leopard waiting to pounce on your prey."

"That's about right," Catherine replied.

Bridie smiled and shook her head. "I had Jack repair and clean the rowboat yesterday. Don't forget to take the picnic basket with you."

Catherine didn't open the door until Brian rang the doorbell. "Good afternoon, young man. Are you selling something?"

Brian closed the door and wrapped his arms around her. "No, I'm giving you something free." They embraced and melted into a long, tender kiss. When Brian opened his eyes, he saw Bridie sitting on the sofa, watching them. Somewhat embarrassed, he stepped away from Catherine. "I didn't know you were there."

"Obviously. You can kiss her again, if you like. I'm sure she won't mind." Bridie stood and walked to the stairs. "I'm going up to my bedroom and read. Enjoy your picnic and ride around the pond."

Catherine took Brian's hand and led him through the house, grabbed the picnic basket from the kitchen table, then went out the back door and into the yard. "Jack has the boat ready. All we need to do is have fun."

Brian paused to survey the pond. It was the size of a city block. He slid the back of the boat into the water before helping Catherine get in. Once she was seated, he lifted the front of the boat and pushed, jumping in at the last second.

"Nice launch, Captain Brian. You must be an old salt."

Brian scowled at Catherine, "Ye just sit aft' and relax, Matey. Cause any trouble and I'll have ye walkin da plank."

"Save me! Save me!" Catherine shouted across the pond.

Brian laughed, as he rowed. Catherine's humor was one of the many things he enjoyed about her. He rowed at a leisurely pace to the far side of the pond and started back again.

Catherine brushed back a stray wisp of her hair and leaned forward, closer to Brian. "Many times, I look at the homes in our neighborhood and think about how lucky we are. We could have ended up on a farm like Monica, or be slaving for a family with eight kids, treating us like a servant." Catherine looked directly into his eyes. "How often do you think about where we are, and how we are living?

"Every day, every day, every day," he answered. "Do you know what I feel luckiest about?"

"What?"

Brian stopped rowing and let the boat glide on the water. "Finding you."

The sounds of the pond seemed muted, as they looked at each other, believing they should always be together. "I love you, too," Catherine said. "Actually, more than before–more each day."

Brian wanted to hold and make love to Catherine. He wanted her forever. His guilt for being with Nerine surfaced again. He loved Catherine, but was having sex with another. He considered confessing his affair and promising not to go to Nerine again, but decided to wait and think it through more carefully. He didn't want to hurt, or lose Catherine. "I'll always love you," he replied.

Knowing they could be seen from every house near the pond, Catherine pointed off into the distance. "Bridie said there was a good picnic area by those Weeping Willow trees. She said it's romantic when the right people are there. We can go when your arms get tired rowing."

"I'll row there now, so my arms *aren't* tired when we get there."

Bridie was in Catherine's bedroom, sitting in the rocking chair watching Catherine and Brian cruise around the pond and picnic by the willow trees. She was pretending they were, Bridie and John.

It was late afternoon when Brian pulled the boat on shore and tied the bow rope to a little birch tree. He took Catherine's hand and they went through the house again, returning the picnic basket to the kitchen table. They held each other and kissed.

"Always," Brian repeated.

"Me, too."

They stepped out onto the front porch and Brian gave Catherine's hand an affectionate squeeze, before starting down the stairs. A short distance away, he looked back at Catherine and waved. When she turned to go into the house, she saw a white envelope sticking out of the mailbox. It was sealed, and Catherine's name was printed on it. She sat on the porch steps and opened the typewritten note. Her eyes went directly to the bottom of the page to see whom it was from. The name, Monica, shocked her. Catherine's heart began to beat a little faster, as her eyes raced over the words.

> *Dear Catherine,*
>
> *I ran away because I had to. Sorry if I caused you to worry. I'm doing fine and I am being well cared for. I intend to sneak back to Newberry this summer and see you to explain what happened and why it took me so long to write you. The person I'm living with is teaching me to read and write and type with one finger. He's helping me with this letter to you.*

You can tell Pina I wrote to you, but don't tell anyone else. I don't want to be sent back to the Peters' farm, or any other home. I'm happy where I am. I love you and miss you. MONICA

Catherine folded the letter and put it inside her blouse before going into the house. She looked at Bridie coming down the stairs. "Do you mind if I got to Kitty's with Pina? We'd like ice cream and girl talk."

"Talk about your afternoon with Brian?" Bridie asked.

"That and other things. I'll call her, now."

Bridie paused, her hand resting on the stair rail. "I talked to Eileen today. Pina can go to the Scottish Festival with us. I'm sure she'll mention it when you call her."

She smiled at Bridie. "Thank you, again."

"Happy Birthday."

Catherine and Pina were at Kitty's sitting at a table in the farthest corner of the room. "Read it now before she brings our ice cream," Pina demanded.

Catherine lifted the letter from her white, beaded purse and unfolded it. She whispered the words, as she read. When she read the sentence; *He's helping me type this letter to you*, the girls paused and looked at each other.

"He?" Pina questioned, with excitement. "Do you think?"

"I would guess so, unless *he* is old."

"It sounds absolutely sinful. Our imaginations can run wild until we learn the truth."

"Remember," Catherine reminded Pina, "Don't tell anyone about this."

The following Friday, Catherine worked at the Bradbury School, helping clean the chemistry laboratory in the basement. It was volunteer work she had agreed to do the last day of school. Two of her classmates, Lee Ann Zulkie and Mary Milloy, worked with her. Their work seemed less toilsome by joking and teasing about boyfriends, other students and teachers, and what they would do during the summer months. At three o'clock, they completed their work and were given tortoise shell hair combs, a small gift from the Principal. Walking away from the school, they tried to think of someone they disliked enough, to give them to.

When Catherine got home there was a horse and buggy tied up in front of the house. She wondered who was visiting. It was a buggy similar to what the Holmgrens had, large enough for three people with a storage compartment under the seat. The color was polished burgundy, with a black interior and black retractable hood. The horse was dapple gray, with a black mane and tail. She believed it was the most beautiful rig she'd ever seen.

Catherine entered the foyer, attempting to appear mature, and ladylike, in case it was someone important. She peeked into the parlor and dining room before entering the kitchen. "Bridie?" she called, in a controlled, proper voice.

"I'm on the porch."

Catherine stepped from the kitchen anticipating an introduction to a stranger, but found Bridie alone, reading the newspaper. She continued to the porch railing, searching the yard.

"Are you looking for something?" Bridie asked.

Catherine turned to Bridie. "Who's visiting?"

"Visiting?"

"Yes. There's a horse and buggy tied to our hitch."

"Oh, that old rig," she replied, trying to keep from smiling. "It's something I ordered weeks ago."

"You ordered? Are you telling me what I think you're telling me?"

Bridie couldn't hold back her smile any longer. "Yes, that's what I'm telling you, without saying it directly."

Catherine clasped her hands together. "Oh, Bridie. It's the most beautiful horse and buggy I've ever seen. We'll be the envy of all Newberry."

"I told you a while back I would do this when you were accomplished enough at handling a horse. Margaret lent us their buggy many times so you could learn, so don't forget to thank her. My main concern was how you would perform in town with other traffic around you, and you've done very well. Riding through the country is less of a challenge."

"I feel very confident driving a buggy." She stepped closer to Bridie. "Let's go for a ride around town."

Bridie laughed. "I guess that would be the logical thing to do." She raised herself from the wicker chair and followed Catherine through the house. "Jack cleaned the coach house last week and we kept the doors closed, so you wouldn't get suspicious."

Catherine went directly to the horse to pet it. "What's its name? Is it male or female?"

"Female. It would be nice if you could name her, but she's three years old and her name is Bree. I don't know why, or what it means, if anything."

"I like it," Catherine said, repeating the name and petting Bree's nose. "It's a gentle name."

"According to the people at the stable, she is just that. I insisted on a gentle horse." Bridie raised her skirt and stepped up into the buggy. "Let's show her off."

"Gladly!" Catherine squealed. She looked into Bree's big black eyes saying, "I love you already."

"Where shall we go?" Bridie asked, settling into the corner of the seat.

"First, we'll go past the Holmgrens' house with my nose in the air. Then we'll show our buggy on Main Street before going back for the Holmgrens,' in case someone would like a ride in the most beautiful rig in town."

"That sounds terribly pretentious," Bridie said, waving her arm forward. "Let's do it."

When they passed the Holmgrens' house, Catherine stuck her nose in the air as she said she would. They didn't see anyone out front, but she did it on the chance that someone may be looking from inside. Catherine enjoyed the ride down Main Street, delighting in the attention from people who noticed their rig. She directed Bree to the train station, looped around the statue of Abraham Lincoln, then back through Main Street on their return to the Holmgrens' house.

"I wonder if they're home?" Catherine mumbled, tying Bree to the hitching post. "Brian went fishing this morning with Todd Hogan. Maybe he isn't back yet?" She gave Bree a kiss, while Bridie climbed out of the buggy. As they started for the house, Tom and Brian stepped out onto the porch.

"Congratulations!" Tom bellowed. "Margaret told us that you were getting a rig. I didn't know it would be so handsome."

Brian came down the porch stairs and took Catherine's hand, walking her back to the buggy. "You must be thrilled."

"I am, and it was a complete surprise." She cuddled up against Brian, as he put his arm around her.

"You can kiss her," Bridie yelled.

"Who can kiss who?" Margaret asked, rushing out of the house. "I heard voices out here, so I assumed I was missing something." She stopped at the edge of the porch. "My Goodness, it is beautiful!"

"Who wants to go for a ride?" Catherine hollered.

"You and Brian," Bridie answered. "There will be plenty of time for us later."

They watched Brian help Catherine into the buggy. Margaret pointed to them. "See, my son is a perfect gentleman."

"He's perfectly in love," Tom declared. They waved to the happy couple, as Bree pulled them away from the house.

"Have either of you thought about their wedding yet?" Bridie asked. "Brian graduates in two years."

"We can't be sure they'll marry," Margaret replied.

Bridie and Tom turned and stared at Margaret, without saying a word.

She pretended not to notice. "We could have it in our garden."

Chapter Fourteen

Two weeks later, they stood on the station platform, waiting for the train to Cambridge, Illinois, and the Scottish Festival. It was a half-mile away chugging towards them, leaving a trail of black smoke. Bridie looked across the tracks at the field of healthy young corn, recalling the day Catherine arrived, unaware of the harvest she was about to reap.

Bridie was standing next to Tom and Margaret, Pina stood closer to the tracks with Catherine and Brian. As the train pulled into the station, the children stepped back, waiting for people to disembark. After boarding the train, Bridie reached over the seat in front of her, giving Catherine and Brian their passenger tickets. She laid one on Pina's lap next to her.

Pina looked up at Bridie. "Thank you so much for taking me with you. I'm about as excited as I can get."

"Don't thank me, thank Catherine. She's the one who gave up a birthday present, so you could come." Immediately, Bridie could tell by the expression on Pina's face she wasn't aware of that fact. "I'm sorry, dear, I thought you knew."

"No, I didn't. Catherine is such a good friend." The train pulled away from the station and Pina turned to look out of the window.

"My life is so much better than what it was," she continued. "I love my parents … the Campbells."

Bridie believed Pina was facing the window, fighting off tears. "I imagine you do. They are very nice people. They love you deeply and are much happier because of you." When Pina looked at her again, Bridie could see she wasn't crying, but was close to doing so.

"The Campbells aren't wealthy people, but I have all the dresses and bonnets I'd ever want. All I wanted was their love, and I believe I have that." Pina turned to the window again. "They treat me better than my own ever did."

Bridie elbowed Pina. "What Catherine doesn't know is, I was planning to invite you to come with us this weekend, but when she made her offer to forego her birthday present, I had to let her feel her generosity."

Pina patted Bridie's hand, "Thank you."

Bridie chuckled to herself, amused by the pats on her hand. She settled back into her seat, feeling good about her own generosity.

When the train pulled into Cambridge Station, they saw flags, signs and banners draped above the streets, on buildings and in store windows. Catherine and Pina squealed enthusiastically seeing five men at the station wearing Wellington boots, kilts and matching tam-o-shanters. "They even have knee socks," Pina wailed.

Brian pointed. "Look, they have purses on their hips."

Bridie and the Holmgrens laughed at the children's excitement. "Do you want a kilt?" Tom shouted to Brian.

"Maybe for the next two days," he answered.

"You'd look adorable in a kilt," Catherine remarked.

"If I'd look adorable, forget it."

Leaving the train, they saw a long banner hanging from the station's roof. It read, WELCOME CLANSMEN.

"Follow me," Tom shouted, "I saw for-hires over this way."

On their way to the carriages, Catherine and Pina noticed three women wearing green and red plaid skirts with white blouses. Being as warm as it was, they were carrying their plaid jackets over their arms. They watched Tom and the driver load the luggage onto a rack at the back of the black carriage.

"To the Erlanson Hotel," Tom said to the driver.

"It's the McErlanson Hotel this weekend," the driver responded, with a chuckle.

They rode slowly, avoiding clansmen meandering in the street, strolling from one side to the other. A sign in a restaurant window advertised, *Clan Chowder*. A Pub sign read, *Scottish Whiskeys*. "Look at that sign," Bridie said, pointing to a barbershop. *Bonniest Shaves and Haircuts.*

"What does "Bonniest" mean?" Brian asked.

Bridie smiled at him. "Bonniest means the best—the best shaves and haircuts."

Pina turned to look at Bridie in the seat behind her. "You mean as in, Catherine is Brian's bonniest girl?"

"That's correct. As a matter of fact, there is a Bonniest Knees Contest Sunday. The men who compete line up in their kilts and blindfolded women decide who has the bonniest knees. They tweak, pat and shift the knee caps to decide which knee she thinks is the best."

"You're kidding?" Brian uttered.

Catherine and Pina looked at each other, nodding. "We *must* see that."

At the hotel, Tom and Bridie registered at the desk, while the others stood outside watching the festivities. Soon, a young man came outside, piled their luggage onto a cart and pushed it back into the hotel. Tom came out and signaled the others to follow.

Bridie had a suite, with an adjoining room for the girls. Margaret and Tom had the same arrangement with Brian. Both suites overlooked flower gardens in a park, with a mixture of brick and frame homes beyond.

At eight o'clock, they went down for dinner at the hotel restaurant where all the waiters and waitresses were wearing tams. During dinner, Catherine and Pina were amused by the variety of plaid outfits worn by different clansmen, and that they wore skirts.

After dessert, Bridie looked at her watch, "It's almost 9:30 and we will have an exciting and exhausting day tomorrow. We need to get a good night's sleep."

"I'm tired from just thinking about the walking we'll be doing," Margaret said. "Are you wearing the McDonald's plaid tomorrow?"

"No, but I would be, if the moths hadn't had their way with it. I still have it, but due to the holes, I can't wear it and never got around to buying another."

They walked up to the second floor and Pina followed Bridie into their suite. "Where is Catherine?" Bridie asked.

"She's in the hall with Brian."

"Of course," Bridie replied, walking back to the door. She stuck her head into the hallway. "You can kiss her, if you like." She walked to her bed, smiling.

"You like to tease them, don't you?"

"Oh, a little bit, I guess. I suppose it's time to quit, but I do love them both. I can't imagine either one of them being with anyone else."

"I don't think they can, either. I hope I have a relationship like theirs some day."

"Be patient, you will. When the right man comes to your door, you'll know it and feel as they do."

The morning was warm and sunny, perfect for a day of festivities. The Fair Grounds were four blocks from their hotel, just beyond the Tomes River. Walking from the hotel, Bridie thought of John McTavish, and the days they spent at the fair. She was proud when she was with him. He was one of the strongest and most popular of the clansmen.

"The bridge is just ahead," Tom announced. "I can see the livestock pens on the far side of the field."

"The sheepdog competition will be over there," Bridie added.

"What's a sheepdog competition?" Brian asked.

"It's a contest to see whose shepherd dog can gather and corral sheep into a pen with the greatest skill and speed. They are very clever dogs."

On the other side of the river, boys in kilts were in a small corral, leading ponies with children riding them. Next to it, a foot race for children was being organized.

Bridie stepped to the side of the crowded gravel path and signaled the others follow. "I should give you information about the Scottish people before we begin the exhibits of their prowess." Bridie straightened her back and clasped her hands together. "To be a Scot is to be fiercely proud, patriotic and competitive. These Highland Games are taken very seriously. Each Clan wants to prove they are the best, or most worthy. These games trace their origins back hundreds of years when Highland Chiefs selected the best warriors through a series of competitions. Rejection by a Chief could be a humiliating disgrace, so to be the best is important." She lowered her hands and looked at the children. "It's almost 10:30. Let's go have fun."

"I'm enjoying all these colorful tartans," Margaret said, continuing down the path. "I've never seen so many colorful people at one time."

"Only about a quarter of the people here are in uniform," Bridie replied, "Imagine if everybody wore a Tartan."

"What are they throwing in that clearing over there?" Tom asked.

Bridie looked to where he was pointing. "That's a sheaf-toss. It's a jute sack filled with hay. The sack represents something, but I can't remember what."

They walked over and watched three contestants toss a sack. Unimpressed with the event, they moved on.

A few yards ahead, Catherine noticed another competition where a woman was tossing a man's boot. A banner hanging above the event read, *Wellie Toss*. She pointed in that direction. "And that is?"

Bridie waited for the others to move closer before explaining. "That's a witty competition between women. It's just for fun … but they do want to win. Scottish men wear heavy Wellington boots with their Tartans, so this competition is to see which woman can toss her husband's boot the farthest. Hence, the name—Wellie Toss. It's as simple as that, but it is a competition and all contestants want to win … for their own pride and their clan."

"I'm beginning to see what you meant, when you said, 'they were very competitive,'" Brian remarked.

"This is nothing compared to what you'll have seen by tomorrow night." She stood on her toes and looked into the small Wellie Toss clearing. "This woman is the last contestant, let's watch her toss and see which clan won the event."

They moved in among the crowd of people. The contestant gripped the top of the boot and rocked back and forth, swinging the boot like a pendulum. When her hand came back a fourth time, the boot slipped out of her hand and flew into the crowd behind her.

"Ya canna win that way, Lassie," one man yelled among the laughter.

"That was a good one. Turn around and toss it backward," hollered another.

Catherine and Pina were laughing. They considered the lady's misfortune quite funny.

The boot was thrown back and the judge handed it to the woman. "This is your second and last try," he said.

The woman was still laughing, taking the boot from the judge, her face red from embarrassment. She started rocking again, swinging the boot. This time, she was late in releasing the boot and it went straight up in the air and landed eight feet in front of her. She buried her face in her hands.

"She must be English," one lady shouted.

"Glad she ain't a'wearin' my colors," shouted another.

"You did fine," the judge said, laughing. He looked at the sheet in his hand and said, "The winner of this event is Martha McInnis of …" People started hollering and clapping so loud, that they couldn't hear the name of her clan.

"As you can see," Bridie said, "They're serious about winning, but they do have fun doing it."

"Thank God we have you to explain the events," Tom said.

Bridie looked at the festival program she picked up at the hotel. "It's almost one o'clock and the Caber Toss starts at two o'clock. The Highland Fling and Sword Dance is starting now, so let's watch them." Walking across the field, Bridie asked, "If anybody wants to roam on their own, say so. We can meet at the bridge later." She looked at the children, waiting for a response.

"We'll stay with you," Brian said. "Maybe tomorrow we'll spend time alone."

The sound of bagpipes passed over the grounds, drawing hundreds of people to the dancers. The men were performing at the center of a large, grass-covered sinkhole, providing higher ground for spectators to watch from. The bagpipes wailed louder and quick stepping, clansmen danced between crossed swords lying on the ground. It was a lengthy performance, and for some spectators, it was exhausting to just watch. There was a fifteen-minute break before the men returned to dance the, "Highland Fling," another spirited dance of high-stepping and swirling kilts. When they finished, the crowd showed their appreciation with a robust round of applause that included screaming and shouting.

"These men are a strong, hardy bunch," Tom remarked. "If I had them at the quarry, I wouldn't need machinery."

"If you want to see them again, they'll be dancing this evening and tomorrow," Bridie said. "We should go over to the caber toss now … *that* is impressive."

Pina took quick steps to catch up to Bridie. "What's a caber?"

"A caber is a tree trunk about fifteen feet long, with the bark removed. It generally weighs 180 pounds and the challenge is to toss it, while keeping it in the most vertical position possible."

"A fifteen-foot tree trunk? And they toss it?" Pina questioned.

Bridie laughed. "Yes, but I won't try to explain. You'll see it soon enough." Bridie looked to see that all could hear what she was about to say. "My fiancé, John McTavish, won the event twice in three years. Rarely does anyone win more than once."

"I wish I could have met him," Catherine said. "He must have been quite a man, if *you* loved him."

Bridie and Margaret glanced at each other.

Bridie put her arm around Catherine. "I wish you could have met that man, too."

"Catherine said, you have a picture of John on your fireplace mantle," Brian reflected. "I would like to see it next time I'm at your house."

Bridie looked at Brian. "Thank you. I'd like you to see his picture."

"We're getting closer to the livestock," Tom announced. "It's becoming rather evident."

"We'll have to ignore the aroma, if we want to see the sheep-dog competition tomorrow," Pina replied.

"Come this way," Bridie said, pointing. "The ground by the trees is a little higher. There we can get a better view and be in the shade. Besides, there's a tree stump I can sit on. My feet are starting to hurt."

People were gathering behind a rope fence, anxious for the caber toss to begin. Thirteen contestants filtered out of the crowd and stood off to the side. They only wore their Wellington boots, colorful kilts and an undershirt. They were huge, muscular men.

"My God," Tom said. "They look as strong as oxen. I'd hate to get punched by one of them."

"If that happened, I would give you a lovely funeral," Margaret commented.

"Look at their arms," Brian gasped. "They're bigger than my thighs." He turned to Tom. "Talk about men replacing machines at the quarry–these, are the men."

"Imagine," Catherine uttered. "They've grown from a few pounds at birth–to this. That's scary." She looked at Pina, "Can you imagine cooking for a man like that?"

Pina rolled her eyes, as she and Catherine sat in the grass.

Bridie sat on the tree stump, tugging at Margaret's sleeve. "Give me a few minutes and you can sit awhile."

Brian noticed a thick, fifteen-foot log lying on the ground in front of the husky contestants. Suddenly, he realized what it was. He looked at Bridie and pointed. "Is that big timer the caber?"

"Yes."

"And they're going to toss that huge thing?"

Bridie smiled. "Big men play with big toys."

A man with a thick, red beard stepped up to the caber that was placed on end by assistants. He lowered himself and lifted the caber from the bottom, letting it rest against his chest and shoulder. The man staggered forward, bent his knees a little and heaved up and out, tossing the caber a few feet in front of him. A judge stepped forward and marked the spot.

"Ouch!" Tom grunted. "If I tried that, something would have dropped from under my kilt."

Margaret poked Tom's arm. "We have young ladies present. Be careful with your comments."

The next contestant stepped up, staggered with the caber, tossing it a bit short of the first mark. A third man tossed it about a foot-and-a-half further than the first contestant. When the fourth contestant staggered forward, he dropped to his knees, letting the caber fall to the ground. He reached for his back, obviously in pain. Two men ran to help him onto his feet and walked him away.

It was almost four o'clock when the contest ended. The third contestant, the man wearing a gray and white plaid kilt, won the event.

Bridie thought how magnificent John looked, when he won the caber toss. *He would have won today.*

"That was interesting, and unforgettable," Tom said. "It's hot. Let's have something cold to drink. The refreshment tent is a short walk back toward the bridge."

"I agree," Margaret said, rising from the stump. "Thanks for sharing the seat with me, Bridie. My feet feel much better."

"That was a *bonnie* show," Brian said, attempting to be clever. "Ready for a *bonnie* drink, girls?"

"I'm more than ready," Pina answered. "The temperature must be over eighty degrees."

At the refreshment vendors, Tom selected a picnic bench under the tent so they would be out of the sun. "Here's some money, Brian. You and the girls go for the drinks." Tom paused to look at the sign listing the beverages. "Get me an iced tea."

"I'll have the same," Margaret echoed.

Bridie raised a finger, "Me, too." She watched the children, as they walked to the makeshift counter. "Remember how dull our lives were before these children arrived? Today, it would be the three of us, as usual, doing whatever we do, but without any meaningful purpose. Now, every day is fulfilled."

Tom sat down between them and faced Margaret. "Remember? Recently we discussed the same thing." He turned to Bridie. "It isn't just having children that has made us happy, it's having *these* children. We took a chance and could easily have adopted children that became a problem. Pina, too, she was a great find for the Campbells."

"Monica is a little different," Margaret chimed in. "A nice girl, but not quite all together."

"I wonder where she is?" Bridie added. "I'm curious as to what really happened at the Peters' farm."

"Three iced teas, two root beers and an iced ginger," Brian said, returning to the bench.

"I'm having the ginger," Pina said. "I had it once, a long time ago, and I really liked it."

Brian lifted his arms and stretched his back. "It feels bonnie sitting in the shade, with a nice breeze and a bonnie cold drink."

Catherine glared at him. "One more "bonnie" out of you, and I'll give you a bonnie kick in the pants."

The adults laughed at Catherine's attack on Brian's jokes.

Bridie was still smiling at Catherine's remark, while removing a white handkerchief from her straw purse. She dabbed at the moisture on her face and neck. "I could use a bath and a nap before dinner." She looked at the others around the table. "It's almost 4:30. When we finish our drinks, we can walk back to the hotel and rest, then meet for dinner at seven o'clock. Is that good for everybody?"

Everyone agreed.

The next morning, they went directly to the sheepdog competition, the first major event of the day. There were bleachers, so spectators could get a good view of the dogs working in the open field. Thirty sheep were released from a pen and a dog ran back and forth, keeping the sheep together and directing them into another pen a hundred yards away. Two judges followed with clipboards, writing down the dog's good and bad points.

"I'm impressed," Brian said. "I wonder how difficult it is to train a dog to do that?" He stood to look where the dogs were coming from. "How many dogs are entered in the contest?"

Bridie looked at her program. "Eighteen dogs. Nine begin here, and nine start from pens on the other side of the field. The sheep are herded between the two pens."

Bagpipes began playing in the distance. "I guess it's time for the Highland Fling and Sword Dance, again," Bridie stated.

"Look, they're opening the pen on the other side," Catherine shouted. "See how quickly the dog runs around the sheep, guiding them one way and then another."

While the eighth dog was performing, a sheep broke away from the herd, somewhat confused as to where it should go. The dog quickly ran past it and turned it back to the others. "My God, they're fast," Tom, uttered.

"Bonnie show," Catherine declared.

The others turned to her. "You said that naughty word."

"Yes, I did. It seemed appropriate, not abusive."

Tom looked at Brian. "That can be your excuse."

During the tenth performance, Brian sighed. "I don't know how they can pick a winner. From what I can tell, all of the dogs have performed perfectly."

When the winner was announced, Bridie shook her head. "You could have fooled me. I thought they all won."

"That was a wonderful way to spend the morning," Margaret stated. "What's next?"

"The Bonniest Knees Contest," Catherine and Pina chimed, quickly.

"It's almost one o'clock," Bridie said. "The Bonniest Knees Contest is at two o'clock. We have one hour to eat and get over there."

After eating Scottish meat pies, the three children ran ahead to be in front of the crowd that would amass for the contest. It was a favorite event because of the sensitivity of it and the humorous remarks made by spectators. They stood near the judge's table watching ten men, wearing different colored kilts, come out of the crowd and line up on the grass. As more spectators arrived, they eventually formed a wide circle around the contestants. Bridie and the Holmgrens were standing a few feet behind the children.

Two women judging the event waited in the grass clearing, while an elderly woman guided five blindfolded ladies through the crowd to five chairs near the judging table. The judge, who would record their decisions, carried a scoring paper on a thin, wooden board. She addressed the crowd, as loud as she could.

"The fun is about to begin." She pointed to the women sitting in the chairs. "Here are five women who must be very desperate for a man, or they wouldn't have volunteered for this contest. And standing over there, are ten men desperate for attention. Let's see what happens."

One-by-one, a judge escorted four women past the line of men lifting their kilts, fully exposing their knees. In turn, each blindfolded woman felt the men's knees, dimples and muscles around them, while shouts and laughter abounded.

"You're getting a bit too high with your hand, Lassy," a husky voice bellowed through the crowd.

"Someone should arrest her," a woman screamed.

"She's using that blindfold as an excuse," another woman called out.

The contestants blushed and giggled when they went from man to man, trying to decide who had the bonniest knees. While the fourth woman was telling the judge whose knees she thought were best, a gust of wind blew the score sheet from the judge's board, landing a few feet in front of Pina. She picked it up and carried it over to the judge.

On the other side of the clearing, a pretty girl with wavy blond hair took three steps out of the crowd, staring at Pina. Slowly, she took three more steps, and called loudly, "Pina?"

Pina turned, looking across the clearing at the girl. They stood like pillars, staring at each other. Then Pina, in disbelief, recognized the girl. She shouted back, "Hillary?"

"Yes!"

The girls ran to each other and embraced, crying and laughing at the same time. They looked at each other, then kissed and embraced again.

Pina placed her hand against Hillary's face. "I never thought I'd see you again."

"I can't believe this is happening, either," Hillary replied. She placed Pina's hands in hers, took a step back and looked at her. "You look wonderful. So often, I wished I could write you or see you." Suddenly, a thought popped into her head. "Wait a minute, if we're both here at the festival, we can't live too far from each other. Where are you living now?"

"In Newberry, south of here. And you?"

"I live near Galena, north of here." Another expression of surprise quickly covered Hillary's face. "My God, I just realized you're speaking English. We've got to talk, talk, talk. I want to hear everything about you, what you've been doing, where you've been."

As the crowd watched the girls, the judge turned to the men lined up behind her. "Drop your skirts men, I believe we're witnessing a special moment."

Pina and Hillary looked at the people surrounding them and realized they were holding up the contest. Pina yelled to Catherine, "I'll be back, soon." Embarrassed, they held hands and ran through the crowd of spectators to where they would have privacy, in the shade of some Birch trees.

"Pinch me," Hillary said. "I can't believe we're sitting together, touching each other again. When I saw you on the Orphan Train in Alton, I was sure I would never see you again."

"When I saw you crying and running alongside the train, I realized how much we meant to each other. We must try to stay together."

Hillary nodded in agreement. "As I think about it, I don't see why that should be a problem. Being that we don't live that far from each other, we should be able to take a train and visit, occasionally."

"You're right," Pina responded, enthusiastically. She looked over her shoulder toward the contest. "I want to meet your mother. Mrs. Gretsch told me she was very nice, and very pretty."

Hillary looked down at the grass. "My mother died last year. That's why I live near Galena."

Pina leaned toward Hillary and kissed her on the cheek. "I'm sorry."

"I feel bad about you losing your mother, too," Hillary added. "I don't understand why it happens, especially to people who aren't old."

They were silent a moment before Pina went on. "When we met, both of us had a mother but no father. Now, we have neither." She hesitated again. "Did you come on an Orphan Train like I did?"

Hillary straightened her back and replied eagerly, "No! Remember Kate, Mr. Dragus' secretary?" Mentioning, Frank Dragus' name, still bothered her. The thought of him made her feel unclean.

"Sure, I do. She was nice to me."

"I live with her. Kate was my mother's best friend. She married John Hanley, who I'm sure you don't know, and they bought a farm near Galena. John was raised there and wanted to go back." Hillary grinned. "Kate said, she'll need me to help care for her babies. That sounded good to me."

Pina's broad smile showed she agreed.

"They bought me a pony to practice riding, and now they feel I'm ready to have my own horse. I've always loved horses, so this is a dream coming true."

"Will you pick your horse, or will they pick it for you?"

"Actually, my uncle Biff will take me shopping for a horse. He isn't really my uncle, but I call him that. Biff is John Hanley's cousin. He came to Alton a few times … on business. I think he fell in love with my mother and wanted to marry her. Obviously, that didn't happen."

The girls looked up, startled by the sudden trill of two yellow and black finches in the tree above them. "What about you, who are you living with?" Hillary asked.

"Richard and Eileen Campbell. They've been wonderful to me. So much so, I feel they really are my parents. I have great friends, too. They're here at the festival. My friend, Catherine, and her … adoptive mother, Bridie, brought me here. Catherine is my best friend in Newberry. You'll love her."

Screaming and loud applause interrupted their conversation. "I guess they've decided who has the bonniest knees?" Hillary laughed, looking over at the festival. "Now, best of all, I found you. If I ever meet Bridie, I'll have to thank her for bringing you here."

"I'll introduce you," Pina said, pointing to the spectators. "Bridie and Catherine are right there."

"Good!" Hillary replied, eagerly. She folded her hands on her lap and asked, "I'm curious, what was it like riding an Orphan Train, not knowing what would happen to you?"

Pina looked down at her hands. "It took three days to get here, and I was scared every day, wondering what kind of people would adopt me, where I would be living, or whether anyone would adopt me. All orphans imagine scary things that could happen to them." She looked directly into Hillary's eyes. "I was so lucky. I feel Newberry is where I belong ... with the Campbells."

Hillary smiled, "I'm happy for you." She hesitated, "Is your brother in Newberry?"

Pina ripped a dandelion from the ground and tossed it over her shoulder. "I don't know where Marcello is. He wasn't adopted in Newberry, so he went back to the train. As they were leaving the train depot, Marcello looked back at me with sad eyes. All I could do was throw him a kiss. He knows what town I'm in, so I keep hoping to get a letter from him. It's been eighteen months, but nothing yet."

Kate was almost upon them, before they noticed her coming. "Pina Sasso, I never imagined we'd see you here."

"Isn't it wonderful," Pina replied, standing to face Kate. "My name is Pina Campbell now."

Kate placed her arm around Pina's shoulders. "You look happy and healthy. Am I right?"

"Completely right," Pina answered. "I was telling Hillary ..."

"Wait a minute," Kate interrupted. "You're speaking perfect English."

"Thank you. I practiced constantly. Now I can speak two languages."

"Good for you." Kate said, touching her shoulder. "Whatever you do, don't give up your Italian. You may need it some day. It's good to know more than one language."

"Where's John?" Hillary asked.

Kate backed away from Pina. "He met another farmer and they went to the McBeer Tent to have a bonnie glass of beer and some farm talk. He's waiting for us, but I'm sure he's in no hurry to leave."

"Great!" Pina responded. "Then I can introduce you to my friends."

"I would love to meet the Campbells," Kate remarked.

Pina turned to Kate. "They aren't here. I came with friends."

"They all live in Newberry," Hillary added, quickly. "That's not far from us, right?"

Kate laughed. "I think I know what's coming." She looked at the two girls. "It's about a five hour train ride and Pina is more than welcome to visit us."

The girls looked at each other and squealed. "Thank you, Kate."

"Don't get too excited girls. We must talk to Mr. and Mrs. Campbell about this."

"Come, I'll introduce you to the others," Pina said, anxiously. "I'll tell you about them, as we walk." Pina positioned herself between Hillary and Kate. They're all nice, friendly people, and both of you will definitely like them." Pina continued at a slow, methodical pace, to avoid confusion as she explained. "I came here in February of last year. The following June, Catherine and Brian arrived. It seems a miracle, because Catherine and Brian met at the orphanage in New York City, fell in love, and were adopted in the same town. How's that for fate? They're both sixteen and it appears they'll be getting married in two years, when Brian finishes college."

"Does Bridie have a husband?" Kate asked.

"No. Catherine told me Bridie's fiance'e, John, drowned only weeks before they were to be married. We came to this festival because Bridie is a Scot. Bridie said he was very strong and won many events here. You can tell by the way she talks about John, she still loves him."

"Well, Bridie and I have one thing in common, we both love a man named John."

Pina pointed to the clearing ahead. "That's them standing there."

Catherine and Brian began walking toward them, with the adults following. Catherine went directly to Hillary. "I assume you're Hillary, from Alton, Delaware?"

"Yes, I am."

"Watching you and Pina discover each other was absolutely magical. Everyone could feel your excitement."

Hillary smiled. "I couldn't believe my eyes. I forced myself to believe I was looking at Pina."

"Pina mentioned you many times, so I'm glad we're getting a chance to meet." Catherine stepped to the side and took Brian's arm. She looked at both Hillary and Kate. "Before we say more, I'm Catherine and this is Brian."

"Nice to meet you," Hillary said. "You make a handsome couple."

Brian only smiled.

Kate's eyes scanned the others. "I'm Kate Hanley. Hillary's mother, Laura, was my dearest friend. When she died last year, John and I brought Hillary west with us. It wasn't a difficult choice, for I've been in love with Hillary since she was an infant. She has been a pleasure."

Hillary playfully fluttered her eyelashes, acknowledging the compliment.

Bridie stepped forward, with her hand extended. "I'm Bridie McDonald and Catherine has been *my* greatest pleasure."

Kate took Bridie's hand. "I'm pleased to meet you, and I'm sure Catherine *is* a pleasure. I'm impressed with her already." She looked beyond Bridie and smiled.

"We're Tom and Margaret Holmgren. Brian is *our* greatest pleasure."

"Stop!" Brian belched. "You're making me sick with all this 'we're your greatest pleasure' stuff."

The adults laughed.

"We're just having fun with our little darlings," Margaret teased.

"Little darlings, now," Brian uttered in disgust.

"Why don't we go to the refreshment tent and rest our feet?" Bridie suggested.

Kate agreed. "It'll give Hillary and Pina some time together."

"We may be spending a lot of time together," Pina said, with fervor. "It's only a five hour train ride from Newberry to Galena."

"Galena?" Bridie repeated, as they began walking. "Is that where you live? I've been there many times, to attend the theatre. Lovely town, and the DeSoto Hotel is a wonderful place to stay."

"Do you live in town?" Tom asked.

Kate looked over her shoulder. "No. We live a mile outside of Galena."

"They'll be starting a family soon and I'm taking care of the babies," Hillary announced, proudly.

Kate noticed Catherine lean forward and look at her.

"No, Catherine, not that soon. Probably next year."

"The Campbells won't be having babies," Pina pouted, "So I'm stuck with me."

Bridie snickered. "They're quite satisfied. You're exactly what the Campbells wanted."

"Are you staying in Cambridge tonight?" Bridie asked Kate.

"No. We're leaving on the 6:15 train, tonight."

"It's almost 4:30 now," Hillary announced. "I won't have much time with Pina."

"I understand that," Kate replied, "but John has an appointment with Biff in the morning. If we had known we'd meet Pina, we would have stayed another night."

Bridie smiled at Pina. "Think of this as a new beginning, my dear. You girls found each other, so get each other's address and telephone information. I'm certain your parents won't mind exchange visits."

At the refreshment tent, there were only three small tables available and they were scattered. "You children sit at that table by the tent post," Tom suggested, pointing. Tom handed money to Brian. "Bring us iced tea and get whatever you four want."

"I'm afraid we'll only have a few minutes with you people," Kate said. "Fortunately, our luggage is packed and stored in the hotel luggage room, or we'd be gone already."

"And you need time to find John at the McBeer tent," Margaret added.

"True," Kate laughed, "The McBeer tent. I could look for John now, but by the time I found him, I doubt we would have these minutes together." Kate glanced over at the beer tent on the chance she would see John. "This is our first time attending the Scottish Festival and we certainly had a bonnie time."

"We must get together again," Bridie suggested. "Maybe you and John could bring Hillary to Newberry? I have an extra room at my house."

"Thanks for the offer," Kate replied. "We just might do that."

Brian brought their four iced teas and said to Tom, "You're sitting at a table with three beautiful women and I'm sitting with three beautiful girls. I like this festival."

"Remember who you came with."

"I often wonder what their lives would be like today, if we hadn't found them?" Margaret queried. "I know our lives have improved because of Brian."

"We've been a good match, all of us," Bridie said. "Some adoptions can be a mistake."

"Like Monica," Tom remarked.

"That's true," Bridie said, meeting Kate's eyes, gravely. "Monica arrived on the same Orphan Train, as Catherine and Brian. She was adopted by a couple who lived a mile from town. After a few months, she disappeared. The people who adopted her said she ran away. I'm not going to speculate, for I feel we'll learn the truth eventually."

"We've all heard stories about children being abused," Tom said. "We also know there are ugly incidences we'll never hear about."

Kate immediately thought of Hillary's experience with Frank Dragus. "I agree. We'll never learn about many of the abuses children have suffered." Kate took a last sip of her iced tea and rose from the table. "I'd better look for John, so we don't miss our train."

"It's a shame we don't have more time together," Bridie said. "We can talk later."

"Good," Kate responded. "Maybe all of us can go to the theatre in Galena? Then I can introduce you to John and Hillary's Uncle Biff."

A smile hovered over her lips, staring at Bridie. "You'll love Uncle Biff."

Chapter Fifteen

The following day, Bridie and Catherine arrived home shortly after three o'clock. They were hot, thirsty, and eager for a bath. Both dropped their luggage in the vestibule and walked directly into the kitchen for a badly needed glass of ice water. Bridie poured water into two glasses, while Catherine went to the icebox and chipped away at the block of ice. Both sighed after taking their first drink.

Bridie walked to the back door and unlocked it. "Since you're sleeping at Pina's house tonight, take your bath first, while I sip my iced tea on the porch." She stepped through the doorway, "Put your dirty clothes in the basket, you're washing clothes tomorrow."

A half-hour later, Bridie carried her luggage upstairs, placing them at the foot of her bed. She cranked the telephone and waited for Cora to respond.

"Welcome back, Bridie. How was the festival?"

"Wonderful, Cora. Everyone had a grand time. I believe we may go again in two years —that's if it doesn't interfere with family wedding plans."

"Catherine and Brian are eager to marry, aren't they?"

"Young, and in love, of course they are. Actually, it may be the safest thing for them to do, if you know what I mean."

"I understand exactly," she whispered. "You know the Belcher boy … Charles? I heard he ran off and married some young chickadee, probably a student of his. Not exactly ran off, but did it sudden-like."

"Charles Belcher?" Bridie gasped. "When did this happen?"

"From what I heard, about two months ago, and it was kept a secret."

"Will there be a church ceremony, celebration, or something?"

"I doubt it. By the rush of it all, my guess is the girl's pregnant and it shows. If there is a celebration, it will probably be some time after the child is born, so they can claim any birth date they want. His parents are very religious, so aborting is out of the question."

"Charles Belcher," Bridie laughed. "Can't wait to tell Catherine."

"I'd better break off," Cora said. "Who do you want to talk to?"

"Ring the Newberry Times, please."

That night, still excited over their trip, Catherine and Pina lay in bed reliving their weekend at the Scottish Festival and Pina's chance meeting with Hillary.

"This afternoon, I asked my mother about having Hillary here for a few days. She thought it was a good idea, but I would have to ask my father. He loves flapjacks, so tomorrow morning we'll make them for breakfast and I'll ask him then. Besides, it would be difficult for him to say, 'No,' with you sitting there."

"That's devious," Catherine laughed, "But a good idea. It would be fun having Hillary here. There are a lot of things we could do, and I'd probably have the use of the horse and buggy, at least some of the time."

"You're right! I didn't think of that. We could ride around town and into the country." The girls laid in the dark discussing all the possibilities of what the three of them could do until they fell asleep.

It was eight o'clock before Catherine and Pina woke. "My God!" Pina muttered. "My dad will go down for breakfast any minute now." They stepped into their slippers, wiggled into dresses and raced out of the bedroom. Running past her parents' bedroom, Pina shouted, "We'll make breakfast." Entering the kitchen, they found Eileen cradling a bowl in her arm, mixing batter. "Mom! I didn't hear you go downstairs."

"You girls were asleep." She placed the bowl on the table and placed a scoop of lard into the hot frying pan. "I made the batter. Now you make it into flapjacks. When your father comes down and sees you two making them, he'll think you did it all. He'd like that."

"Our secret," Pina whispered, scooping batter into the fry pan.

Catherine smiled at Mrs. Campbell. "Thank you for your help." Catherine took plates from the cabinet and began setting the table.

Minutes later, Richard came down wearing his dark brown suit, ready for work at the bank. "Good morning, everyone." He looked toward the stove. "Flapjacks. What a pleasant surprise." He stepped up behind Pina and kissed the top of her head. "You're a good daughter. That's why I love you so much." He turned to Catherine, placing silverware around the table. "She knows I love flapjacks. I thank you both."

"You're welcome," Catherine replied, with a smirk. "Pina says she lives to please you." She cast a brief glimpse at the other two, wondering if they recognized her contribution to softening him up.

"Oh, she does, does she?" Richard responded. "I have no complaints about Pina, but that sounds a little exaggerated to me."

Pina looked over her shoulder at him sitting at the table. "We've got butter and molasses, too."

"Great!" he said, enthusiastically. He glanced at Eileen. "Now that school is closed for the summer, you get to spend much more time with Pina than I do. It doesn't seem fair."

Pina carried a plate with three large flapjacks to her father. "I'll save most of my evening time for you … if you're a good boy."

Richard began cutting his flapjacks into little squares. "What determines that I'm a good boy?"

Eileen sat at the table, pushing the jar of molasses toward him. "I think being a good boy means, you'll allow her friend Hillary to come and stay with us for a few days."

Pina brought Eileen her flapjacks and gave her father a coquettish glance. "That would be a good start."

Richard laughed. "A good start? What would be the finish?"

Eileen smiled at the two girls. "Is there ever a finish?"

"None that I know of," Pina answered.

"I'd better get to the bank. I'll be safer there … I think."

Pina began putting more batter into the fry pan. "In my letter, I'll ask Hillary to pick a time she could come. It would be nice if she could be here for our Fourth-of-July celebration, but that's next week already."

Richard hesitated before putting another bite of food into his mouth, then looked at Catherine. "The way those two are glaring at me, you'd think I was an ogre." He squinted at Eileen. "Why would I object to Hillary coming here?"

"We really didn't think you would," Eileen answered. "But, we want to hear you say it."

Richard looked at Pina. "Hillary can stay here a few days."

That afternoon, Bridie returned home after a morning at the newspaper. Catherine was in the kitchen baking a variety of cookies. An open cookbook was lying on the table. "Well, aren't you ambitious … and thoughtful."

Catherine appeared very pleased with herself. "Yesterday, you mentioned having a taste for homemade cookies, so I decided to make them. I made extra peanut butter cookies for Jack, since they're his favorite."

Bridie watched Catherine slide another tray of cookie dough into the oven. "He's been bringing you flowers and you bake him cookies and tarts. Is there something going on between you two that Brian and I should know about?"

"Absolutely. We're passionately in love."

Bridie pulled a chair from the table and sat down, opening her high-button shoes. "Seriously, I'm very pleased with your acceptance of Jack and the relationship you've developed with him. Jack needs to feel he belongs."

"Sometimes, I pretend he's my new father, when I watch him do chores around the house."

Bridie remained silent, dwelling on Catherine's statement.

Catherine lowered the oven door to inspect the next batch of cookies. "Are we all going to Getty's Field for the Fourth-of-July celebration?" She decided they weren't baked enough and closed the door.

"Tom will be on a business trip, but Margaret and Brian will be with us."

"Brian will be with me," Catherine assured her.

"I guess that would be a better way to say it," Bridie laughed. "I'm going upstairs and change into a dress that's more comfortable than this thick, clothy thing."

"That's the trouble with dress clothes." Catherine frowned. "They're so cumbersome and uncomfortable, especially in this warm weather."

Bridie stood at the table. "You and Brian have a birthday coming soon, so we'll have to plan something quickly."

"I received my present, remember?"

"I know," Bridie answered. "I'm not buying you anything. We'll just invite close friends to celebrate your birthdays." She started to leave the kitchen, then turned to Catherine, again. "It's your sixteenth birthday and that's a special one for a girl."

Catherine placed her hands on her hips. "Nothing else, please."

Pina and her parents spent their Fourth-of-July afternoon with some of Richard's co-workers from the bank, but intended to watch the evening's fireworks with Pina's friends. At 8:30, Richard tucked a blanket under his arm and they left for Getty's Field. When they arrived, they went directly to the trees where they were to meet

Catherine and the others. It was getting dark and the stars were becoming more prominent.

"There they are," Pina said, waving to Catherine. A glowing kerosene lantern illuminated the four of them sitting on two blankets. "Good, they brought a lantern this year," Pina commented.

Pina sat with Catherine and Brian, while her parents unfolded their blanket next to Bridie and Margaret.

"I have some fruit, if you're interested," Margaret said. "Bananas, apples and pears."

"No, thanks," Richard replied. "We've been eating all afternoon." He looked at Brian. "I imagine you're working at the quarry all summer, building up your muscles."

"Yes, and I love it. I think about the structures I could build with all that stone. Working there stimulates my imagination."

"Are you studying three, or four years of engineering?"

"Three. What I learn first-hand at the quarry, more than covers that extra year."

A loud explosion and a gigantic ball of white sparks appeared overhead, followed by more exploding fireworks. The crowd squealed and applauded, with each beautiful display of color and powerful eruption. Bridie noticed Eileen looking at the children, instead of the fireworks. She leaned close to her. "They've made it a wonderful year for us, haven't they?"

She realized Bridie knew what she was thinking. "Yes, they have."

At the end of July, the temperature had been in the eighties for six days. Catherine and Pina planned a breezy, afternoon buggy ride to cool themselves and explore the nearby countryside. When Catherine returned home from shopping, she found a note from Bridie on the kitchen table, requesting her to meet Carol Swane at Winnemac Park at two o'clock.

"I don't know a Carole Swane ... unless it's Carole Cobane from school," she muttered. Catherine put the groceries away, while trying to figure out which girl it might be, and why she would want to meet at the park. She went upstairs and washed, then went to her bedroom window and looked down at the pond. Roper was walking along the edge of the water sniffing the brush. He wagged his tail, looking skyward, hoping for the two ducks to return. To her left, she could see Jack putting the bridle on Bree for her. *It is such a beautiful rig,* she thought.

Catherine walked to her dresser and looked at herself in the mirror. She spun around and decided the yellow cotton dress she was wearing was appropriate. She went down to the pantry and took three peanut butter cookies from the cookie-jar, then went to the carriage house.

With reins in his hand, Jack pointed to Bree and mumbled, "Ready." He noticed the cookies in Catherine's hand and smiled.

"Thank you for getting Bree ready for me, Jack." He gave her a nod and presented his upturned palm, accepting the cookies. Catherine climbed into the buggy, taking the reins Jack was holding up to her. She held up three fingers to Jack and said, "I'll be back in three hours."

He nodded again, with half of a cookie sticking out of his mouth.

Catherine was pleased with the way she controlled the buggy, knowing part of her success was due to having a good horse that responded quickly to her every whim. When she arrived at Pina's house, she was standing at the curb wearing a blue cotton dress. Catherine glanced toward her white frame house and saw Mrs. Campbell at the window, waving to them. Driving away, Catherine waved back.

"We have to go to Winnemac Park before we do anything else," Catherine stated. "A girl called me when I was shopping. Bridie left a note telling me her name was Carole Swane. I don't know a Carole Swane, or why she would want to meet in the park. I find it very suspicious."

Pina looked at Catherine, frowning at the oddity of it all. "That *is* strange. Let's ride by the park and see who's there before we leave the carriage."

"That's what I was thinking. She wants me there at two o'clock and it's almost that now."

Approaching the park, they could see a woman pushing a child in a buggy, and the head of a woman sitting behind a row of bushes. "It must be the person behind the bushes," Catherine said. "With her back to us, I can't tell who she is. Besides, I don't know anyone who wears a black hat during summer."

"It appears safe," Pina decided. "I don't see any evil-looking people around."

Catherine steered Bree to a hitching post opposite the bushes hiding the woman. After securing Bree, they walked carefully toward her. When they got close, the woman must have heard them coming. She stood and turned to face them.

"Monica!" the girls squealed.

"I told you in my letter, I would come one day."

"That's not Monica," Pina joked, pointing at her. "That's Carole Swane."

"I faked that name and altered my voice, so Bridie wouldn't know who I was." Monica stepped from behind the bushes, her eyes darting back-and-forth from one friend to the other, waiting for a response.

Simultaneously, Catherine and Pina cried out, "You're pregnant!"

Monica rubbed her abdomen. "Five months." She held out her left hand and wiggled her fingers, showing her rings. "My new name is Monica Belcher."

Catherine gasped. "You're the girl who married Charles Belcher? Bridie told me he got married."

"Yes. I'm Mrs. Charles Belcher of Knoxville, Illinois."

"Let's sit on the bench," Pina suggested. "This is too much for me to absorb."

They sat with Monica between them. "How did you meet Charles?" Catherine asked, eagerly.

Monica smiled broadly before explaining. She was feeling important because of her marital status. "Every week, Charles, or someone from his family, bought eggs at the Peters' farm. Soon, he was the only one who came for eggs, showing interest in me ... especially my big tits." She laughed. "We liked each other, but I never expected anything to come of it."

"The Peters said you ran away. What's that all about?" Pina asked.

"I did."

"Why?" Catherine questioned. "And how did you end up with Charles, if you ran away?"

"First answer, *why* you ran away," Pina asked, inquisitively.

Monica sat quiet for a moment, debating whether she should answer that question, honestly. "I'll tell you, if you promise not to say anything to anyone ... our secret?"

"Of course, we promise," Pina assured her.

Monica glanced at them in turn, and said to Catherine, "One day, I told you that I thought Mr. Peters always looked up my dress, and I believed he wanted to have sex with me. Well, I was right. The day I ran away he raped me in the hayloft. I said I would tell what happened, and he said if I did, I would be sorry. I didn't know what he meant, so I lied I wouldn't tell. I also knew, that if I stayed, he would do it again. When he went into the field for the cattle, I packed my things and ran down the road toward Newberry." She squinted at Catherine. "I was hoping you could hide me at your house, until I knew where to go."

Monica took a deep breath and rubbed her abdomen. "I had gone a short distance when I ran into Charles, coming to the farm for eggs. He saw me struggling with the suitcase and crying, so he stopped his wagon to help me. I had to give him some explanation, so I told him the truth, with a promise he wouldn't tell. I wanted to get away from Mr. Peters forever and not be involved in embarrassing things with the law."

"Did Charles think you should go to the sheriff?" Catherine asked.

"No! Straightaway, he suggested I go to Knoxville with him that evening and he would hide me. I liked the idea, because I didn't want to try an adoption again. I needed someone to help me immediately, so I agreed."

"Weren't you afraid of living with him, you know, like Mr. Peters?" Pina questioned.

"I thought of that, but I was already raped and there weren't any other choices for me. Like I said, I did like him. And if sex is what it would take for security, I'd do it."

"How long did it take before you … did it?" Pina giggled.

Monica rolled her eyes. "The first two nights he slept on the sofa, but neither of us slept well, knowing we were alone in the apartment. The third night, I was cleaning the supper dishes and he came up behind me and put his arms around my waist. I turned to look at him, knowing what he … we wanted. It took just one kiss, and the dishes didn't get finished until the next day."

"Where is Charles now?" Catherine asked.

"He's at his parents' house, talking to them about our future and how we'll try to hide the facts. They don't know I'm here. I insisted on coming, so I could see you girls and explain what happened to me."

"Where are you staying tonight?" Pina asked.

"We aren't staying in Newberry. We're here for just a few hours, then going home on the 4:15 train. We decided I should stay away from his parents' house, so their neighbors couldn't see my condition. His parents are rather strict and they aren't pleased with our situation. They hope to hide the truth; as if people won't suspect, being that it was a quick marriage and all."

"Are you happy?" Catherine asked. "That's more important than anything."

"Yes, I am. Being that I didn't know Charles that well before we got married, I pray that it lasts."

Catherine made eye contact with Monica, searching for an honest answer to her next question. "How does Charles feel about having a baby?"

Monica smiled and answered immediately. "He's delighted. He appears to feel, extra manly, now that he has a pregnant wife. You know how some men are, the wife goes through the pain and he struts around like he accomplished something, proving his manhood."

Catherine kissed Monica on the cheek. "I hope you have a wonderful life."

"Me, too," Pina chimed in, kissing her other cheek.

"Thank you," she replied. Monica stared out into the park and went on, as though reliving what she was about to say. "Not long ago, we all rode an Orphan Train, not knowing what kind of life we would have, or where we would be living. At night, I sat in the dark as the train went through one town after another, deciding which kind I'd like to live in. I wondered if the people who adopt me wanted someone to love, or just work for them. If they had children of their own, would they accept me or mistreat me? When the Peters adopted me, I wasn't sure whether I should go with them, but I went because I knew I'd have a home, knowing most of the children standing around me would go back on the train. As you can see, it didn't go well for me, so I ran away. Now, at sixteen, I'm married to an educated man with a good job. We have an apartment and I'm expecting a baby." She looked at her two friends and shouted, "It's a miracle."

The girls laughed along with Monica, happy for her situation. When it was time for Monica to leave, Catherine took her to the train station, where they all promised to stay in touch. Driving away, Catherine looked back at Monica standing on the train platform, waiting for Charles. She wasn't fully convinced that he would be good to her. She looked at Pina. "What do you think of her situation?"

"She's never had anything and I believe she's gambling, hoping it works."

Catherine jerked the reins, "I feel the same. We can be there for her, if it doesn't."

Chapter Sixteen

Bridie was reading in the parlor when Catherine came down from her bedroom. "I love you in green. It's the perfect complement for your hair and green eyes."

"Thank you. Brian likes me in green, too."

"Brian likes you, no matter what you wear." Bridie closed the book. "I understand Hillary is coming to visit Pina next month. Is she coming for a weekend?"

Catherine stood by the window, watching for Brian. "No. Since school hasn't started yet, she's coming for a week. She's arriving August, 7th, a Tuesday."

"A week? That's in eight days. I guess they plan to make up for lost time, now that they found each other. Good for them." Bride smiled, watching Catherine peek around the widow curtain for Brian. "What restaurant is Brian taking you to?"

"Being that it's Saturday night, he suggested the Highlander."

"Good choice. They have excellent beef, but they're expensive."

"True. But I don't want a heavy meal, so I suggested Mr. Poon's Chinese Restaurant."

"Mr. Poon's," Bridie wailed, as if in pain. "Brian offers you excellent Scottish cuisine in a beautiful restaurant and you ask for Chinese food?"

"I like Chinese food. Besides, I like the sound of the waterfall they have there."

"So do I," Bridie lamented. "But if a man offers me a fabulous dining experience, I wouldn't turn it down. I'd much rather sit in a room with highly polished wood, stained glass windows and chandeliers, than bamboo furniture, paper lanterns and a three-foot stone waterfall."

Catherine couldn't help laughing at Bridie's comparison of restaurants. "We can go to the Highlander another time. Besides, if we …" Catherine turned and headed toward the front door. "He's coming up the walk now."

When he stepped inside, Bridie yelled from the parlor, "You can kiss her, if you like." There was no response. "I guess he doesn't need coaxing anymore," she mumbled. She heard the front door close and saw them walking past the house hand-in-hand, flowing with smiles for each other. Bridie looked up at John's picture on the fireplace mantle, recalling when they shared the same feelings.

It was after nine o'clock when Catherine and Brian returned from their dinner and a stroll down Main Street. They walked to the back of her house and sat on the porch stairs, looking out at the moonlit pond.

"So many times I've wished my parents were alive, so they could know you," Catherine said.

Brian put his arm around her as she laid her head on his shoulder. "I've thought the same thing. I know they'd love to have you for a daughter-in-law."

Catherine lifted her head and smiled at him. "Is that a proposal?"

"Well no, not yet. I'll do that later."

"Why later?" she asked, disappointed. "Are you shopping for someone else?"

"Of course not. I just thought I'd wait until it got closer to the time for us to marry."

"We could be committed secretly. And besides, you graduate in only two years."

"It's always been understood that we would marry."

"Understood, isn't the same as commitment," Catherine said, lying her head on his shoulder again.

After a few moments of silent thinking, Brian asked, tenderly, "Will you marry me?"

"I'll have to think about it," Catherine replied.

"What?" He roared, pulling away from her.

She grabbed the front of his shirt and pulled him close. "I'm sorry, I shouldn't have teased you. My answer is yes, a thousand times–yes." While still gripping his shirt she looked up at the stars. "Mom, Dad, this is the man I'm going to marry. I love him with all my heart."

Brian looked skyward, too. "Mother, Dad, this is Catherine, the girl I'm going to marry and love until the day I die. I hope you can enjoy her with me."

Tuesday evening, August 7th, at 6:22 p.m., Hillary's train pulled into Newberry station. Catherine watched Pina hurry down the platform and embrace her. "Welcome to Newberry," Catherine greeted, as they walked toward her.

"Thanks, I'm very excited about spending a week here … with both of you!"

"Good!" Catherine responded. "We'll make it a fun week."

Pina carried one of Hillary's two suitcases to Bree and the carriage. She noticed Hillary admiring the rig. "That's Catherine's horse and buggy, and it's ours to use for most of the week. Isn't that great?"

"It's not really mine," Catherine assured her. "It belongs to Bridie McDonald." She stepped into the carriage and opened the lockbox under the seat.

Hillary passed her luggage to Catherine. "When I go somewhere, I either ride my horse or a buckboard, nothing fancy like this for us country folks."

Pina squealed, "You got your horse?"

"Yes!" Hillary squealed back, with a smug expression. "That's why I couldn't come last week." Hillary climbed into the buggy, telling about her horse. "Uncle Biff was negotiating a price for the horse I wanted, but I had to be there in case I had to pick another."

Pina untied Bree and boarded the buggy. "It must have been difficult for you to leave, especially after just getting it."

"It was, but coming here was more important."

"What's its name?" Catherine asked, shaking the reins.

"Knickers," Hillary laughed. "If you could see him, you'd understand why he's named that."

"I think it's a cute name for a horse," Catherine insisted. "Why do you laugh?" She guided Bree around the statue of Abraham Lincoln, and up Main Street.

"Yeah! What do we need to understand?" Pina asked, giving her an inquisitive look. "Does the name have something to do with the horse's size or coloring?"

"It definitely has to do with his coloring. He's rusty brown to just below his knees, and his lower legs are black. It looks as if he's wearing brown knickers and black stockings … but he is beautiful, especially with his long, shiny black mane and tail."

"He does sound nice," Pina agreed. "I hope to see him sometime."

"You can when you visit me," Hillary replied. "You can come, too, Catherine. I've already asked Kate and John and they thought it would be a good idea for both of you to come and enjoy a few days of farm life."

"Me?" Catherine cried out. The huge smile on her face revealed that she was delighted with the invitation. She gripped the reins a little tighter and glanced at Hillary. "Thank you. I'd love it. I'd like to see Galena, too. Bridie thinks it's a wonderful town."

At Pina's house, Eileen and Richard greeted them at the door. Eileen smiled, "It's nice to see the face of the girl we've heard so much about."

"Thank you for inviting me. Finding Pina again is a dream come true." She removed a package from one of her suitcases and handed it to Eileen. "Kate, my guardian, baked an apple cobbler and two loaves of wheat bread. She made the bread from the wheat we grow on our farm."

"That was nice of her," Richard said. "A personal touch, using your own wheat. We'll certainly enjoy it."

"Are you girls hungry?" Eileen asked.

Pina folded her hands in front of her, and with pleading eyes, asked, "We'd like to go to Kitty's, have a sandwich and … girl talk, if you don't mind?"

Richard chuckled. "I'll take the luggage to your room. Be home by nine o'clock."

Eileen smiled at the girls, as Richard walked away. "Men don't understand the importance of girl talk. Have fun. We'll be up when you get home."

The girls sat at a corner table under a slow turning ceiling fan, scanning their menus. "Your letter is the first one I've ever received," Hillary said to Pina. "I was so excited it made me feel important."

"Yours was my first letter, too." She lowered her menu to look at Hillary. "I knew you'd be sending me one, yet when my mother told me I had a letter, I didn't think of you, I thought of my brother, Marcello. After waiting for so long, I thought of him immediately."

"Don't give up," Catherine said, thoughtfully. "Believe it will happen." She leaned toward the center of the table and lowered her voice. "Did either of you notice a posting at the train station that an orphan train was coming to Newberry this Saturday?"

"I didn't," Pina answered, quickly. "Do you want to be there when it comes?"

"Yes! I've wanted to do that, but they rarely stop here." Catherine looked at Hillary. "Would you like to see how children are offered for adoption? It would be interesting to see—especially for us, after our experience."

Hillary nodded, solemnly. "Yes, I would. When I lived in Delaware, my friends and I would watch orphan trains pass through town on a Sunday. It never stopped in Alton, but we would stand by the tracks and wave to the orphans, throw kisses to them and wish them luck. I always feared for them, not knowing their future." A hint of pain settled over her face, turning to Pina. "That was how I saw Pina for the last time. I was scared to death for her." She settled back in her chair and faced Catherine. "Yes, I would like to see what happens at this end of their train ride."

Catherine rapped her menu on the table. "Good. I know Brian will want to be there."

Kitty came to their table carrying three glasses of water on a tray. "I see a new face at the table. Permanent or visiting?"

"Visiting," Pina answered. "This is my friend, Hillary. We lived in the same town before I came here."

"Oh! The girl you met at the Scottish Festival. Bridie told me about that miracle." Kitty felt a sudden rush of tenderness for them. "It must have been a thrill for both of you. God must have thought it important you two be together."

"I'm here for a week," Hillary beamed, "and Kitty's is our first stop."

"I'm flattered," Kitty said, giving the girls their water." She held the empty tray against her chest and walked away. "I'm sure you have a lot to talk about, so take your time."

That night, storm clouds hovered over Newberry. Rain was imminent. Pina and Hillary were in bed, lying in the dark talking about their lives in Alton. Ever since she left there, Hillary was determined to find a way to contact her friends, Iris and Vera, without giving away where she lived. She reached for Pina's hand. "I need your help with a problem I have," she whispered. Hillary heard Pina's head turn on the pillow.

"Of course, if I can," Pina responded.

"It's another, 'promise not to tell anyone,' request. And I strongly mean, *No One*."

"I promise."

She gave Pina's hand a gentle squeeze. "Remember my friend Vera, who worked with me at the mill?"

"The girl you always ate lunch with. Right?"

"Yes. I'd like to get a letter to her and another girl, but they can't come from Galena. I can't tell you why, but where I live must be kept a secret from certain people in Alton. I haven't done anything wrong, of course, but no one must know. I can't explain it now, maybe someday."

"It sounds so mysterious I want to be a part of it," Pina giggled.

"I'd like to write a letter to Vera and Iris, but have them mailed from Newberry. I can mail the letters to you, already addressed, and you can mail them from here. I'll have them send me mail the same way, through you."

"I could do that. Give me their addresses tomorrow and I'll hide them somewhere."

"I can't send it to them directly," Hillary insisted. "I'll address a letter to a Mr. Thompson at his grocery store. He was always kind to us girls, like a second father. I'll explain everything to him in one letter, then there'll be letters for each of the girls."

Pina squeezed Hillary's hand in return. "It sounds a little complicated, but I understand what you mean."

Raindrops began rapping on the roof and tapping the windowpanes. The girls continued to hold hands and whisper, until the rhythm of the beating rain lulled them to sleep.

The next morning, Eileen Campbell surrendered her kitchen to the three girls, so they could make their own breakfast. Catherine arrived at nine-thirty with a jar of orange juice she squeezed that morning. She entered the kitchen, as Pina turned strips of sowbelly in the frying pan.

"You're right on time," Hillary commented. "I'm putting butter on the hominy now."

Catherine placed the jar of orange juice on the table. "What's hominy?"

"It's boiled white corn. It tastes good when it's hot and buttery like this."

Catherine walked to Hillary and looked in the bowl. "I've never heard of it, but it looks inviting."

Hillary sprinkled a little salt into the bowl and began stirring. "Hominy is new to me, too. It's a popular southern food John introduced to me. He's traveled all over, being that he worked for a shipping company, sailing to hither and yon."

"Where's Yon?" Pina yelled, with a strip of sowbelly dangling from her fork. "It sounds like an interesting place."

Hillary walked over to Pina, placing the bowl of hominy at the edge of the stove to keep it warm. "It's about 1,000 miles east of Hither, and I'd like to send you there."

Catherine laughed at their antics. "Is there something I can do?"

"Yes," Pina replied. "Get six eggs from the icebox. I'm about ready to fry them."

"I'll set the table," Hillary said, rushing to the dish cabinet.

Catherine reached into the icebox, placed five eggs in a bowl and carried them to Pina. "Here's, five eggs. I only want one." She sniffed the air and sighed. "It sure smells good in here. Maybe you should own a restaurant."

"Actually, I've thought of that," Pina admitted. "Not an all-day restaurant, but one downtown that only serves breakfast and lunch for business people. That way I'd be home by evening."

Eileen entered the kitchen, anxious to see how the girls were progressing. "It sure smells good in here."

Catherine chuckled. "That's exactly what I said a minute ago."

She smiled at Catherine, then gazed at the table and stove. "I see you girls are ready to eat. I'm going to the library for an hour or two, so enjoy your breakfast and don't forget to clean the kitchen."

They drew their chairs to the table and Catherine tasted a spoonful of hominy. Its warm, buttery flavor pleased her. She closed her eyes and said, "This hominy *is* good. I'll bet it's even more enjoyable during cold months, you know, like soup is in winter. I must tell Bridie about it."

Hillary glanced at her friends a couple of times before asking a question she thought may be sensitive to them. "I'm curious about something," she started. "I've known Kate and John all of my life. Being that I live with them now, I continue to call them by their first names. Yet, both of you were adopted by strangers. Pina calls them mother and father, while you and Brian call them by their first names. Why is that?"

Pina glanced at Catherine, unsure of her reasons. "Let me answer first," Pina asked, politely. She sat back in the chair. "I believe it's because of our family backgrounds. Catherine's relationship with her parents was warmer and more loving than mine. All I knew was work and making money. We didn't have free time to enjoy as a family. My parents were strict with me and Marcello, never allowing us time to play with friends." Her face saddened looking at Hillary. "That's why I never invited you to my apartment, like I promised. Remember?"

"I remember," Hillary answered. "When I learned that after working six days at the mill, you had to make paper flowers all day Sunday, I knew it would never happen. But, it would have been fun strolling through the Italian neighborhood, and you teaching me things about Italy."

A faint smile appeared on Pina's face. "When the Campbells adopted me, they showered me with genuine love. In no time, I felt like they were really my parents, as though they returned from some far-off place and were making up to me for being away. It was like my real parents were the guardians, taking care of me until the Campbells returned. I know that isn't being fair to my parents, because we were poor and they didn't have time or money for us. I guess it was their strictness, and not showing us physical love. That helped me accept the Campbell's, quickly."

"All of us were poor," Catherine added. "Now we have more than we need. I had loving parents and they're still part of my life, and always will be. I love Bridie, but she can never be my mother and she knows that. When she first adopted me, she admitted she could never replace my mother and didn't expect she could. We love each other deeply, but it's a different kind of love. She's been so good to me, I could never pay her back … except by giving her grandchildren to play with."

The girls laughed. "How many are you and Brian going to give her?" Pina asked, inquisitively.

"It's true," Catherine insisted. "Bridie said, when she first saw me, she knew I needed to be in her life. She pretends that I'm the daughter she and her John McTavish never had. We're both giving each other something we need, so that's good."

Hillary picked up her fork to begin eating. "What about, Brian?"

"He feels the same as me," Catherine answered. "His mother and father can never be replaced. Even though he loves the Holmgrens, and appreciates what they're doing for him, they'll never be his parents. Tom Holmgren adores Brian. He's the son Tom always wanted and enjoys having him work at the quarry. Anyone without the facts would never guess that Brian wasn't his son."

"Thank you for explaining," Hillary said. "I was curious."

That afternoon, the girls took a buggy ride into the country. A mile from town they came upon the Peters farm. Mr. Peters was leaving the house, heading for the barn, taking long hurried steps. He looked in their direction just before entering the barn.

Catherine got a chill and goose bumps when he looked their way. She tapped Pina's ankle with her foot, and Pina responded in kind, neither wanting to mention Monica and her situation in front of Hillary.

"There's a farmer going back for an afternoon's work," Hillary commented. "Just like on our farm."

Catherine shook the reins, so Bree would whisk them away from *that* farm. "I'll take Kutter's Road back to Newberry. That way Hillary can see Fox Valley."

Pina elbowed Hillary to get her attention. "It's beautiful there. You'll love it." Next, she elbowed Catherine. "We should picnic there one day this week."

Catherine nodded in agreement. "You're right, we should."

Hillary began singing her favorite song, "Buffalo Gal." Soon, Catherine and Pina joined in. The three of them began swaying and singing as they rode to Fox Valley to see the colorful patches of flowers, birch and weeping willow trees and a stream that meandered through it.

Chapter Seventeen

Friday afternoon, Brian delivered a wagonload of foundation stones to a farm in Tomah, three miles east of Newberry. Tom Holmgren told him to end his day there and go home for the weekend. At 2:30, he rode the buckboard into town to see if Nerine was home. He could bathe there, as he had done before, and have an hour or two with her.

Riding north on Main Street, he saw three young ladies peering into a shoe store window. He noticed the attention they were getting from young men walking past them. He stopped the buckboard and shouted, "Do you lovely, young ladies want a wagon ride?"

Catherine recognized his voice immediately and turned to him. "What do you think we are, young man—easy ladies you can lure off the street?"

Pina placed her hands on her hips. "If you drag that filthy wagon through a river and clean it out, we might."

Brian smiled at Hillary. "And you, young lady, do you have anything to say?"

"Yes," Hillary answered, firmly. "I have my own buckboard and I don't need a ride from a stranger, especially someone as strange as you."

"That's telling him," Catherine laughed. She waved her hand forward and yelled, "Move on, stranger."

Brian shook the reins. "Remember girls, train station tomorrow." He looked at Catherine. "I love you."

Catherine blew him a kiss. "I love you, too."

"We all love you," Pina yelled, waving.

Three blocks ahead, Brian turned left onto Temple Street, thinking about how much he loved Catherine and what a wonderful life they should have together. He recalled the night he and Catherine sat on Bridie's rear porch, looking at the sky, declaring his unending love for her to his parents. Once again, he felt guilt-ridden, approaching 170 Temple Street, first floor front. He loved Catherine, but was going to another woman. A decision had to be made.

Nerine arrived home minutes before she saw Brian ride his buckboard past her apartment. He didn't have that lively, eager face that she thought made him adorable. His face was somber and he was looking down, not ahead. She sensed what was bothering him. Nerine sat for a half-hour in one of her stuffed chairs reading a dime novel, waiting. When he didn't come to her, she knew she had been with him for the last time. *He's a very nice boy*, she thought.

Saturday morning, Brian arrived to walk Catherine to the Orphan Train. Once inside, they kissed and held each other until they heard Bridie close her bedroom door upstairs.

Bridie descended the stairs, putting her driving gloves on. "Do you want a buggy ride to the train station?"

"I'm a little nervous," Catherine answered. "I think if I walk, I'll feel better. I don't know why, but I'm afraid of reliving that emotional experience."

"That's understandable, but I don't believe it will be as emotional for you as you think."

"Nor do I," Brian added. "We'll be watching children's lives change from bad to good. How should that be a problem?"

Catherine kissed Brian on his cheek. "That's a good way of looking at it. I feel better already."

"Lead the way," Bridie said, "I can't leave you two alone in the house, or the neighbors may talk." She followed them outside and locked the door.

Catherine waved vigorously to Jack, waiting by Bree and the buggy.

He responded by raising his hand shoulder-high.

Catherine took Brian's hand and started for Main Street. Passing Carrie's Dress Shop, they could see the train arriving. "Let's run," Catherine said, pulling Brian along. They ran across the street dodging wagons and horses, racing the last seventy yards to the station. Pina and Hillary were waiting on the station steps, waving for them to hurry.

Fifty-five people waited for the orphans to march in and lined up in rows. Catherine counted forty-three children, none older than twelve by her estimation. One tall boy stood out among the others. He was rather homely and had a large purple birthmark that covered his lower left cheek and part of his neck. She pitied him, believing he would never be adopted. She elbowed Brian. "Are you having any emotional feelings?"

"A little. Seeing Mr. Blatt and Miss Hawthorne, brings that day much closer than I imagined. I recall clearly, how I felt when we were lined up for inspection."

"Me, too. Like it was just a few days ago."

Catherine leaned closer to Hillary and whispered, "Only a few people came to adopt. Most came out of curiosity. The people standing on their toes, preening their necks to look at the children, want to adopt. The people standing flat-footed are spectators."

Five couples stepped out of the crowd and began talking to some of the children. A few moments later, two more couples advanced to the orphans, then another. The children were told in advance to smile and appear friendly, giving them a better chance of finding a home. It worked for some, but others stood like sticks, afraid to move, yet forcing a smile. Their eyes revealed their true feelings.

Within minutes, a man picked up a curly-haired boy about five years old. His grinning wife kissed the boy on the cheek and they took him to the desk for adoption.

"One down," Catherine whispered.

A man and woman with olive complexions and black hair took the hand of a light-skinned, blond girl and tried to walk her to the desk. She leaned back, stiffening her legs in an attempt to stay in line. The woman knelt on one knee and talked to the girl, while stroking her head. The woman said something that made the girl smile and loosen her legs to walk.

"Two down," Brian and Hillary said, simultaneously.

"I wonder what happened to Jason?" Catherine questioned aloud.

Brian shrugged his shoulders. "Look over there," he said, pointing to the end of the line. "There goes a happy little girl."

Catherine looked to where he was pointing. A three year-old girl was being carried away with her arms wrapped around a woman's neck. Catherine immediately thought of curly-haired Becky, clinging to her tattered doll and being held the same way when she was loved away from the line-up.

Catherine looked at Pina, to see why she had been so quiet. She noticed a wet trail from a tear that had run down her face. Catherine elbowed Hillary and nodded toward Pina.

Hillary looked at Pina. "Are you okay?"

Another tear emerged, as Pina tried to answer. The only word she could squeeze out was, "Marcello."

Hillary put her arm around Pina's shoulder to comfort her.

After an hour, people began leaving the room, indicating that interest in adopting the remaining children was waning. One couple still walked among the children, hoping to find a child that would suit them.

Catherine noticed a middle-aged man in coveralls walk to the back of the line and look at the bigger boys. The farmer tapped the shoulder of the boy with the birthmark on his face. He turned to face the man, appearing somewhat nervous. Catherine watched them intently.

The farmer didn't feel the boy's muscles or check his teeth, he just talked and the boy responded quickly to each question. Smiles began flashing back-and-forth, as a relationship seemed to be developing. Soon, the farmer led the boy to Mr. Blatt's table. Catherine smiled. *Bless you, Mr. Farmer.*

"End of the line for six children, thirty-seven to go," Hillary commented. She turned to the others. "I'm glad I came. Seeing the love poured out to these children has made me feel better about the orphan trains. Now, I see them as a symbol of hope, not fear."

They went outside and sat in the grass by a flowerbed, sitting in a circle facing each other. Hillary posed a question. "What did each of you feel when you lost your last parent? And how do you feel about your lives now?"

"Desperation," Brian snapped, quickly. "What would happen to me? I felt like a puddle of water lying somewhere." He deliberately avoided mentioning how he lived and supported himself. "When I finally got here, and was lined-up to be inspected, I felt like a pitiful being, hoping someone would be kind enough to take me home with them. When Tom Holmgren came to me, he spoke fast but politely, like he found exactly what he wanted and was afraid he might lose me to someone else. After I met Margaret, I sincerely believed they both wanted me." Brian smiled and folded his arms. "I actually put my hand in my pocket and pinched my leg to be sure I wasn't dreaming. The adoption happened so easily, I wondered if it was a joke. Now I realize that it wasn't a matter of being easy, but a matter of luck." He looked at each of the girls. "The Holmgrens have been wonderful to me, as you know. I can only guess where I would be today, if it weren't for them." Brian drew up alongside Catherine. "You tell next."

"I was concerned," Catherine said, casually, "I knew about the orphan trains and believed I would have a home, at least as nice as the one I had. The love and emotional connection I had with my parents wouldn't be there, but I'd have a place until I got married." She laughed softly, tugging Brian's shirt. "That's where you come in young man."

Brian squinted at her.

"What would you have done if you were placed in a home where you were abused?" Pina asked Catherine.

"I didn't believe that would happen. I was old enough, to where I could tell which people I could trust and who I couldn't. It's the innocent, little children that become victims, because hope is all they have to work with."

"Good for you," Pina commented. "I was like Brian, devastated. There was no one to take care of us, and Marcello and I didn't speak English very well. I was sure I would be in an orphanage for years. I was quite surprised when the Campbells took me home with them. Right up to their taking me into their house, I was sure something would go wrong and end it, even until days later." She looked at the other three in turn. "I love the Campbells. They've given me a new and wonderful life."

"What about you, Hillary?" Brian asked.

Hillary took a deep breath before answering. "For weeks, I watched my mother suffer until she died. My father died six years earlier, and right up to the end, I wouldn't believe that God would take both my parents. When my mother did die, my world came to an end. I even considered drowning myself." Hillary paused, as her emotions started taking control of her. She wiped a tear from her eye before continuing. "The thought of being sent away on an Orphan Train frightened me. Fortunately, just a few hours after my mother died, I learned I'd be living with Kate and John. I was relieved and it changed my thinking completely. I had a reason for living." She wiped a tear again and forced a smile. "I'm very lucky to have them, and Uncle Biff. I love where I live and would like to continue living in the country, or a small town the rest of my life. I don't want to live in an industrial city again." She looked at Pina and Catherine. "Do either of you have a handkerchief?"

"Sorry, I don't," the girls said.

Brian chuckled. "I do, but I don't think you want to use it."

"Thanks anyway," Hillary snickered.

"Four out of four of us have good lives," Pina remarked. "That's a perfect percentage."

"Four out of four because we were lucky," Brian assured her. "If any one of us were unlucky, we wouldn't be sitting here to be counted." He looked at Catherine and Pina. "Where are Marcello and Jason? Have they been as lucky as us? What about Monica? What happened to her and others like her?"

Catherine and Pina glanced at each other, but remained silent about Monica.

"You're right," Pina agreed, quickly. "And if it weren't for Bridie's newspaper article about us, we would still be considered bastards? Thanks to her, we've been invited to parties this last year and Brian has friends to play ball with and go fishing."

"We were lucky with our second families," Catherine agreed. "We weren't lucky with our first families because our parents died."

"True," Brian admitted. "I would love to have my parents back, but that's impossible. Given my present circumstances, I couldn't wish for more than what I have." He looked to the sky. "Thank you, God." He tore a tuft of grass from the ground and threw it into the air, shouting, "My life is BONNIE!" He looked at the girls, waiting for a response.

The girls laughed and followed suit, throwing grass into the air, yelling, "BONNIE!"

Chapter Eighteen

Tuesday morning, Hillary and her two friends went to the train station, sharing hugs and kisses until the train pulled from the station. Hillary sat back in her seat, thinking about the wonderful week she had. When she arrived at Galena, Kate was standing next to their horse, Cokie, and the buckboard. She stepped from the train carrying her luggage in one hand and waved the other.

"How was the train ride?" Kate asked.

"I was away for a wonderful week, and you ask me how I liked the train ride?"

Kate laughed. "Only because you just got off of the train. I have more questions, probably more than you want to hear."

Hillary threw her luggage into the wagon and climbed aboard. "How's, Knickers? I can't wait to see him."

Kate got into the wagon and reached for the reins. "Knickers is doing fine … and so are me and John, if you're interested."

"I'm sorry. I should have asked about you and John first … and Biff."

Kate flipped the reins and looked at Hillary. "You appear excited. Tell me about your trip."

It was a grand week. Catherine was with us the whole week, and we had Bridie's, absolutely beautiful, horse and buggy much of the time. We rode into the country and had a picnic in a beautiful valley, shopped around town, visited some of their friends, played croquet in Bridie's back yard and rowed a boat around a big pond behind her house." Hillary sat pensively for a moment before continuing. "Saturday, we went to the train station and met an Orphan Train, watching people adopt six children. It was very interesting, but sad for those who weren't adopted. The love given to some of the children was beautiful. It was an emotional morning for all of us."

Kate flipped the reins and looked into Hillary's face. "If I remember correctly, all three of your friends rode an Orphan Train, right?"

Hillary gripped the bench seat, bumping through a rut in the road. "Yes, but now they're secure in good homes. This time they were on the outside looking in at the orphans. It was especially upsetting for Pina. That was the train station where she and her brother, Marcello, were separated. She still doesn't know what happened to him. She keeps hoping to get a letter from him."

Kate shook the reins again, hurrying Cokie along. "What are Pina's parents like?"

"Very nice. They loved your wheat bread and apple cobbler." Hillary patted Kate's leg. "They wanted me to be sure I thanked you." They hit another bump and Hillary bounced into the air. "I'm so glad I have Knickers to ride," she said, sarcastically.

Kate laughed. "I'm heavier than you, so I don't bounce as much."

"If you ever go to Newberry and stay at Bridie's house, you'll love it. She and the Holmgrens have big, lovely homes. Pina's house is much smaller, but Eileen and Pina keep it spotless." She sighed a moment. "I loved everything about my visit. We must have them come to Galena. Us girls can stay in the bunk house and the adults can sleep in my bedroom and the guest room."

"I doubt all of them would come at the same time," Kate assured her. She pulled back on the reins. "Hold on … ruts in the road." They both shook side-to-side until they passed to smoother ground. "Don't tell them about our roads. It may keep them away."

Twenty minutes later, they turned onto the path leading to their house. John came out of the barn and walked over to them. Hillary jumped from the wagon, right into his arms. "You smell like a farm," she joked, hugging him again.

"I should," John chuckled. "Did you have a good week?"

"Wonderful! But it's good to be home."

John lifted Hillary's luggage from the wagon. "I'm surprised you haven't asked about Knickers, yet."

"You and Kate are much more important than a horse," Hillary replied. "I'll see Knickers in a few minutes." She looked slyly at Kate for her response.

Kate leered back at her, with one eye closed.

That evening, after Hillary visited Knickers, they sat down for a dinner of fried chicken, buttered corn, sliced tomatoes and potatoes. Hillary told about her week in Newberry.

"When will Pina and Catherine be coming here?" John asked.

"Hillary and her friends start school in three weeks," Kate interrupted. "I doubt they'll be coming here until next summer–unless they come for an extended weekend."

"That's better than waiting until next summer," Hillary responded, quickly. "We should plan for their parents to come, too."

John put a spoonful of butter into his hot potatoes. "They're working people. I doubt they'll all be able to come."

Kate nodded toward Hillary. "That's what I told you. It will always be difficult for the Campbells to get away, but Bridie is in a position where she could come most any time." She sipped her tea before continuing. "I thought it would be nice if Bridie met Biff."

Hillary glanced at Kate. "Why would you want Bridie to ... oh?" She looked down at her plate and mashed her potatoes.

"So, you want to play matchmaker?" John questioned. "What makes you think they'd match up?"

"I think they'd be a good match," Kate said, confidently. "Biff is a very handsome man and Bridie is an attractive woman. They are about the same age, financially secure, and both of them lost the person they loved. Therefore, they never married but wanted to be. I believe they're ripe to find someone to make a home with."

John sat back in his chair. "Biff lives in the country where *his* business is. Bridie lives in a big fancy house a couple hundred miles away, where *her* business is. How can you imagine that would work out?"

"In a couple of years, Catherine and Brian will be married, so Bridie will be alone, again. Biff is already living alone and we know he's interested in marrying. All I ask is that we bring them together and see what happens."

"Whatever," John said. "I can't imagine a fancy lady moving onto a farm."

Hillary leaned toward John. "Bridie said she likes the country."

"To visit," John responded. "Not permanently, I'm sure."

Hillary laid her knife and fork on her plate. "Wait a minute. Bridie McDonald is Scottish and very proud of it, which was obvious by things she said at the Scottish Fest. Also, she was engaged to a Scottish man." Hillary looked at John and Kate in turn. "Biff's last name is Arley. What nationality is that?"

Kate and John looked at each other. "Scottish."

"The name was changed some when his grandfather came to this country," John added. "But it is Scottish."

"What was Biff's mother's maiden name?" Hillary asked.

"Doone," John replied.

"And what is that?" Hillary asked, again.

"Scottish."

"This match-up is looking better all the time," Kate laughed.

John wiggled his fork in his hand. "I still don't believe a rich lady will leave a town to live on a farm."

"She didn't appear to be snobbish," Kate insisted. "Bridie said she likes Galena, very much. Besides, they could have a big house on a farm."

"I just remembered something," John said, suddenly. "When I was in town today, Paul Johnston told me the Lantinos have a buyer for their farm. Couldn't give me a name, though."

"New neighbors?" Hillary squealed. "How exciting. I wonder how many children they have and how old they are? It's always interesting when you get new neighbors. They're like a surprise package."

John chuckled. "It depends on what's in the package. I'll try to find out what I can before they move in."

Ten days later, Eileen handed Pina a large, thick envelope from Hillary. "I got a *Thank you* note from her, too. Not as big as yours, though. Girl talk, I guess."

Pina believed there were other letters in that envelope, not just one for her. She smiled at her mother. "Yeah, a bunch of girl talk." She immediately went to her room and opened the envelope, picking out the letter that was for her.

Minutes later, Pina put the envelope with three letters to Alton, Delaware, into her purse. She went downstairs, yelling, "I'm going to mail a letter."

"You wrote to Hillary already?" Eileen shouted from the kitchen.

Pina lied. "Yes. Girl talk is very important, you know."

"More important than in my day, I guess."

Pina walked to McKenna's Drug Store, where they had a postal station at the back of the pharmacy. She walked through the store, imagining herself a spy, veiled in mystery, as though she was doing something illegal, like sneaking letters to an enemy agent. Ahead of her was a dark, wooden cage, with black bars at the service window. To the left of the window was an oval, brass slot for outgoing mail. Pina unsnapped her purse and slid the envelope containing three letters through the brass opening, then hurried out of the store.

The following day, Brian was leaving for Illinois University. On the way to the train station, he and Tom stopped to pick up Catherine waiting on the front porch. Bridie came out of the house and gave Brian a kiss on the cheek. "We'll miss you until Thanksgiving … then we'll miss you again until Christmas."

"I'll miss all of you, too," he replied. "Only two more years of school and I won't need to leave again."

"I can't wait for that day," Catherine said, with a big smile. She took Brian's hand and they started down the porch stairs.

Bridie watched them board the carriage and drive away. "It's wonderful to be in love and loved in return," she muttered. Her thoughts were interrupted, as the telephone rang. She hurried inside. "Hello?"

"This is Eileen Campbell. I called to tell you that Kate Hanley just telephoned me. She wanted to thank us for the wonderful time Hillary had here. It appears Hillary is still talking about it."

"She was a delight to have," Bridie added. "When I watched the girls playing around my house, I enjoyed them so much, I had an urge to join in the fun. But, I'm sure that wasn't what they had in mind."

"I believe you're right," Eileen laughed. "I have other exciting news, especially for our girls. Kate has invited us to her farm, preferably before the school year begins. She asked about the weekend after next. But, before you answer, I must tell you, Richard and I can't go. He has to work and I have a teacher's meeting that Saturday. Would you mind taking Pina with you, if you go?"

"Not at all." Bridie pondered the coming days before answering. "I don't have anything special to do that weekend, and if Catherine does, I know it wouldn't keep her from going."

"Good. I'll call Kate this evening and tell her."

"When you talk to Kate, tell her I'll call her in a few days to discuss whatever needs to be discussed."

A half-hour later, Catherine entered the house with the demeanor of a sick puppy. Bridie gave her a pout-face and said, "Cheer up, he'll be back in three months."

"That's almost a lifetime," Catherine moaned.

"For a butterfly, maybe." Bridie pointed towards the deacon's bench. "There's a letter for you. That should lift your spirits … for now, anyway."

A smile blossomed on Catherine's face, rushing for the letter. "It's from Hillary. I knew I'd be getting one soon."

"I received one, too—a *Thank you* letter." Bridie followed Catherine into the parlor and they sat opposite the fireplace. Bridie sat quietly until Catherine finished reading her letter.

Catherine folded her letter and put it inside the envelope. "Hillary has ridden Knickers every day since she got home. One day, her Uncle Biff took her for a ten-mile ride along the Galena River."

Bridie folded her arms across her chest. "I rode horses when I was a young girl, and with John a couple of times. I never owned a horse, just rented them. I enjoyed riding, but not enough to be bothered caring for them."

"Maybe Biff would take you for a ride, if we go there."

"I don't think I'd do well on a horse at my age."

"At your age?" Catherine questioned, loudly. "You're a young woman."

"Not exactly," Bridie responded. "But thank you for the kind words. I'd probably fall off and break something. Besides, I may not want to be around this … Uncle Biff, person. It's possible, I may dislike him."

"As for this … 'Uncle Biff, person,' as you call him, Hillary wrote that he is Scottish, through-and-through, top-to-bottom, inside and out."

Bridie nodded. "Then he has something going for him." She leered at Catherine. "I hope you aren't scheming for a romantic relationship between Biff and myself." Bridie pointed at John's picture on the fireplace mantel. "He's the man I love, and that isn't going to change."

Catherine stood. "If we ever go to Galena, we'll probably meet him. I'm not scheming. I was thinking that he take you for a ride, just something for you to do while you're there."

Bridie unfolded her arms and clasped her hands together on her lap. "Don't walk away. I have something very exciting to tell you. While you were at the train station, Eileen Campbell called. We are planning an extended weekend visit to Galena the weekend after next."

Catherine dropped onto the sofa again, grabbing Bridie's wrist. "Don't tease me. Is that true?"

"Yes, it's true. It'll be just us, and Pina. Her parents won't be able to go."

Catherine released Bridie's wrist and fell back into the sofa. "This is wonderful. I never thought I'd be going there this soon, if at all."

"I'm about as excited, as you are. I don't know why, but I feel good about this trip. I hope we can see a play while we're there."

Catherine rolled her eyes. "I'll have to go through my clothes to see what I have to wear on a farm."

Bridie looked at Catherine. "We have clothes shopping to do. Just a few things for visits to the country."

"Do you mind if I call, Pina?" Catherine asked, anxiously.

Bridie smiled at Catherine's enthusiasm. "Seeing that eager face of yours, I'd be a cad if I deprived you."

Catherine raced into the kitchen and cranked the telephone.

"Destination, please?"

Catherine paused. "Destination, please? What happened to, 'Who do you want?' "

"We have a new company policy," Cora whispered. "We operators are to be more professional. Between you and me, it means I'm to be prissy and unfriendly … 'I'd be more than happy to connect you, Ma'am.'"

"Ma'am?" Catherine questioned. "Since when do you call me, Ma'am?"

"I can do that for you, Ma'am."

"Do what for me?" Catherine asked. "Is your Supervisor standing near you?"

"That would be correct, Ma'am."

"Please, Ring Pina Campbell for me, Ma'am."

"Thank you. I'll connect you now, Ma'am."

Catherine leaned against the wall, tapping her shoe against the floor.

"Campbell residence."

"Pina, it's Catherine."

"Catherine!" Pina shouted. "I was about to call you. Did Bridie tell you about us being invited to Galena?"

"Yes. That's why I'm calling. I'm sorry your parents can't go."

"They would like to. My parents are quite fond of Hillary and they believe a few days on a farm will be a nice experience for me."

Catherine cupped her hand around her mouth and whispered, "If your parents aren't going, it should make it easier for us to get Bridie and Biff together."

"You're right. They can concentrate on each other. I'm anxious to meet Biff. Hillary says he's handsome, as well as being a great person."

Catherine looked over her shoulder to see if Bridie was coming to the kitchen. "We'll do what it takes to get them together, but we can't be obvious about it. Bridie is suspicious, already." She dropped her hand and began talking a little louder. "We're going clothes shopping Saturday morning. Do you want to go with us?"

"Good idea. I'll need a few things for the trip. Let me know what time and where we will meet?"

Bridie was talking to Jack in the back yard, while Catherine washed the supper dishes. She returned to the kitchen carrying two bunches of wildflowers, one in each hand. "Flowers for you and me," Bridie chuckled. "You should have seen Jack. He was walking toward me with one large bouquet of flowers, then stopped and turned his back to me. When he faced me again, he had two smaller bouquets, one for you and one for me."

Catherine smiled. "That was sweet of him."

"I think all of the flowers were intended for you, but when he saw me, he decided to give them to both of us. You know, like I was an afterthought."

Catherine wiped her wet hands on her apron and took a bunch from Bridie. "I'm sure half were intended for you. He's given you flowers before."

Bridie grinned. "True. Almost as often as you." She laid her flowers on the kitchen table and took two small vases from a cabinet. "I'll put one bunch on the fireplace mantle and one on the dining room table."

Catherine smelled her flowers before laying them next to the others. "You go read on the porch, or talk to Jack. I'll take care of the flowers."

"Thank you, Catherine. If you need me, you'll find me outside."

Catherine tended to the flowers before drying the dishes then went to her room to write Brian a letter. She looked out of her bedroom window and saw Bridie standing at the edge of the pond, looking out over the water. Black and gray clouds drifted overhead, occasionally exposing a bright, three quarter moon reflecting on the surface of the water. Lantern light and a moving shadow revealed Jack was tending to Bree in the coach house. Catherine went to her closet and removed the quilt of the "flying geese" from the shelf. She unfolded it partially while walking to the rocking chair, spreading it across her lap before writing her letter.

At 9:30, Bridie was sitting in a wicker chair on the back porch, imagining the wail of bagpipes coming from the darkness, crossing the pond toward her. Her meditation was interrupted when she saw two ducks paddling to shore. She knew why. Bridie saw Jack's dark silhouette carrying a small paper bag that contained pieces of bread. The ducks knew him by his bent body. He got down on one knee and began feeding them. His broad shoulders blocked Bridie's view of the ducks, as if they were for him only.

Catherine came out of the house and sat next to Bridie. "I thought I'd find you out here." She leaned forward to look up at the sky. "We should have a full moon in a few days."

"Were you in your bedroom?" Bridie asked.

"Yes, writing a letter to Brian. I wanted to tell him about our trip to Galena. I hope we can go there together, sometime."

"Has he expressed an interest in going to Galena?"

"Not really, but I can't imagine he wouldn't want to go. I believe he thinks the farm and Galena are something separate from him, you know, like it's for Pina, me, and Hillary. He never discusses Galena unless I mention it."

Bridie looked toward Catherine and asked, cautiously, "Have you and Brian had any discussions about marriage yet?"

Catherine looked at the porch stairs where she and Brian had promised themselves to each other. She giggled. "We have, but that's a couple of years away."

"Do you want to marry as soon as he finishes school?" Bridie didn't want to lose Catherine so quickly, but she understood their need to satisfy their love.

"We want to and Brian will have a good job with Tom. Can you think of a reason we shouldn't? I realize we'll only be eighteen then."

They were quiet, watching Jack feed the ducks. Bridie broke the silence. "A bride needs someone to give her away. Have you decided on anyone?"

"I've thought about it, and can think of only one person. Outside of Brian, there's only one other man in my life, and I want him to give me away."

Bridie looked at her through the darkness. "This should be interesting. Who is that?"

"The man in front of us feeding the ducks."

"Jack?" Bridie gushed, completely surprised by Catherine's choice.

"Yes! I've learned to love him for the man he is. He probably won't understand what he's doing that day, but I will. I know he has feelings for me, in his own way, or he wouldn't bring me flowers. One day, he charged toward Charles Belcher when he got aggressive with me. I understood then, that I was important to Jack, enough so, that he would protect me, if need be." She looked at Bridie and noticed a wet streak on her cheek, shining in the moonlight. "Why are you crying?"

"You don't know anything about Jack, yet you've accepted him into your life so thoroughly. That's why I'm crying. I've never told you the truth about Jack because I wanted to see what kind of relationship you would develop with him, especially after he frightened you your first night here."

"All I know is that he is a handicapped man who works for you. Why would my relationship with him be so important to you?"

Bridie wiped away a tear with the back of her hand. "He wasn't born handicapped. He was a healthy man. His last name is McTavish."

"Jack McTavish? Your John was a McTavish." Catherine gasped. "He's John's brother?"

"No, my dear, Jack is the informal name for John, like Bill is for William and Bob is for Robert. Jack *is* my John McTavish."

Somewhat confused, Catherine stared at Bridie. "How could that be? You told me John drowned."

"No, I didn't say that, though I admit, I deliberately misled you. What I said about Jack was, 'it was too late.' The little boy, David, had drowned that day, but John was still alive. After being under the water for so long without oxygen, John's brain was damaged. That's what I meant when I said, 'it was too late,' and too late for John to be my husband."

Catherine reached over and held Bridie's hand. "Now I understand why you've been so kind and understanding with him. I love you and wish I had the power to bring John back to health." Catherine squeezed Bridie's hand. "I'm sorry. That was a senseless statement. Everyone wishes it never happened."

"It wasn't senseless. I know what you meant, and realize it's difficult to express feelings about something you can't change. All I could do, at that time, was readjust my life and go on. When I watched you standing in that line of orphans at the train station, I knew immediately that you were the kind of girl John and I would love to have for a daughter. As I've said, you look very much like I did when I was your age, so the logical thing was to have a daughter that looks like me. But your looks weren't the main reason I wanted you. I saw in you … how do I put it … a nice girl from a good home; a charming girl that I could love. It was obvious to me that you weren't a girl from the streets. I was determined to have you as our daughter. Now, you tell me you want Jack to give you away when you marry. How perfect that is for me. That's why I'm … emotional."

They watched Jack stand, throwing the last scrap of bread into the water and walk back to the carriage house.

"Why do you call him, Jack?"

"It was his mother's idea. Doreen wanted to remember John as the strong, handsome and powerful son he was. In her mind, Jack would be another son, the impaired one. Even though he's the same man, it's her way of keeping John's memory alive, because no one could replace him. I couldn't see any harm in her request, so I agreed to her wishes."

Catherine began rubbing her thumb across the back of Bridie's hand. "I wonder if Jack confuses me with you, the girl he loved?"

"I believe he does." Bridie took a deep breath. "Since you arrived here, I've seen Jack watching you, looking at you the way he's never looked at anyone else, as though studying you. I believe somewhere in the depths of his mind, there is a little spark that tells him you are important to him. He doesn't know why, but he accepts it and lives it."

"And that little spark would be you, not me," Catherine added, quickly. "Being that I look like you when you were engaged. I'm just stirring his memory of you."

"I believe that's correct," Bridie said, smugly. "Because of the way he responds to you, I know he hasn't forgotten me."

O0O0O

978-0-595-43629-3
0-595-43629-3